THE **RED LEDGER** REVENGE

THE RED LEDGER REVENGE

VOLUME THREE
PARTS 7 - 8 - 9

MEREDITH WILD

WATERHOUSE PRESS

*This book is dedicated
to everyone who's ever
tried to fuck with me.*

TABLE OF CONTENTS

THE RED LEDGER

part 7

1

TRISTAN

Boston, Massachusetts

Bare trees thrash in the wind, but otherwise the streets are quiet. I speed through the greenway, ignoring the biting chill against my skin, the beginnings of a freak spring storm that seems to have shown up precisely as we did.

My lungs burn from the cold. As my rapid footfalls on the sidewalk mark the seconds, the pendulum of my heart is a constant reminder that I have someone else's heartbeat to worry about now. Isabel Foster's. She's become my reason for breathing, even if she's trying to hide things from me. I tighten my fists and run faster, causing my heart rate to hammer from the added effort.

I follow the map in my head, turning down a narrow

street that leads me toward the wharf and our home base for the time being. I slow my stride in front of a long stretch of brick building and gaze up at the carved stone archway that's collecting snow along its edges. I stall there, catching my breath and regretting the run wasn't longer to give me more time to think. But night will fall fast under the storm, and no matter the weather, I have plans I can't cancel.

I punch the code onto the door's keypad, climb the stairs to the third floor, and enter the apartment. Isabel is perched by the window seat, a blanket wrapped around her. Her chestnut hair kisses her shoulders, framing the face I've come to love. Her stormy eyes are darkened, almost sullen. The light has left them a little more each day since I set our course for Boston for reasons I won't explain to her.

"It looks like it's getting bad out there," she says.

I pull my shirt over my head and walk to the kitchen for water without saying a word. Shutting her out is so easy sometimes, but it rips me apart to do it as well as I do. It's like volunteering to have a vital organ extracted while I watch in determined silence, knowing once it's gone I'll die. Without her, I would. That fire to survive and kill and protect would taper off until someone had a gun to my head, and I'd find myself wishing for it to all go black so I didn't have to think a second more about losing her.

I guzzle down a glass of water and half of another, my back to her all the while, even if I can feel the heaviness of her stare. The emotions she whips up in me are more than I can handle sometimes, so I shove them down, run them off, or hide them among the sins of my recent memories, tucked away with a version of me who wasn't as vulnerable.

Then she's behind me, a brush of chenille throw and her cheek warm on my back. She curls her arms low around my waist, which activates the one part of me that I'm willing to share with her lately. Long into the night, I feed the demon in me with her willing body, her whispers and cries filled with all the things we don't say. All the things we feel.

"You're freezing." She roams her hot palms over my chilled skin, methodically trying to warm me up. The gesture is sweet and selfless and makes me hate myself.

I grasp her hands and gently untangle her from my body. "I have to shower. Then I'm heading out for a while."

To kill your ex-boyfriend.

When I turn, her eyes are shadowed with hurt as if she somehow heard my quiet desire. If Kolt Mirchoff gives me a good excuse to rid our lives of him forever, I won't hesitate to act on it. It probably won't come to that, but if it does, Isabel may never forgive me.

"You shouldn't go out in this weather." Some of the warmth has left her voice. "The city is probably going to shut down once the snow really starts coming down."

"This is Boston, not DC. I doubt everything is going to come to a standstill over a little winter weather."

She folds her arms across her chest, still covered by her blanket. "Where are you going? What's so important?"

When I don't answer, her countenance relaxes under a strange calm. "It's okay. You don't have to tell me."

I don't believe her, but she leaves, resuming her seat by the window before I can make up some bullshit excuses for why I need to leave our cozy apartment in the middle of a blizzard. Excuses she's apparently not interested in hearing. I should be relieved, but suddenly I'm questioning all my red rage over Kolt's communications with her and wondering if I should have confronted her about it and thrown all of it into the light instead.

Not really my style. Pressing the muzzle of a gun to his temple and threatening his life for everything he knows about his murdering family is more what I had in mind. The fleeting vision of a scenario like that spurs me toward the bedroom, where I shower and change, discreetly stowing my Sig Sauer in my jacket along with anything else I'll need to make my point.

When I return, the window seat is empty. Her blanket hangs off the edge. My heart thuds heavily in my chest because I can feel that she's gone. A scrap of paper is pinned to the mullion of the door.

I walk over and yank it free.

Went out for coffee. See you later.

I glance at my watch. It's almost five o'clock. I never confirmed an exact time Kolt could expect to meet with Isabel when I hijacked her email account, which gives me an undetermined window to scope out the area, watch, and wait for his arrival. I don't have time to track Isabel's coffee run or psychoanalyze her reasons for leaving, though as I start the short walk toward my destination, I imagine it's her way of telling me to fuck off for leaving her behind and keeping her in the dark.

I accept this, push Isabel out of my thoughts, and make my way toward Faneuil Hall. The snow falls heavier once I arrive at the pedestrian-friendly promenade. Tourists slip and laugh as they maneuver the cobblestone streets, arms heavy with shopping bags.

I pull my cap down my forehead a little farther and move quickly toward the green-faced pub on the corner, scanning the cross streets on my way. Nothing's tripping my radar. I decide to head right inside, too eager to see if he's beaten me here.

A blast of warm air and traditional Irish music greet me when I step inside. I don't have to wait long. My mouth is nearly watering when I see Kolt appear at nearly the same moment. He's across the restaurant, hovering at the end of the bar. He brushes the snow off his jacket and runs his hands through his dark-blond hair. He doesn't notice me. The fool can't feel me watching him like he's prey. Something else holds his attention.

I follow his gaze to the opposite end of the bar. And that's when I see her. Her sullen eyes are suddenly brave, brimming with determination as she slices a look my way that stops me dead in my tracks.

ISABEL

We've been fighting this war for days. Something snapped back in Miami. I felt him change, transforming back into the cold, calculating Tristan bent on a mission. Next thing I knew, he was making plans for Boston. That's when I figured he had set his sights on Kolt.

I found the email messages he thought I'd never find—the emails he trashed after confirming a meeting only he was supposed to know about. In retrospect, maybe I should have never answered Kolt's plea to begin with. But while the guilt of the evasion ate at me, so did the unspoken murder in Tristan's eyes whenever I opened doors for him to tell me the truth. He never did.

Now there's nothing to say. The bar is busy with patrons. While Tristan seems pinned in place at the opposite doorway, Kolt takes long strides toward me. I tense, bracing myself for danger. But the second I meet his eyes, I know he's not here for that.

His snow-damp hair is overgrown, the tips curling against the collar of his black peacoat. He still looks rich in his designer jeans and expensive boots. He reaches out to embrace me when he's arm's length away, but I hold up my hand, stopping him before he can.

He doesn't get to touch me that way anymore. Judging by the stung look in his eyes, I think he understands this. I've been harboring my anger for weeks. Seeing him in the flesh borders on overwhelming because it's with new eyes, knowing everything I do.

"It's good to see you." His voice is quiet, almost apologetic as he slips onto the stool beside me. "Is everything okay?"

I swirl a spoon through my coffee a few times. A couple of months ago, I would have had a very different answer to that question. The hole Tristan left in my heart is nothing compared to the death-defying journey we've endured since he came back into my life. Worse, the blank innocence in Kolt's expression dashes any hope I've been clinging to that he may actually be able to help me.

"Why did you want to meet so badly?"

He looks past me like he's steeling himself for something, but he doesn't speak.

"I don't have a lot of time, Kolt. If you have something to tell me, I need to know now."

He licks his lips and tentatively looks me over. "Are you safe?" He studies me that way for a long time, his whole body tense, like he's trying to find something that's different. I may seem the same on the outside, but on the inside everything's been rearranged for survival.

I peer over my shoulder and scan the restaurant. I can't see Tristan now, but I know he's here somewhere— watching, waiting, and definitely fuming over this shift in plans. I'm not sure I want to know what his actual plan was. Any latent affection I had for Kolt incinerated the second I found out he was sent to Rio by his family to get close to me, but I still don't want him dead.

I turn back to Kolt. "I'm not like you anymore. I can't stay in one place for too long. It's never safe for me."

"I want to help you." I can barely hear his offer over the murmur of patrons and restaurant music. "I'm just in a tough situation."

"*You* are? I lost my whole life over this. And all this time, you knew I was in danger and you never warned me, never tried to help me. Why should I believe you want to help now?" I curl my fist on my thigh, renewed anger flooding me at his betrayal—deceit that led me into his bed too many nights, creating memories that make me cringe with regret now.

"Just—" He closes his eyes a moment and exhales a deep breath. "You don't have to believe me, but I hope that you do. I didn't go there to hurt you. I didn't go for any other reason than to get the hell away from my life here. I was failing at school, cracking under the pressure, and I was ready to jump at any chance to get away and have some fun. My uncle said I could help him with a work issue in Rio. All I knew was that your family was in a dispute with the company. He wanted me to keep an eye on you and see if you knew anything about it that might help. Honestly, I didn't care about any of that. I asked you a couple of questions about your family when I met you, and I knew right away that you had no part in whatever was happening. Then it was over. I had nothing to report back, so I was just living my life in Rio and getting to know you." He reaches across, grazing his fingertips along the outside of my fist as if willing me to unfurl it. "As much as you'd let me."

I swivel toward the bar, torn over whether to believe him. He sounds genuine, but he fooled me before too.

"So you never thought getting close to me might cause problems?"

"I figured it was a lawsuit or something that would blow over. And once it did, who cares if our families had issues? You love who you love."

"That's obviously not how it works in your family."

"No kidding. I was way off base. I'm lucky I'm alive." His next words are hushed, like he doesn't want to risk anyone hearing him. "I want to help you in any way I can, but if I turn on my family, they might come after me next."

"You're their flesh and blood."

He shakes his head like I'm definitely wrong. "They don't know why Tristan didn't kill you the first chance he got. He had clearance to—" The notch in his throat moves when he swallows. "Let's just say if I happened to be collateral damage, it wouldn't have been a total tragedy for them."

I wince at the thought of his family caring so little about his life. "That can't be true."

"I'm pretty sure it is. I overheard my uncle talking on the phone about it one night. He didn't like that I'd gotten so close to you, something he wouldn't have had to worry about if Tristan had taken care of us both that night."

I'm too stunned to respond. Seeming to sense this, he continues.

"I'm their blood, but they'll never trust me to take over the company, Isabel. I'll just get some pointless job with a fancy title because I'm part of the family, but no power and no responsibility. And instead of living in blissful ignorance, I'll have to spend the rest of my life knowing they never gave a shit if I lived or died."

My heart hurts over Kolt's new reality, but I'm past family heartache. I have enough of my own. I've been trying too hard to survive to dwell on the shortcomings and well-meaning betrayals of my own parents.

Kolt's soft brown eyes dim a little. "You don't want to hear about this. I get it. Honestly, I can't imagine what you've been through."

"I've lost count of the number of people who've tried to kill me. Strange thing is, I think I might be getting used to it."

The weight of what's been lost and everything that's changed adds more tension to the air between us. A part of me wishes I could spill all of it to Kolt, a man who'd once been a lover but also a friend. Someone I could talk to. I wish he could understand all the brushes with death, the unthinkable things I've had to do to keep myself alive, the people I've lost.

"Disappear with me." A glimmer of hope hits his eyes. "They want us gone. Why don't we just fucking leave and never come back? I've got enough money in my trust to float us for a long time."

"It doesn't work that way."

"It doesn't? That's what you've done."

"And they'll keep trying to find me until I'm dead. Extinguished. A slash through my name for real, not just on paper."

His lips thin. "What do you want me to do?"

I let his question linger between us a moment, almost waiting for him to draw it back right away. He doesn't.

"Can you get me more information from the inside? Something that will give me leverage or any kind of advantage?"

"What if they find out I'm helping you? Then I'm

fucked and you're no better off."

"You're smart. Just be careful. You know them better than most."

"I used to think that...until they tried to kill the girl I was falling in love with."

I avert my eyes to escape the pleading in his. He talks like maybe there's a chance I'll say it back. It'll never happen.

"I should probably go."

"Isabel. Stop. Please." He places his hand over mine, breaching the space between us again.

This time I don't move. "What?"

He hesitates like he's trying to find the right words. "You *know* how I feel."

"Yes. I do. It doesn't change anything."

"Maybe it changes what I'm willing to sacrifice."

Everything inside me tenses. "What is that supposed to mean? I thought you wanted to help me. Now you have conditions?"

"Are you still with him? And I don't just mean under his protection."

I keep my body perfectly still, not allowing myself to scan the room again for Tristan or give Kolt any reason to believe I'm not here alone. The less he knows, the better.

"Are you seriously worried about whether or not I'm sleeping with Tristan when I have a bounty on my head?"

"Yes."

His answer is so hasty, I'm momentarily stunned by it.

"He was the one, wasn't he? The one you talked about who you could never get over."

My silence is my answer. I don't have time for these confessions. Kolt and I are over. We never really started. But I can tell he's not letting it go.

"He's a murderer. Have you considered that? God knows what he's capable of."

"You have no idea what you're talking about."

"I know that I want you back. I know this isn't over between us. No doubt these are severely messed-up circumstances, but I think once the dust settles, once you don't need him to be your bodyguard anymore, you'll realize he's not actually the right person for you."

I pull on my jacket and stand.

"Isabel, wait—"

"Do you love me?" I level him with my stare.

His lips part and his eyes glitter under the bar lights. "You know I do."

"Then help me. Or I'll walk away right now, and I promise you'll never see me again."

Pain washes over his face. He reaches for me again but stops himself. "Don't say that, okay? We can figure this out."

"Then let's keep things simple. This isn't Rio. This is life and death. All I can give you is my trust. Even that…" I shake my head, knowing I could never really trust him again after what he's done.

"You don't trust me. I get that. All I can do is try to earn it and pray I can win you back somehow. I'll take whatever you can give me."

A long moment passes. Something compels me to touch him, on my terms. I bring my fingertips to his cheek and draw them slowly along his jaw and fine stubble. He feels familiar and strange. Time and experience will do that—twist the things you used to care about to become things you can hardly stand the sight of.

"Save your prayers, Kolt. You'll need every one of them if we go down this road together."

2

TRISTAN

By the time she walks out the door, I'm pent up with a thousand things I want to say to her. Scolding, scathing things. Warnings and detailed, harrowing scenarios of what could have happened if she hadn't been so lucky. Thankfully Kolt's nothing more than a desperate fool chasing after a woman he'll never deserve. As soon as I realized he wasn't here to hurt her, I scoped out the perimeter of the building more thoroughly, suddenly worried about Isabel's vulnerabilities over my own.

She took over the whole plan without telling me. She could have gotten herself killed on the way here.

Her warm breath billows in the air, illuminated under the street light. I think she's going to walk my way when the bar door swings open behind her. She spins and Kolt's there, his hands fisted at his sides like he wants to touch her but knows he can't.

"Isabel, wait a minute."

She doesn't speak. For a prolonged moment, they simply stare at one another. I can't help but wonder how the conversation started back in the bar, but I'll have to wait to find out.

"I overheard some things. I don't know if they'll help," he says. He looks pained by some invisible force. "Will you just promise me something first?"

She hesitates, and I curl my hand over the rough handle of my gun, sensing her tension.

"Whatever goes down, wherever we end up, whether or not you decide to give us another chance, I just want to know you're safe. Will you let me know that you're okay? That's all I want. I realize I don't have the right to ask for a lot more."

"What did you hear?" Her voice is clipped, lacking the affection he's probably longing for, which infuses some satisfaction into my frustration with her right now.

"Your mother and her friends were accessing deeper parts of Chalys. Killing you would have been more than a warning shot. Your death was meant to be a distraction from whatever they were digging into so they would back off. There was too much on the line to let it go further."

"What didn't they want her to find?"

He licks his lips and glances around as if someone could be listening. I keep still, hiding myself where the edge of the building meets an alleyway, shadowed in the dark.

"Have you heard about Felix?"

She frowns. "No."

"It's short for felixedrine. It's a new synthetic drug they've been working on. Right when all this shit was going on, they were trying to push it through the last stages of FDA approval."

"What does that have to do with me?"

He taps his foot nervously. "Isabel…"

"Kolt, just tell me. What does Felix have to do with me?"

"When your mother's friends started going after the accounting records, it was the last straw. They were getting too close. This Felix drug… It's big. It's like everything Chalys has achieved over the past decade is peanuts next to what this drug is going to do to the market. They're branding it as the 'opioid cure.' The answer to the epidemic. We're talking about billions of dollars here. And now that it's approved, it's setting off a bunch of other initiatives."

"What kind of initiatives?"

"I guess you could call it a next-level marketing plan. A lot more than a campaign of commercials with happily medicated people vacationing on a lake. They're talking about government contacts opening the floodgates at ports of entry for more heroin to hit major cities next month. Concentrated efforts so that a wave of overdoses across the country will be top news at the same time Felix starts shipping out."

Her lips part with something like shock. I feel it too, which makes it all the more difficult to stay put and not insert myself into their conversation.

"They're setting themselves up to cure the national crisis they're fueling."

He nods. "They want to make sure they're the one and only true answer to it. Billions, Isabel. More money than God."

Snow swirls silently around them and collects on their shoulders. "And you really don't want any part of that? All that money?"

He laughs. "I've got ten million dollars in my trust. I don't need half that for a whole lifetime in Rio. I like nice things. I like my life, and I thought I loved my family. But this is too messed up. They tried to *kill* you. They wouldn't have blinked an eye if I'd been killed too. And what they're doing... A lot of people are going to die so Chalys can be the savior. That's not forgivable white-collar crime. That's murder."

"I don't even know what to say."

"Promise me you'll be careful. This is bigger than a family grudge. They'll destroy anyone and everyone who gets in their way with this."

"Then you should be careful too. If they truly think you're expendable..."

"Trust me, I've considered it. My uncle's been missing for a while. No one's heard from him for days. They're acting like it's no big deal right now, like maybe he's on a bender with some hookers in Miami or something. They don't want to turn it into a media spectacle, but I can't help but wonder if he got in the way of things somehow."

I tense, silently praying Isabel stays quiet. Thanks to me, Vince Boswell's life ended on a yacht last week, and it'll be a miracle if they ever find his remains tied to the end of an anchor. I have no regrets, only that Isabel had to witness it. Knowing he's gone after all his violent promises fills me with nothing but calm that the world is rid of him. But Isabel's a better person than I am. Face-to-face with Kolt, she may be tempted to tell him the ugly truth.

The silence stretching between them makes me uneasy. I'm tempted to reveal myself and end their conversation when he pulls her against him, hugging her tightly. He whispers something in her ear that I can't hear. It's better than her telling him about his dead uncle, but it's killing me to see them this close.

She pulls away first, taking a step back. The tension I'm holding from watching their conversation and interactions doesn't ease up. It's like I can't take a breath until she's away from him.

"I have to go. Thank you for telling me all this," she says.

"I'll reach out if I find anything else that might help."

She lays her palm against the lapel of his jacket. "Thank you. I mean it."

I exhale as she turns and walks away, leaving him to watch her go, hopefully for the last time. I wait until Kolt disappears in the other direction and she passes me. Then I fall into step several feet behind her.

When her pace picks up, I know she can hear my footsteps following her down the street. I gain on her, hoping she feels me before she sees me. She pauses to look back just as I lasso my arm around her torso and trap her against a granite-walled building with my body. I cover her mouth with my hand to muffle her scream, lifting it away only when it dies with her recognition of me a few seconds later.

Her pulse is thrumming at her neck. Her breathing is ragged. If her meeting with Kolt didn't give her an adrenaline rush, I just did.

"Scare you?"

She narrows her eyes and tries to push me back, but I won't budge. I'm pissed off, but I want to feel her against me too.

"You have no idea how scary it could have been," I speak through gritted teeth. "What the hell were you thinking?"

"I wasn't going to let you hurt him." In her eyes lies the challenge that I would have done worse than hurt him.

"I didn't realize he meant that much to you." I can't help baiting her to deny it and convince me that he doesn't own any part of her affections. After what we've been through together, I demand all of them.

She turns her head. "Let's go back. I'm not doing this with you right now."

I give her a little space, but we're not through. "You should have told me when he reached out to you."

"The way you flipped a switch the second you found out is exactly why I didn't."

I do my best to ignore the pulse of fury that runs

through me as I replay that night in Miami, one that could have been memorable in so many other ways. One second we were at the club and I was deep in fantasies of taking her back to the penthouse and losing myself in her until night bled into morning. Then I saw the email and wanted to possess her for different reasons rooted firmly in my hatred for her ex-lover.

We could play this game all day, but it's a dangerous game.

"So you went rogue? What if they had people waiting for you to show up? There are a hundred places people could have been hiding, waiting for a chance to get a clear shot."

"I was careful. I always watch my back. Plus I knew you'd show up eventually."

"It was sloppy. Don't do it again."

Her glare is more intense this time. "I took a gamble that Kolt wanted to see me for the right reasons. I wasn't wrong."

Just because Kolt wasn't leading her to her death doesn't mean he wanted to see her for the right reasons. But I force myself to take a full breath to keep myself from berating her about it anymore.

"I heard everything once you were outside. What else did he have to say?"

"Just that he overheard Vince saying they wouldn't have been heartbroken if he'd died in Rio along with me. His world has been turned upside down. He knows they don't care about him, so he's more inclined to help."

"Especially if it comes with a chance to get you back."

She holds my silent stare, confirming what I assumed brought Kolt through the doors of the Black Rose to begin with—to win her over.

"Just because he's in love with you doesn't mean you can trust him."

"I don't. I'm even wondering if I should trust you."

She slides past me, and I watch her walk away, a little stunned, because she's hit her mark.

ISABEL

Tristan shuts the door behind us. I strip off my coat, hoping I can avoid more lectures from him tonight. I have too much whirling through my head right now. Kolt dropped more on me than I expected, and I need time to work through it all.

Before I can disappear into another room, Tristan takes my hand and pulls me toward him.

"What?"

My tone is sharp, but he's gentle, his expression unexpectedly even. He laces our fingers together, and I can feel my anger begin to thaw.

"What if we both said we were wrong at the same time? Would that be an easier way to end this?"

I blink up at him, surprised but undeniably relieved. "Are you admitting that you were wrong to set up a meeting with Kolt without me?"

"I'm suggesting that because you made a bad call by

not telling me about the email, I was triggered into also making a bad call."

I do my best not to smirk at his indirect attempt at an apology. I try to turn away before he can catch it, but he cups the back of my neck, drawing me close. Our gazes tangle. His warm breaths tickle my chilled skin.

"If anything happens to you, I'm never going to forgive myself, even if it is your fault. I don't want to live without you, so you need to talk to me. About everything."

I try to balance the way he riles me with my overwhelming desire to end the tension that's been gnawing at us all week. He's right, of course. We were both wrong, even if neither of us wants to admit it.

"Then you need to stop worrying about Kolt. He's not a friend, but he's not the enemy either. I think tonight proves that. If he's right and Chalys has this whole plan in motion, we need to figure out how Simon's involved. This has Company Eleven written all over it."

"How am I supposed to game-plan with you when you could be keeping secrets from me? You want to trust me, and I want to trust you. That means we need some transparency."

I huff out a sigh, frustrated but convinced he won't budge until we can agree on this point.

"Fine. No more secrets. But it goes both ways." I lift my chin with a defiant flare because I'm still angry with him for trying to see Kolt and for scaring the hell out of me after I beat him to it.

I expect something fresh to come out of his mouth, but

instead he lowers his lips to mine. It's a simple kiss. Soft and thoughtful. And when he pulls away again, it feels like we've sealed the deal.

"No more secrets," he murmurs the affirmation, walking to the window. He stands there for several minutes, hands in his pockets, staring into the quiet storm.

I follow him. "What are you thinking?"

"I'm thinking about all the reasons Kolt might have to lie, but I don't think he did. If what he said was true, the circumstances behind the hit on you make more sense. Something always felt off about it... It seemed too simple, like the punishment never fit the crime in a way."

"Is that why you hesitated?"

He looks down at me, and I search for the answer in the blue of his eyes. His hesitation—whatever instinct convinced him not to pull the trigger—is the only reason I'm alive.

"I didn't completely understand the hit, but that never stopped me before. One second I was ready to go through with it, and then I couldn't. Something about you felt familiar. But I didn't give it any weight until you said my name. I don't think there's any way I could have convinced myself to do it after that. Not until I knew more about you."

His choice came down to seconds. I look out the window, trying not to think about the alternative—the end of my life, as innocent and ignorant as that life might have been.

"The money trail is almost always the best way to the truth," he says, interrupting my troubling thoughts. "We need to get a hold of those records if that was their breaking point. Maybe it's time you reached out to your mother to see what they found. Lucia probably wants to know you're okay anyway."

I tense and internally sidestep the guilt that comes along with all the time that's gone by with no contact with my parents. But maybe I've punished them long enough for the hand they had in Tristan's enlistment.

"If Halo was involved, they'll have the information banked, right?"

"Maybe. Who knows what Martine did with everything she dug up on people or if it's even accessible now that she's gone."

"Martine and my mother never knew about Company Eleven. If Simon's involved, other people in the Company are probably in on this too."

"If there are billions of dollars at stake, I can guarantee you there are plenty of fingers ready to get into that pot."

Every time we think the problem is one size, another layer is revealed. The only thing that has stayed the same is the Boswell family. My grandfather was convinced of their malice all those years ago, and they've done nothing but prove him right ever since he left their company and blew the whistle on their practices. His voice was too small to matter. My sister's death too insignificant.

I press my fingertips against my eyelids with a tired groan. "This is more than anyone bargained for, Tristan. What could we possibly do to keep this from happening?"

"The bigger question is how many more people will we piss off trying to send it off track? We thought taking

Simon out would send the Company into chaos and they'd disassemble. Even if a few of them are invested in this scheme, removing Simon from the equation may not even matter."

"Then maybe Mateus was right. Maybe he can get close enough to help us fill in the blanks."

"I have a feeling they're going to want him closer than he realizes. They took an interest in him for a reason. This is a global project, and he has something they want. They're not inviting him to the party just because he's charming."

I smile a little. "He is charming, though."

"Let's hope so, because they'll kill him if they smell deceit."

I wake before Tristan does. I've been staring at the phone in front of me for the better part of an hour. I know what I should do but wish I didn't have to do it. Being at odds with my parents is the last thing I need when I'm running for my life, but a stubborn and wounded part of me doesn't want to be the one to extend the olive branch.

I finally force myself to pick up the phone and dial my mother's number. As it rings, I hope it'll go to voicemail so I can do this another time when I feel more ready for it.

"Hello?"

"Mom, it's me." My voice is small.

Her breath catches. "My God, Isabel. Are you all right?"

"I'm fine. Everything is fine."

"I'm so glad you called. After what happened to Martine, I've been so worried about you."

I close my eyes as a fresh wave of guilt hits me. Martine may have been my mother's friend and a trusted accomplice when it came to revenge on the Boswells, but in the end, she made her own choices—dangerous choices that ended up getting her killed.

"I'm sorry, Mom. I know you were close."

She sniffs quietly. "Thank you. I'm glad you at least got to know her. It still feels so surreal. Halo will never be the same without her. She touched so many people."

I bite my tongue because I know better. Halo may not ever be the same. It can only be better, but my mom's heart can't take the truth right now.

"That's one of the reasons I called. I'm not sure where things stand with Halo at the moment, but I really need your help with something."

"What is it?"

"Right before I left Rio, Halo gained access to Chalys Pharmaceuticals' financials. It's what triggered the hit on me. You were getting close to something important. I need to see what you found."

"That was Martine's operation. She kept whatever they found. We never had time to look at everything because you came home. That's all I cared about."

"Halo's been storing up information on people for years. Tell me you still have access to everything."

She doesn't answer right away. My stomach does a dive. A lifetime's worth of blackmail couldn't have died with one woman. She couldn't have been that conceited.

"I came to town for Martine's funeral. Papa and I

managed to make sense of things. So, yes, the information is safe. I can send you the financials if that's what you need."

I chew the inside of my lip, wondering how I should outright ask for what I really need. *All of it.* My grandfather already padded my account with a hefty sum of Halo funds should I ever need them, but the real fortune is the incriminating information Martine kept on people. Right now, it could be the key to unlocking whatever Company Eleven has planned for this operation.

"I need more. This is bigger than Kristopher Boswell, and we don't have a lot of time to be kept in the dark on anything."

"What are you asking?"

"Mom, I need all of it. I need as much as I can get my hands on if we're going to connect the dots on this."

"You're talking about thousands of files. Extremely valuable and potentially dangerous information if it gets into the wrong hands."

I know she's talking about Tristan. The man who's kept me safe. The lover who's killed for me. The assassin who could have ended my life but somehow ended up making me fall in love with him all these years later, under the worst possible circumstances.

"If this is about Tristan…"

"This is about keeping you safe. If you think you're in danger now, you have no idea how much trouble you could be bringing yourself if someone knows you have those files."

I clench my jaw and will myself not to groan in frustration. My mother's persistently narrow way of thinking is at least part of the reason we're in this mess. In the spirit of making peace with her, I don't tell her this.

"Mom, please, I'm begging you to trust me. Believe me when I say I've been through hell and all I want is to end this once and for all. If I don't find what I need in Halo's files, I promise I'll destroy everything. But you've been trying to bring them down for years. I'm going to do more than try this time."

"What do you know? What's going on?"

There's a mix of panic and eagerness in her voice that worries me. I love my mother, but I don't entirely trust her instincts when it comes to this mission. No doubt I'm emotionally invested, but she's let her thirst for vengeance blind her before. My grandfather's seen it, and Martine twisted it to her advantage for years.

"I don't have the big picture yet. That's where I need your help."

She sighs heavily. "Fine. But please don't make me regret it."

We spend the next few minutes figuring out the logistics of giving me access to the Halo database. Focusing on the details is a welcome break from negotiating for the information itself, or worse, dwelling on the days of silence between us and the resentment I still harbor.

"I wish your father were home right now. He'd love to hear your voice," she says once we've finished.

I'm hit with a pang of missing him, but I can't forget he campaigned the hardest to rid my life of Tristan years ago. Reconciling with him will be a tougher bridge to cross.

One day I will, but it won't be today.

"I'll call again soon," I say.

She keeps me on the line, trying to keep me talking. She doesn't want to let me go, but I promise her again that I won't let so much time go by before reaching out again. Whatever I find and however Tristan and I can use it, I hope I can keep that promise to her.

3

TRISTAN

When I join Isabel in the living room, she barely notices.

"Morning," I say, drawn to the half-empty coffee pot sitting in its cradle.

"Hi," she mutters absently, her attention glued to my laptop screen. She's sitting cross-legged on the floor, using the coffee table as a makeshift desk.

"Anything new?" I drop onto the sofa behind her and peer over her shoulder.

When she doesn't answer, I lean in for a closer look. She's scrolling through what looks like document scans.

"What are those?"

"Letters between Michael Pope's attorneys and dozens of women."

"Who's Michael Pope and why do we care?"

She turns to face me, lifting up a piece of paper with her handwriting scribbled all over it.

"I made a list."

I sit back and sip my coffee, trusting she has a lot more to tell me.

"Back at the yacht party, Simon's wife sat me with the other girlfriends. Ramsey Paulson's girlfriend said there were eleven of them in this 'club,' but maybe more now that Mateus is about to join them. Anyway, she rattled off a few of their names. Michael Pope was one of them. I'm not sure if he was on the boat, but he was definitely on the list."

"And?"

"And until his son finally went to the slammer a couple of years ago for raping and beating his ex-girlfriend, he'd been paying off a bunch of women who came out against him or threatened battery charges."

She seems so focused, I hesitate to interrupt her, but I have no idea where this is going. "Those are the letters?" I nod toward the screen.

"Yes, all negotiating hush money. His son's a vicious bastard, and Pope's paid out hundreds of thousands to keep him out of trouble. It's disgusting."

"How does this affect us? He's in the Company, but this isn't tying him to Chalys."

"All of this"—she gestures to the screen—"is too much and not enough. The accounting records are partial. The bookkeeping is limited to last quarter, and that's what I was hoping would narrow things down. Everything else… There are at least a thousand folders and then thousands of documents on top of that. It'll take weeks to sift through it all, and by then Felix is going to be skyrocketing to success. We don't have that kind of time."

"How much coffee have you had?" I can't help smiling at her infectious energy. "And more importantly, where did you get all this?"

She blinks. "Oh. I talked to my mom. I convinced her to give me access to all the Halo files."

My smile slips with this realization. "You're kidding." I reach around her and pull the computer onto my lap.

I can hardly believe it, but she's right. There are endless files, and probably not easily searchable, like the fuzzy scans she was looking over.

"What else did you find? Anyone else from the list?"

"Other than Chalys, no. A lot of their stuff is pretty dated, though. Remember, this is a twenty-year-old grudge, so there's a mountain of things that probably aren't helpful. But I have an idea."

She lifts herself to sit on the edge of the table to face me.

"Michael Pope. I think he's our key. He has enemies."

"They all do, Isabel. Comes will the territory of being a billionaire captain of industry."

She smirks. "Yes, but he has a really smart one." She lifts up her paper again and points to one name written in capital letters and underlined several times.

BLAKE LANDON

"Who's Blake Landon?"

"He's a hacker."

"I can hack into things too, you know."

"I'm sure you can, but this guy is next level. Rumor has it that he hacked into some big-time Wall Street accounts when he was thirteen and almost did time. Instead, he got scooped up by Michael Pope to develop some kind of next-generation banking software they sold for a ton of money. But they parted ways around the time Pope's son, Max, went to jail. The ex-girlfriend's wasn't the only charge against him. He assaulted Landon's wife too. Attempted rape. Trust me, he *hates* this guy."

"So what's your plan?"

"Okay. The best part? Landon's right here in Boston. He runs a handful of tech companies and an angel fund with his wife. His office is a few blocks away. I say we get a meeting with him, tell him just enough to whet his appetite for a chance at payback against Pope, and see if we can get him to hack into whatever else we need."

I drink my coffee and consider everything she's said. I have no idea who this Landon guy is or who his connections are. Her proposition isn't terrible, but she's made a lot of assumptions.

"What if you're wrong and he's still affiliated with Pope in some way? If Landon was in business with him for that long, they may have meaningful ties no matter what Pope's kid did. If you lay all this out for him, you could be bringing attention to us for no reason."

Her lips thin and she nods. "That could be the case, but I don't think it is. Either way, I think I could feel him out to see where he stands before I completely tip our hand."

I lift a brow. "*You* could feel him out before *you* tip our hand? Were you going to invite me to this party, or are you considering another rogue mission?"

"I would be happy to invite you, but I get the feeling this Landon guy walks the straight and narrow most of the time. A meeting at his office should be safe." She reaches behind her and hands me my phone. "Besides, Townsend isn't happy. I wouldn't normally care, but I don't think we should risk pissing him off when we could still use his help. Or Jay's, for that matter. You should probably figure out how to talk him off the cliff."

I glance over the few texts he sent. Most of them threaten my life if I don't stop stringing him along with Crow's whereabouts. All of them are riddled with profanities. I curse under my breath.

"Fine. I'll deal with Townsend. Let me go call him before he blows a gasket, and we'll figure the rest of this out."

Her smile is full of giddy satisfaction, probably because I haven't totally shot her down like I have so many times before. Suddenly it's the strangest sensation to know that she's here, not just *with* me but *beside* me.

I rise and step outside to call Townsend. It's a Saturday morning, and the streets are quiet. Most of the sidewalks are still covered with last night's snowfall. I was hoping to scope out the Boswell estate north of the city today, but the weather's thrown a wrench in that plan until the city plows catch up.

Townsend picks up on the second ring.

"About *fucking* time, Red. Where the hell are you?"

"Where are *you*?"

"Well, I've spent a lot of time around a certain strip joint in New York where I was told I'd find Crow. Not having much luck."

"Could be worse places to be hanging around, I suppose."

"Where the fuck is he, Red? We had a deal. I helped you, and you were going to give me Crow. I've been here for days. Nothing."

"He didn't answer my last couple of texts. He's probably busy chasing down the leads Jay gave him. And if you're prowling outside his favorite haunt, he might be suspicious and keeping his distance."

He cusses again, followed by the fierce sound of him sucking down a cigarette that's probably doing nothing to ease his nerves.

"You talk to Jay about this yet?"

"Don't worry about it," he snaps.

"Is she all right?"

"She's fine. You worry about your business, and I'll worry about mine."

As much as I'm glad not to be in charge of Jay's safety, she still feels like my business. And Isabel's right. We may still need her. She was the right hand of the Company for too long. She knows a lot more than she ever told us.

"I might be getting close to something," I say.

"Simon? You going to let him slip by you again this time?"

I ignore his taunt. Mateus let Simon Pelletier go, not me. If it were my call, Simon would have swallowed the aconite Townsend gave us and died on the yacht right along with Vince. Unfortunately Mateus thought it'd be a better idea to join the Company Eleven ranks instead.

"I think I found the connection between him and Boswell. Have you ever heard of Felix?"

I walk up and down the pavement, waiting for any acknowledgment. The silence is too long. It doesn't feel right. "Townsend…"

"What about it?"

"What do you know about it?"

"Fuck you. Find me Crow."

I grind my teeth together. Damnit, he's so difficult. "Fine. I'll ask Jay. She's probably due for an update, right?"

"Red, stay in your fucking lane."

"Then stay in yours. Tell me how you know about Felix. I thought you only dealt with underground drugs."

With his black bag of tricks, Townsend would be the one to know about the dark side of any new drug on the market. It hadn't occurred to me that Felix would have a dark side, though.

"Listen, Crow's flown the coop. I'm wasting my time here. I might as well come to you."

I'm anxious to press him more about what he knows about Felix, but something tells me I won't get very far on the phone, especially with Townsend's present mood. Bringing him to Boston brings its own challenges, but right now nothing is more important than unraveling the

Company's involvement with Felix.

"I'm in Boston."

He snickers. "I should have guessed that."

He's not stupid. He knows I'm here for the Boswells.

"Can you keep your mouth shut? I'd rather if they didn't see it coming."

"I want to get on their radar about as much as you do. This is your fight, not mine. Didn't think you were going to move right into their backyard, though."

"When have I been known to back down?"

"One particular instance comes to mind," he offers with no small amount of satisfaction.

Isabel. I roll my eyes, irritated that I gave him an easy opening.

"Let me know when you get into town. Then we'll talk," I say.

"I'll be there tonight. Tell cupcake to lay out the welcome mat for me."

ISABEL

"Are you sure you don't want me to come in with you?"

Tristan and I linger outside the entrance to Landon's downtown office.

I shiver and hug my coat tight across my middle. "I can handle it. Promise."

He purses his lips and looks me over. His silence makes

me edgy. The confidence I've been building up all afternoon leading to this meeting starts to waver. I'm not sure how this is going to go, but I've mentally prepared myself for every scenario I can think of. Getting Blake Landon on our side would be a coup for our cause, but if he goes the other way and still holds allegiance to Pope, we could lose critical ground. Every move matters, and I'm in the driver's seat on this one.

"Tristan, I can—"

He touches his finger to my lips, stopping me as he takes a step closer. "I know you can handle it. Periodic questionable judgment aside, you continue to impress me with the things you're capable of. And if I don't tell you enough, it's because I'm an asshole. It's not on you."

I lift my lips into a smile. "You've been a little distracted."

"A little." He slides his fingertips to feather over my cheek, his expression growing serious again. "Don't let anyone make you question your strength. Not even me. Don't give anyone that kind of power."

Our gazes lock for a long moment. I nod, feeling bolder, because right now Tristan does have that kind of power. I know I can be strong on my own, but having Tristan's faith in me makes me feel stronger, no matter what he says.

I glance to the door and back. "I should go in. His assistant said he had a small window of availability today. I don't have a lot of time."

He frowns a little. "Listen to your gut. That little voice in your head. If something feels off, get out of there."

"Got it." I squeeze his hand once more before turning

and passing through the doors.

I expect a fancy corporate reception area, but most of the office serves as an open-concept bullpen, where at least a dozen people are wired into their computers, tapping away like I don't exist. I walk quickly through the aisle that leads toward a young woman behind a large desk.

I smile politely when I reach her. "Hi, I'm Isabel."

When she looks up, her short, pink-tipped spiky hair doesn't move an inch from all the product in it. "Oh, hi. I'm Cady. We spoke earlier."

"That's right. Is Mr. Landon still free now?"

"He just finished up a conference call. You can head right in. He's expecting you." She gestures toward the closed office door behind her.

My stomach does a nervous flip, but I try to stifle any outward signs of my anxiety, no matter how justified it may be. Landon is an important man regardless of what I need from him. I take in a deep breath and walk to the door, eager to get face time with him.

I step inside the office. It's completely quiet except for the subtle taps of fingertips across a keyboard. I can only see the side of Landon's face, which is glowing from the multiple monitors taking up a second desk.

I clear my throat. "Mr. Landon. Thank you for seeing me on short notice."

He doesn't look up. "Take a seat."

I do, and another awkward moment passes as his fingers fly over the keys. Finally he turns, rises, and extends his hand, which I shake firmly. The gesture is formal, unlike the man, who's sporting mussed hair, a vintage T-shirt, and worn jeans. That and the black-rimmed glasses he wears do little to distract from the fact that he won the lottery when it came to genes. His hazel eyes zero in on me with an intensity that tightens the knot in my belly.

He doesn't smile, only drops back into his chair and continues studying me. "What can I do for you?"

I swallow hard and prepare to dive in, praying the script I've prepared will sway things in my favor. "I understand that you have extensive history with Michael Pope. I was hoping to speak with you about that."

His laser beam doesn't break. "Yes, Cady mentioned that. Anything regarding Pope tends to get my attention."

I smile a little. "That's what I was hoping for."

"How do you know him?"

"I don't really. I know of him, and I've recently come upon some information that I thought might be of interest to you."

"Why would it be of interest to me?"

"It has to do with his son."

If I've touched a nerve, I can't tell, save the subtle tightening of his jaw.

"I've cut them both clean out of my affairs. They're toxic people. Max is a monster, and his father is a soulless power monger. I'm not sure what else there is to illuminate."

A little part of me registers relief hearing his brutal assessment. If he truly feels this way about the Popes, half the battle is already won.

"I heard about what happened between Max and your

wife. That must have been devastating for both of you."

His jaw ticks and his nostrils flare. "Erica was drugged. Then he tried to rape her. It was at a family party in my parents' home."

I wince, feeling the full force of that ugly tidbit of information. The barely harnessed wrath behind Landon's words is heavy in the air. It's so heavy that I almost wish I didn't have to say what I need to next.

"She wasn't the only one. There were others."

"I don't doubt it. He's behind bars now, though. It doesn't feel like justice to me, but what can I do?" He glances toward the televisions broadcasting the news silently on the adjacent wall, pretending to be interested, but I suspect I have his full attention.

"Maybe there is something more you *can* do."

He returns his gaze to me, a silent invitation for me to continue.

My heartbeat picks up speed. "I'm not sure if you realize how involved Michael Pope was in all of this."

He frowns. "Excuse me?"

"These women that Max assaulted, they were paid hush money that kept him from facing charges all that time. Everything went through Michael's attorney. He helped him cover up what he was doing for years before he ever laid a hand on your wife."

He becomes eerily still, then leans forward, resting his forearms on his massive desk. "How do you know all this? Were you one of the women they paid off?"

"No, thank God. But I have…a file…that's come into

my possession recently. I was looking for something else and came across some document scans. Confidential letters between the women and the lawyers. Dozens of them. A little online research linked both of the Popes to you, which is why I wanted to reach out."

"What do you want me to do about it?"

"These cover-ups are unconscionable. Wouldn't it feel good to expose him for what he helped do?"

He lets out a dry laugh. "I think you know the answer to that. But I'm getting the feeling you want something from me. Is it money you're after?"

It's my turn to frown. "I have no interest in your money, Mr. Landon."

God knows I have plenty of my own.

"If you don't want money, then explain to me why you're sitting in my office dangling a Michael Pope-shaped carrot in front of me."

"To be completely honest, I'm interested in your... skillset. These letters weren't what I was looking for. I was hoping you could help me find what I am."

"Listen, I've got a reputation. Unfortunately, it's stuck with me ever since I was a kid. But I'm not in the hacker business anymore."

"I'll admit, I read up about it a little."

He shrugs. "I thought I was doing the right thing. Correcting some of the injustices that were keeping me up at night way before I should have cared about things like Ponzi schemes and corporate abuse of power. You don't know the half of it. Trust me, I learned my lesson. That part of my life is over."

He slices his hand through the air for emphasis. I'm losing ground. My thoughts whirl. I can't accept a simple refusal. He needs to know what's at stake.

"Mr. Landon."

"Blake," he corrects.

"Blake… This isn't a personal vendetta for me. It's a matter of survival. For me and a lot of other people who don't realize they're about to play a part in a much bigger plan. I need to stop it from happening, but I'm not sure how I can without your help."

"A bigger plan?"

I hesitate, uncertain how much I should say when he's been so resistant to helping.

"Will you help me?"

"Do I come across as someone who takes up illegal favors for complete strangers?"

I cringe a little inside because he's right. I've been banking on him wanting revenge on Pope enough to justify the fact that what I need from him involves him breaking the law.

His intercom beeps. He turns to answer it. "What's up, Cady?"

"Erica is here."

He glances at his watch briefly before rising and circling the desk. "Listen, you seem like your heart's in the right place. I wish I could help you out with this thing, but I just can't."

I blink up at him, desperation racing through me

now. "What about what Michael did? Doesn't that mean anything to you?"

He closes his eyes a moment before opening them again. "It burns. No doubt about it. Not like I needed another reason to hate him, but I've known long enough that he was never who I thought he was. I already ripped the mask off."

"And what about justice?"

He shakes his head, a nearly imperceptible motion, as if he's fighting a war inside his own head. Quietly I root for the side of justice, the side we could both be on if he could only understand the magnitude of its importance.

"I'm sorry. I just can't help you."

When he walks away, opens the door, and disappears through it, I jump up and follow him out. I'm ready to spill everything about Chalys and the Boswells and this whole twisted endeavor—at least the parts I know. Except I fear the window has closed when I see Blake with another woman.

"You ready?" he asks her.

"Ready when you are." The petite blonde who must be his wife beams up at him, her features glowing.

The stone-faced man I just met seems transformed— softer, vulnerable even, as he glides his palm gently over her swollen belly, no doubt the source of her glowy energy.

Seeing them together sends a shockwave of emotion through me. Jealousy. Disappointment. Understanding.

He glances over his shoulder to me. Something unspoken passes between us.

This is why.

Judging from the look of pure devotion on his face

when he turns back to his wife, I feel certain that nothing could be more important to him. No grudge or vengeful wish.

I should go. The opportunity has passed. I move past them toward the exit. I shove my hands into the pockets of my jacket. The hard edge of the thumb drive scrapes against my hand. I halt at the door. I breathe. Close my eyes. Listen.

Giving it to him would be stupid. He's already said no. Who knows how many bombshells there are on this drive that could create problems for me down the road. I can't seem to push through the door and leave Blake Landon and his refusal behind, though. My mother's warning rings through my head, but it's not the only voice there. There's another one daring me to take a gamble.

I turn on my heel and head back toward the beautiful couple. Blake looks up as I approach.

"Here."

His brow wrinkles when I hold my outstretched palm to him.

"What is this?"

I shrug. "I suppose it's whatever you want to make it."

He exhales a quiet sigh before lifting the little device from my hand. "I have a feeling I'm going to regret taking your meeting today."

"Why?"

"You're giving me dirt on one of the people I most despise. That's like offering a free hit to a drug addict."

"Funny you should say that." I huff out a sad laugh at the quip only I can understand.

He lifts an eyebrow, but I only shake my head because it's too much to explain now, especially with an audience.

"If you change your mind, Cady has my number."

He replies with a curt nod, the only assurance I get that there may still be a chance.

4

TRISTAN

"He's not staying here." Isabel bangs the wooden spoon on the edge of the pan without making eye contact.

"What's the difference?"

She shoots a narrow glare my way. "The difference? Townsend tried to kill me. Did you forget that tiny detail?"

I gently grasp the spoon from her and take over the task of pushing vegetables around the pan.

I haven't forgotten. Killian Townsend joined us on the Company's hit list by way of protecting Jay. That doesn't mean I'll ever trust him after he nearly plunged a lethal dose of heroin into the woman I love.

"He knows about Felix, and our last lead just turned us down."

She shifts away and pulls two plates out of the cupboard.

Her lips are pressed tightly together. I know she wants to say more. She was tense leaving Landon's building but hopeful he'd change his mind and help unravel the Company's plan. We can't wait around for Landon to have a change of heart, though.

"Why couldn't he just tell you what he knew over the phone?"

"Because he wants to bargain with me. People like Townsend don't give up anything without getting something in return."

"Further reason why he shouldn't be sharing a roof with us."

"What about that saying…keep your enemies closer?"

She rolls her eyes. "I think our enemies are plenty close. We don't need to invite them inside."

A loud, fast knock causes us both to look toward the door. Another series of impatient raps, and I'm certain it's Townsend. I pull my gun from my waistband anyway and go to the door, confirming our visitor's identity with a brief glance through the peephole.

When I swing the door open, Townsend walks in without ceremony. A half-burned-down cigarette dangles from his lips. He tugs off a knit winter hat and runs his hand over the blond fuzz on his head.

"Home sweet home." He nods to Isabel. "Hey, cupcake."

I cuss inwardly.

Isabel stands motionless, a steel wall of opposition on the other side of the room, arms crossed, her shoulders tense. "Don't you have someplace else you can stay?"

He chuckles and saunters her way. Leaning over the pan, he plucks out a sliced carrot and pops it into his mouth. "You know, if you missed me, you can just tell me."

His smirk might be endearing if he wasn't such an evil prick. Too bad we all know better.

Isabel turns and angrily pulls out another plate. She lets it clang on the counter beside the stove. "Help yourself."

Dinner is quiet and strange. Townsend is ravenous and unaffected. Isabel barely eats. I'm about to start grilling Townsend when Isabel shoves up from the table and goes to the kitchen, easing the strain a fraction.

I push my emptied plate to the side and lean forward as Townsend releases a satisfied sigh.

"Not going to lie to you, mate. The hospitality here is unmatched."

"Don't get used to it," I say, mostly for Isabel's sake.

He snickers and rubs his hand over his freckled cheek absently. "Right."

"So what do you know about Felix?"

He purses his lips and fishes out a fresh cigarette, buying him a prolonged pause. "The miracle drug," he finally says.

"How do you know about it?"

"I'd hardly be an expert in my field if I didn't know these things." He exhales loudly, sending a plume of smoke between us. "You see, every time a new drug is developed, there are the castoffs."

"Castoffs?"

"Mistakes that end up in my bag. Like Elysium Dream. You think these Big Pharma guys are paying a bunch of lab nerds to cook up drugs so I can blast away people's memories? Of course not. But shit happens, and the mistakes don't necessarily go to waste. It was originally supposed to be a breakthrough drug for treating severe neurological disorders. PTSD among them. The stress of war, early abuse... Those kinds of things can cause long-term changes in the circuits in your brain. The idea was to remap the circuits, turning severe trauma into pure fucking bliss. Except early trials showed that the drug didn't play well with the body's natural neurotransmitters. Test subjects were complaining of memory loss. Make a few modifications, and you could give someone a blank slate with one treatment. Pretty fucked up, but useful in my line of work." He takes another drag of his cigarette. "I guess you could say I'm a collector of castoffs."

I fist my hands tightly. The casual way Townsend talks about the drug that robbed me of my past is enough to make me want to wrap my hands around his throat and rob him of his future. He seems to sense this, lifting the corner of his lips into a wry grin.

"Sorry, mate. No hard feelings, all right? Just doing my job."

His words echo in my brain until logic overrides my anger.

I'm no better than he is. I spent years killing for hire. He used a needle. I used a gun. Our paths crossing now doesn't change the reality of these things. I unclench my fists and will myself to focus on what's important. My muddled past is something I'll have to sort out another time.

"So what does this have to do with felixedrine? It has FDA approval. It's legit."

He smirks. "Finally got the recipe just right, I suppose."

I still. Did I hear him right?

"Wait… The drug that wiped my memory is a failed version of Felix?"

He sucks in a long drag of his cigarette, an odd mirth glittering in his gray eyes. That's when I feel Isabel behind me, her hands resting on my shoulders. A quiet comfort. I circle one of her wrists in my hand and stroke my thumb over her soft skin. I never know how devastatingly powerful her support can be until she offers it.

"It makes sense when you think about it," he continues. "Drug addicts and broken veterans. Both trying to escape something that's hurting them. Trying to chase happy, except it never lasts long. A whole generation of people whose families just wish they could stop. Feel better. *Be* better."

"Remap the circuits."

"That's the idea."

"I'm afraid to ask about the side effects."

He shrugs. "Couldn't tell you. Development takes years. I got my hands on Elysium Dream long before Felix started going through trials."

Isabel moves to my side and takes a seat. "They're going to market it as the opioid cure. Millions of people are going to be rushing to get their hands on it. Do you think it'll actually work?"

"It'll do something. Wouldn't get this far without some results. But I wouldn't fucking take it," he says.

"You also suck down cigarettes with no regard for what they're doing to your body."

He lets out a dry laugh. "I'm not expecting to live long enough for a cigarette to kill me. Until then, I'd like to know who the fuck I am." He shoots a knowing look my way like I'm the only one who can appreciate his dark humor.

Nothing is funny right now. The cyclone of fury I felt earlier is morphing into something else. Something like horror. Maybe Felix really is a cure. But maybe it's not and it's about to be unleashed onto a nation desperate for an answer to an epidemic. I'm not wired to care, but for some reason I do.

"They're going to push shipments through the ports. Flood the market with drugs," Isabel says.

"Create a crisis. Feed the demand. Smart thinking. I almost wish I'd thought of it first."

"Simon has to be behind it," I say before she can lay into him. "Chalys is a powerful company, but pulling off something of this magnitude is bigger than one corporate giant. Only someone like Simon could orchestrate an operation at this many levels."

"Sounds about right. But you're fucked if you think you can change any of it."

"Why couldn't we?" Isabel bristles as if we haven't been wrestling with the same inevitability.

Townsend holds her in an amused stare. "You might think you're a warrior princess now because you sliced through Bones in the heat of the moment, but you and your killer boyfriend here are no match for whatever's about to go down. There could be hundreds of people involved in this. Even if you succeed in crippling some piece of it, it won't be enough to stop this train."

"Then help us."

Townsend laughs loudly and pushes upright. He saunters into the living room. "This isn't a three-man job."

"Then we build a team," she presses, seeming intent on convincing him.

Townsend swivels to face her. "You going to amass an army now?"

"We know people. I'm sure you do too," she says.

"Everyone I know is out for themselves, same as me. They don't fuckin' care about your cause."

"Then why are you here?" I interject.

Townsend pauses and takes another drag. "You know why."

"I gave you everything I have on Crow. The rest of the hunt is yours."

"So maybe I'll hang around in case he comes back on the radar. I have a pretty strong feeling he will. And when he does…" He slices his index finger across his neck with an eerie smile. "Until then, I'll play along."

Isabel's eyes go wide, no doubt at the prospect of keeping close company with Townsend for any prolonged period of time. When I look back, Townsend's plopped himself on the couch, head back, eyes closed, feet propped on the table, like he intends to stay that way awhile.

Isabel and I clean up quickly. With Townsend claiming the couch, we find privacy in the bedroom. I come up behind her as she changes out of her clothes. Her movements are jerky, like she's still working off some of her anger. She tenses a little before relaxing into my embrace.

"Hey," I whisper against her ear, marveling at how natural she feels in my arms every time. "Don't let him get to you. We'll work this out. With or without Townsend."

"If he's not going to help, I really wish it could be without."

"You're setting the bar too high. You can't expect friendship when we're traveling this road. Alliances, yes. He may be a chronic pain in the ass, but he brings his own assets to the table."

She doesn't acknowledge this, but I take her silence as frustrated acceptance. When we crawl into bed, I tug her close again. I kiss along her shoulder and nibble at the sensitive spot just below her ear. Goosebumps break out on her skin, and her nipples pebble through her tank top. The responsiveness of her body only adds fuel to this never-ending fire that burns for her.

When she releases a soft sigh, I roll her to face me. She seems distracted, though. Her eyes don't reach mine, so I tip her chin up, hoping to force a better connection.

"What's going on? This can't all be about Townsend. Something's been off since you saw Landon. Did something happen in there?"

She tries to roll away, but I won't let her. I need her eyes on me. Need to read the expressions that are beginning to form a language all their own.

"Isabel. Transparency."

"Jesus, Tristan, it's nothing. It's stupid and couldn't be more unimportant next to everything else we're dealing with."

She turns her head away from me like she's afraid to show me what's hiding behind her eyes. I brush my lips down her neck, desperate to soften her or at least take her mind off whatever's bothering her.

"If it's taking up space in your thoughts, it's important," I say softly. "I'm not great with feelings, but you don't have to hide anything from me, okay?"

"I just had so many dreams for us, Tristan. And I locked them away when you left. I tried so hard not to think about them, but sometimes they rush back and I can't help the way it makes me feel."

Her eyes gleam when I lift my gaze to hers.

"Tell me."

After a long moment, she finally speaks. "Landon's wife is pregnant. I saw them together as I was leaving. It's why I didn't press him after he said no. He has too much to risk."

I don't understand the relevance right away. But then it hits me. When it does, I'm frozen, seemingly unable to respond or move until Isabel laces our fingers together. Somehow I can feel her pain holding space in my chest as if it's my own.

"The way he looked at her and touched her. Everything hit me all at once," she says. "I couldn't help but wonder what it would feel like, you know? To have something like that with you one day."

And just like that, her vision seems to sail right into my

own thoughts. Then the intoxicating and equally alarming possibility of her carrying a child. *My* child.

I swallow hard and concentrate on her fingers sliding back and forth between mine. I'm too overwhelmed to respond. I know I'll say the wrong thing, because her dream is impossible. I'm not going to pour salt on the wound and tell her that.

When I brave a look into her eyes, a tiny tear journeys down the side of her face. Something happens in my chest. A tightening. A spear of determination, as if somehow I might have enough power to make one of her dreams come true.

I lean down to capture the salty drop with my lips, letting myself taste her sadness.

"I love you," I whisper.

I can't save her from the truth. This is the life we've committed to. But I can be here for her. I can love her as much as I know how to.

She folds her arms around me, and we stay that way a long time. Breathing each other in. Kissing and feeling and falling into the intimate rhythm we know well. Except when I make love to her this time, the dreams she's held tight are infused in the act. The regret and hope and sorrow swirling between us inspire me to love her harder and hope that on the other side of the crest, those dreams can fade away. That this can be enough.

ISABEL

Trying not to make a sound, I take my spot in the window

seat and warm my hands with my mug. The snow outside has melted, and pedestrians are in motion again, making short, fast strides up and down our side street. A part of me despises them in their dark jackets and side-slung bags, with jobs and friends and bills. I resent their simple problems.

The click of Townsend's lighter interrupts my quiet survey of the street below, but I refuse to look at him. I hate him more than the morning commuters walking toward the rest of their blissfully normal days.

"So I was thinking last night," he starts, his familiar British rasp like a bristle across my nerves. "I was thinking about you worrying over all those unsuspecting degenerates ready to inhale Felix the first minute their insurance companies clear the payments."

"They're not all degenerates."

"Course not. But that doesn't mean I care about them any more than the next person." Of course he wouldn't. He's a murderer. Not the kind who's on the path to a better life, either. "But you care, don't you?"

I finally face him, if only to match the hint of thoughtfulness in his voice to the condescending look I expect to see on his face. Except his crooked smile seems oddly genuine.

"Jay is like that, believe it or not," he says.

"You must be joking."

"She did some good work at the Trinity House."

I wince, disgusted at the suggestion. "That was a cover. Hitman brainwashing disguised as veteran rehabilitation."

He frowns. "Wasn't all like that. Every sorry fuck who

wandered through those doors was someone she wanted to help. Maybe not in the traditional sense. But Tristan's life would have been over when he reentered society. Discharged. Dumped back into his shitty life."

"I was part of that shitty life, you know."

"No you weren't. You were in Rio fucking Boswell's nephew."

I grind my teeth and clutch my mug tightly. The steady simmer of hatred I feel for Townsend threatens to go into a full boil. He doesn't seem to care.

"You don't know a fuckin' thing, with your privileged life," he keeps on. "You think everyone's got a fighting chance, don't ya? Everyone's got the same opportunities to live a cushy life like your parents gave you, right? News flash. The world ain't fuckin' like that. The life he was coming home to… Hell, he'd be better off dead anyway. Jay saw his potential and knew it'd be wasted if she hadn't done what she did."

"She ruined him. *You* ruined him."

He jumps to his feet and goes to the kitchen, slamming the cupboard after retrieving a mug and filling it to the brim with coffee. He stands there a long time, his back to me. My heart hammers in my chest, and my eyes sting with emotion that never has anywhere to go lately. There's no justice for the past. No stealing back what was taken away— the memories of our life together before Townsend drained them.

He finally turns and walks my way. Defensive, I swing my feet to the floor and set my mug to the side. His expression is hard. I don't trust him. He stops several feet in front of me. His lips are pulled tight in an unpleasant wrinkle.

"You know, most of the time we do the job and walk away. We don't have to face the ones we're paid to deal with after the fact."

"That's touching," I mutter, risking more of his anger.

He takes a harsh drag off his stub of a cigarette and points at me with it. "Nolan Mushenko. You think you want to save the world? Maybe figure out if it needs saving first."

"What are you talking about?"

"All the big guys have someone like him. They keep him on the books for 'research and development'"—he emphasizes the title with one-handed air quotes—"but they're just shady lab rats cooking up potions for people like me. If Felix isn't what they're promising it'll be, that's who will know."

"Why are you telling me this?"

"I just fuckin' told you," he snaps. "I'm not going to war for you, but if you want to put your life on the line for a bunch of junkies, maybe do your research first."

My thoughts whirl, but I don't move, wary of every morsel of information that leaves Townsend's lips.

"Tristan says men like you never give anything up without wanting something in return."

He laughs. It's brittle and reeks of truth. "Maybe I'm holding out for a favor that counts, cupcake."

When he says it, I believe him. But I don't know what we could possibly offer him, short of Crow's head on a plate, which seems unlikely—at least according to Tristan.

Regardless, Townsend's given us a new lead, one that may make it worth keeping him under our roof for a little while longer. After what he told us last night, I'm just as worried about the cure as the wave of overdoses that will put it into the spotlight.

"Where do we find him?"

Just then Tristan emerges from the bedroom, any signs of the passion and understanding we shared last night erased from his features. With Townsend around, I can't do anything to change it. Besides that, his man-on-a-mission mood suddenly matches my own.

Townsend turns his body toward him. "You got a car?"

"Yeah, why?"

"I was hoping to introduce Miss Foster to a friend of mine."

We're at least twenty minutes outside of Boston when Townsend signals Tristan to take an exit off Route 1. We drive a few miles past well-kept neighborhoods with tidy yards, grass deadened from a long winter. As the streets narrow, the houses look more like rundown apartments. Busy convenience stores are positioned on nearly every corner.

"I thought you said Mushenko was on the books," I say.

"Left up here," Townsend says, pointing toward a more promising downtown. "Chalys headquarters is in the city, but since there's nothing regulation about what Mushenko does, they have him set up at a warehouse in Lynn. It's right up here."

Minutes later we're parked on a street shadowed by a graffitied wall that supports train tracks running parallel to it. Like almost everything else I've seen here, new abuts the old and dilapidated. We stroll past a condominium complex advertising brand-new two-bedroom apartments on our way to an adjoining building with no signage. Several of the first-floor windows are shattered and backed with plywood.

I glance around. "This is it?"

"It's not so bad. Don't let the curb appeal fool you." He bangs on the door loudly.

"Hey, man." A young man in shabby clothes crosses the street toward us. "Can you spare a dollar?"

Townsend grimaces like the man's presence revolts him.

After a brief hesitation, Tristan pulls a dollar out of his wallet and hands it to him. "Here you go."

The man smiles, revealing gaps where several teeth should be. "Thanks, man. I just need like five dollars to get the bus, though. I got an interview. You'd really be helping me out. Could you spare a five, man?"

"Heaven help us all," Townsend mutters.

The glaze in the man's yellowed eyes and his dirty clothes betray the lie. Wordlessly, Tristan peels a twenty off his wad of bills and hands it to him, prompting the man to thank him profusely. His words seem genuine, if not his intent, but I look away. His desperation is painful to watch. Townsend rolls his eyes as the man wanders down the street out of sight.

"Felix's first customer. Fuck me, they're going to make a fortune."

"I doubt he'll be able to afford it," I say just as the heavy metal door grinds open a few inches.

Townsend props his hand against the building and leans his face toward the opening. "Hey, Mush. It's me."

"Who's with you?"

Tristan takes my hand and casually guides me behind him so his body is between me and the source of the sound.

"Got a case study for you. Don't worry. They're friends of mine."

The door doesn't move.

Case study. Friends.

Townsend's odd words ring through my head, trying to latch on to meaning and then vanishing when the door opens wider. Mushenko is short, barely my height. His hair is a wiry brown mass that hangs unstylishly over the tops of his ears. His lab coat is more gray than white and speckled with visible stains. His eyes jitter back and forth between Tristan and me as we file inside and into the darkness.

I jolt against Tristan when the door shuts behind us with a loud clang.

"Come in. This way." Mushenko shuffles ahead, leading us to a metal staircase illuminated in harsh white light from the second floor. "What brings you to town?"

"Thought I'd see what you were working on," Townsend says, his tone friendlier than normal.

Mushenko laughs and rushes up the last few steps.

The windows to the outside are covered with huge boards, but the second floor is bathed in light thanks to the dozen or so large fluorescents beaming down on the space.

"I have some new things I think you'll like," he says, navigating between rows of crowded tables, each one covered with laboratory equipment. Some look active, others not.

When we reach his desk, he pushes notebooks and papers across the surface until a handful of test tubes are revealed. They all seem the same, with strips of masking tape and handwritten scribble. I recognize the labeling system from Townsend's bag and shudder with the memory of being introduced to it for the first time.

Mushenko's smile grows broad. He holds one vial lengthwise between his finger and thumb and gives it a little shake. "I call this one the Abyss. A few drops of this will increase your lung capacity by twenty-five percent. Average lung volume for an adult male is about six liters. Bump that up to seven and a half. Makes a big difference on those long swims. Navy is showing some interest in that one." He gives it another shake before grabbing the next one. "Okay, and this. I think you'll like this. It's a lot like Sleeping Beauty but with some fun new twists."

Townsend glances over his shoulder at us. "Gives all the appearances of death without, you know, death."

I nod with a tight smile, like any of this is normal. But something about Mushenko's unfiltered enthusiasm almost makes me want to share it.

"Right. Same effects. Dramatically reduced heart rate, breathing becomes undetectable, subject goes limp as a ragdoll. The difference—" He punches his free hand into the air, pointer finger firmly extended. "Full consciousness."

Townsend's eyebrows lift up his forehead. "Interesting."

"I thought so. Just in case you want to fake it but still be part of the festivities."

He and Townsend share a laugh. When Tristan and I remain silent, Mushenko seems to break out of his show-and-tell trance, shifting his focus to us.

Townsend follows his gaze, landing on Tristan, a secretive look in his eye. "Remember Elysium Dream, Mush?"

Mushenko nods vigorously. "Of course. Was it useful for you?"

Fresh fury vibrates through me, but Tristan wills me silent with another wordless grasp of my hand.

Townsend pitches his thumb toward him. "If you ever wondered how it works, this one's living proof. Knocked out twenty-some years of memories. Blank slate except a few flashbacks from time to time."

Mushenko pauses a moment, seeming to take in this surprising new information. Then he springs forward. Eyes wide, he looks Tristan up and down like a museum artifact. "Fascinating," he says under his breath.

Tristan's tense grip on my hand spreads to the rest of him. His muscles are taut. His palm is hot against mine. Except what rolls off him feels more like panic than rage. "I'd like to talk to you, if you don't mind," he says.

His voice is deceivingly calm.

"Sure, sure. I'd love to take some samples if you don't mind." Mushenko waves him toward a nearby room. If Mushenko knew what the rest of us know about Tristan's abilities, he'd be wise to be concerned. But there's nothing but childlike curiosity awash on his features.

Only then does Tristan release me and follow behind the man who could be our only chance at bringing back the past we lost.

5

TRISTAN

My blood floods the tube, filling it in seconds. My normally steady, patient heart is racing. No amount of mental fortitude will slow it down being this close to the man who designed, or at least manipulated, the drug that wiped my memory. He seems harmless enough. So detached from the gravity of what he produces that he can hardly be blamed for the results. At least that's what I've been telling myself since we walked into this sad excuse for a lab.

"You say you get flashbacks?" Mushenko flickers his gaze up to mine a moment before removing the needle and capping the tube. "Here you go." He hands me a patch of gauze to hold against the pricked skin.

"Every once in a while. Nightmares usually. Except for one time, several of them hit me all at once. Back to back over a couple of days."

He frowns thoughtfully. "Was there something you did to trigger such a rush of them?"

"I was injected with a heavy dose of SP-131 after getting shot by a tranquilizer dart. Got me telling the truth. Also unlocked a shit ton of my memories."

He lowers onto a nearby stool. It squeaks under his weight. I can faintly hear the murmur of Townsend and Isabel in the other part of the lab, but I'm too eager to hear Mushenko's theories to let them distract me.

His gaze pings around the room, like he's connecting a series of invisible dots. When a long time goes by this way, I clear my throat, breaking his concentration. An irrational fear grips me as I work up the nerve to ask him what I truly need to know.

"Can you reverse it? Will enough SP-131 unlock the rest of my memories?"

He shakes his head. "I'm not sure. I don't usually"—he waves his palm in the air—"undo things. I work with a set of test results, usually tests that have gone wrong, admittedly, and then I use the data and alter the serums to satisfy other needs."

"Like forced amnesia."

For the first time since I've been in his presence, Mushenko has the decency to look tentative.

"I—I'm contracted to explore the possibilities. I've done important work."

"I don't care about your accolades. I need you to undo it. I need my memories back. How much is it going to take?"

The prospect of having them back is making my chest tight. It's irrational how much I crave them. I've survived so long without my past. My life can go on just fine, but none of that seems possible right now.

Mushenko rises, arms crossed, and begins to pace around the room. "I'm contracted by my employer. I don't really take on these kinds of assignments."

"You take Townsend's money."

He pauses and gives me a guilty stare. "Those are small exchanges. We have military contracts. I have important work—"

"I don't care if the Pope wants you to cure the blind." I stand. My next words are quiet, threatening, and precise. "You're going to reverse it. I can tell you get off on this shit. I'm throwing a fun problem on your lap. Work it out. Unfuck my brain, or you're going to have bigger, less fun problems on your hands. How much is it going to take?"

"It's not that simple. The work I do... I'm not paid for my precision. I throw a dart and try to get close to the target. I do some testing here. Minimal testing. They have a team that does the rest when it matters. I could try, but I can't promise you the results you want. I can't promise it'll go back to the way it was before the drug was administered."

I breathe through my nose, trying to control my heart rate and the rush of adrenaline coursing through me.

"How much, goddammit?"

His answering sigh is heavy with defeat. I've left him no other choice. "Ten thousand is fine."

"How long?"

He shrugs. "A few weeks, maybe."

"Make it a week and I'll double it."

He shakes his head again. "If I rush it and it's wrong, you won't care how much you paid."

What he's saying makes sense, but I'm not feeling rational right now. I'm feeling desperate. That's the kind of thing that gets a man killed. As driven as I am, I have to question if my memories are worth the risk. Do I trust that Mushenko's Frankenstein potion flowing into my bloodstream won't mess me up even more?

A voice inside me is screaming that I can't walk away without trying.

"Townsend knows how to reach me."

He nods, his energy a dim flicker next to what it had been moments ago.

"What do you know about Felix?"

He lifts his brows high enough that they disappear under his mop of hair. "I haven't worked with it. Not in its final form anyway. They send the winners to a different department. They don't make it here." He chuckles and gestures to the lab outside, an operation that can't be anywhere close to meeting regulations.

"Elysium Dream was an iteration of it, though."

"Years ago. No doubt it's come a very long way since it was given to you."

"Can you find out more about it?"

He opens his mouth to speak, but I cut him off before he can tell me no.

"You said they gave you the failed test results, right?"

"Sure. Some, not all. My God, there are thousands of failures. Tens of thousands."

"Then get your hands on the Felix tests. Surely you have some contacts who can scrape some up."

He licks his lips and cants his head back and forth a few times. "It's possible. It's a brand-new drug, though. It's a Rolls Royce next to anything Chalys has ever put out. Anything related to Felix will be highly sensitive. I'm not exactly"—he waves his hand around again—"you know, top of the food chain."

I walk to the door and place my hand on the knob. "Find me the antidote. Then find what you can on Felix. I'll make it worth your while."

Townsend leaves a large roll of bills with Mushenko and takes vials in return. We step out just as a train grinds loudly over the tracks and heads north, giving me a good idea.

"Take the train back," I say to Townsend. "We'll meet you in the city later."

I can't deal with Townsend's mouth right now. I need time to work things out. Refocus. Figure out our next steps.

"Fine. I have a little business to take care of anyway."

"You on the job?"

He grins at my challenge. "Working for myself now, Red. No one calling the shots but me. Nice try, though."

I don't completely believe him, but I'm too distracted to care. Townsend strolls casually away. The dynamic shifts instantly, and I'm grateful for the break. Not just for Isabel's sake, but the sit-down with Mushenko still has my thoughts in a tangle.

We get to the car. The second the doors close, Isabel begins.

"What did he say to you? You were in there a while. Can he help?"

"I'm not sure."

The possibility of reversing what Townsend gave me is more than a passing hope. It's a loud and all-consuming prospect that changes the shape of everything else around it. The sudden unsteadiness I feel is disturbing and dangerous. It'll be weeks before I have any answers. I have to put this away. Banish it from my thoughts and carry on.

"Well, what did he say?" Isabel presses, making the task impossible.

I start the engine and rest back in the seat. I circle my hands around the steering wheel, letting it chill through my fingers. Isabel's palm gently covers one. She's warmth and affection when I'm doing everything I can to strip myself of the emotions terrorizing me.

"Are you okay?"

No.

But I owe her a better answer than that.

"Mushenko isn't sure if he can reverse it. He's going to try. And while he's at it, he's going to work on getting some files on Felix. Anything that might point to faulty trials. By the time he digs anything up, it could be too late. I don't know."

I don't meet her eyes. She draws her touch up to my

shoulder, then across my chest until she reaches the place over my heart. I close my eyes and grip the wheel tighter. I feel her body shift, her heat at my side, her comfort and her love warming the places in me trying to go cold.

"It's going to be all right," she whispers. "Whatever happens, we have each other."

I shake my head, suddenly furious with her comforting words and whatever they're masking. "Right. All of you and a fraction of me."

"Don't say that." She does nothing to hide the hurt in her voice.

My eyes flash open as her hope clashes violently with mine. I twist to face her, breaking the embrace. "That's what we're talking about though, isn't it? Giving you back pieces of me that you wish you still had. And if this doesn't work, worst case, Mushenko will make soup out of what's left of my brain. Or maybe nothing will change at all. And then there's a slim chance that he'll get it right and I'll be the old Tristan again. Except nothing's ever going to be the same, no matter what."

Her warmth slips away. It's agony in the wake of my words—words that cut me just as deeply. She looks out the window, fingertips pressed tightly to her lips. I resist the urge to tug her back and apologize. But what good would it do? I've already landed the blow.

Her voice is shaky and soft when she finally speaks. "Selfishly, I wish you could remember us and how we were before. But some people waste their whole lives wishing for more than they have. I don't want to spend the rest of my life wishing for you when I already have you."

We seem caught there for a long time, somewhere between grim acceptance and devastating loss. I'm no closer to working it out when her phone vibrates. She retrieves it from her jacket and stares at the screen too long.

"Who is it?"

"It's Blake Landon."

ISABEL

"Why exactly did you bring this to me?"

Landon's pointed question serves as his abrupt greeting. I'm still in disbelief that he's reached out. I was beginning to think he'd accepted the information on Pope for his own benefit and I'd never hear from him again.

I take a few seconds to collect my response, trying to sound steadier than I feel. "I'm looking for something specific. I thought you could help me if I helped you."

"What are you looking for?"

I swallow hard. *Be careful*, I remind myself. "Does this mean you're going to help me?"

"You can tell me what you want, or I can hang up. I'm not putting my ass on the line unless you want to come clean with me about what's going on."

I shoot a sideways look to Tristan, who's staring at me intently. His hands are still wrapped around the steering wheel like a vise. Landon's sharp tone is a slash through my best intentions to take care in what I reveal, lest I put us in even more danger. Because he's listening. He's actually considering it.

"I was looking for financial records for Chalys Pharmaceuticals. There are some in the file I was given, but not enough."

"Why are they important?"

"Chalys is involved in something…big. I was hoping to make some financial connections to other people who are involved."

"Elaborate."

Shit. Here goes nothing.

"They're releasing a new drug called felixedrine, otherwise known as Felix, and branding it as a cure for opioid addiction. The cornerstone of their marketing plan is to flood the streets with illicit drugs and create a wave of overdoses so devastating that Felix will be in every headline across the country as the answer to the crisis. It's…terrible."

A long pause. I pick at a frayed thread on my jeans and hope to hell I've piqued Landon's interest once more. The threat of him hanging up is real and something I'm willing to avoid at nearly any cost. Mushenko may be able to dig up some dirt on the dark side of Felix, if one exists, but he's useless when it comes to the bigger plan.

"Why do you care?" he asks, breaking the tense silence.

I've asked myself that same question so many times since we got here. Even as Townsend drew comparisons between me and a more philanthropic, less murder-oriented Jay, I had to ask myself again why I cared so damn much. With the money from Halo in my account and the man I love within reach, somewhere deep down I still believe we can find a way to disappear forever, even if Tristan doubts we can get away with it. Instead, Felix has become my problem. The Boswells are another day closer to executing their plan, and Company Eleven has to be stopped. Who else is going to do it if not us?

I close my eyes and exhale a quiet sigh.

"Twenty years ago, they killed my sister, and for the past two months, they've been trying to kill me because my family got too close to figuring out what they were doing. Not to mention they're about to facilitate the deaths of God knows how many people with this plan."

When he's quiet for too long, I continue.

"If that weren't enough, the family that runs Chalys is part of a dangerous organization. The underground kind that carries out unspeakable favors and can pull strings at every level to make something like this happen. I'm sure they're behind this, but I need more information to find out how far this goes if I have any chance of stopping it."

"How did you find out about this organization?"

"I can't go into all of that with you right now. But I can tell you that a man named Simon Pelletier is the ringleader. It's a small circle—only about a dozen people who carry enough power in different industries to create a web of connections that's unrivaled."

"And you think you can foil this plan of theirs?"

I gnaw on my lip and let the doubt in his tone mingle with my own fears that this is a fool's errand. "I have to try. Wouldn't you?"

He doesn't answer but says, "You think Pope's involved with them?"

"I think he's part of the organization. I'm almost positive. His name came up along with a few others. Ramsey Paulson. Davis Knight. And the Boswell family, of course. Kristopher owns Chalys, but his son Vince has been involved too." I trail off, not sure how to explain that Vince isn't in the picture anymore.

Landon curses under his breath loud enough for me to hear, but I'm not certain I was meant to.

"Excuse me?"

"This is un-fucking-believable," he says.

I mentally skim over everything I've just laid out, unsure what I could have said to suddenly upset him. He seemed so measured when we met. Calculating but sincere. Something's different now. There's an edge to the way he's talking, like something snapped.

"Is there something wrong?"

"I'll get back to you."

"But—"

The call ends. I lower the phone and stare down at the black screen, momentarily stunned by the severed connection after all I just told him. Short of confessing whose lives have ended because of all of this—and how and why—Blake Landon now knows *everything*.

"Is he going to help?"

Tristan's voice pulls me out of my shock a little. I shake my head, not sure if I should feel defeated or hopeful. Or worse, scared that I just told a complete stranger our whole predicament.

"I have no idea."

"We have to do something," I say.

Tristan pushes his hands deeper into his pockets. The steady breeze coming off the ocean whips his dark hair around messily, but he doesn't seem to notice or care as we walk a long stretch of seaside.

I couldn't stand the idea of being cooped up in the apartment with everything that's happened today. I'm too wrapped up in my thoughts. Too worried about Tristan being wrapped up in his. I can almost see the struggle in his expression, but I feel helpless to bring him out of it.

The prospect of him getting his memories back is too overwhelming to consider. I wish he held more than a few snapshots of memory of us. I think he wants that too. But the more we endure together since he's come back into my life, the less I care about the past. It hurts and it haunts me, but what truly matters is that I have him now and I'm never letting go. I could say it a hundred times. I'm just not sure he'd believe it.

"We're falling into the same pattern Halo was. Do you realize that?" He shoots me a critical stare.

I blink against the sting of the wind in my eyes, forcing my thoughts back to the bigger issues looming. "How's that?"

"I mean Martine and your mother spent years trying to figure out ways to cause trouble for Chalys. Halo picked at the edges, barely penetrating the Boswells' bubble."

"They got close enough to trigger the hit on me."

"After years of trying to hit a nerve. My point is that they weren't aggressive enough."

I'm afraid to ask the former assassin to explain how aggressive he thinks we ought to be. I know he's been waiting to put Kristopher Boswell's name in his little red book, but now there's information we need first.

"What do you suggest?"

"I don't know exactly, but it might be a lot easier to get information from the inside than the outside. Otherwise we're sitting around waiting for someone to drop info into our lap, and who knows if we can even trust it."

We walk in silence for a while. He's right, of course. We're relying on resources outside the organization, and every time we hit a wall, I can't help but worry that we're running out of time. Mateus has a line into the Company now, but he may not know enough until it's too late. We have options. They're just dangerous and probably not high on Tristan's list of last resorts.

"So what do we do?"

Tristan's pace slows to a stop. He turns to face me. Waves roll and crash behind him. Sunrays peek through the cloudy sky and glint off the endless sea. The picturesque backdrop doesn't seem to match the situation we're up against. It's ugly and dark and far from peaceful.

"Breaking into their offices isn't going to be easy. Security in the building will be tight. I'm good at getting past things like that, but I'm not sure it's worth the risk," he says. "But the Boswell estate is close. About a half hour north of here. Until Mateus can clue us in to how the Company is involved, Kristopher is our best bet. I can scope the place out tonight. Figure out what I'll need to get in undetected."

My heart starts hammering. I know Tristan well enough to guess what he has in mind, and I don't like it.

"Then what? Go in with guns blazing?" I can't hide the panic in my voice.

He draws a hand along his rough jaw. "Not unless the situation calls for it."

My thoughts spin. There has to be another way. One that doesn't involve Tristan's lethal skills right out of the gate.

"How about we just get an invitation, walk right in, and find what we're looking for? Wouldn't that be easier?"

His body becomes perfectly still. A jogger whizzes by us. Nothing breaks Tristan's unmoving focus on me. "Whatever you're thinking right now..."

"Kolt can get me in. No systems to bypass. No one needs to get hurt."

"I'm not convinced that's how it'll go."

I force down a frustrated groan. "If Kolt wanted me dead, he would have set it up our first meeting and you know it."

"I'm not as worried about that as someone else in the house knowing you're there when you shouldn't be. Sorry, but I'm not going to rely on Kolt to protect you. He's—"

"He's what, Tristan?"

The corner of his lips lift at my challenge. The tiny movement chips off a little of my anxiety.

"Well, he's not me."

He closes the small space between us and twines his fingers through my hair. My breath catches when I can feel his heat and smell the soap on his skin. I'm not sure he'll ever stop affecting me this way.

"He won't kill for you," he says, his voice raspy and low. "He won't die for you. And he'll always love himself more than he loves you. He'll never know how to be anything else."

I stare into his eyes, letting his words wash over me. His hatred for Kolt is never in short supply, but for once, I don't think that's what this is about.

I'll kill for you. I'll die for you. I'll always love you more than I love myself. I'll never know how to be anything else.

The underlying meaning sinks in deeper, like truth in my bones. I believe it so fully that I struggle to take in my next breath. If he can love me this much without our past…

I lean into his gentle touch. "I know."

"Then let's find a way to do this without giving me a heart attack."

I absently fiddle with the collar on his jacket. "What if you could come with somehow? I'm not sure if Kolt will be as receptive if he knows you're there, but if you were close… You could be close enough to get in if there was trouble."

His expression turns thoughtful. He pulls away, and we begin walking back toward the car. "You really think he's going to let you just come in and poke around? No reservations?"

I shrug. "It's possible. Can't hurt to ask."

I don't voice the possibility that the more hope I give Kolt about our impossible relationship, the more likely he may be to help me. Of course, Tristan's not stupid. He knows this too, but I worry saying it aloud will dash the possibility of moving forward my way.

"Fine. Ask." His tone is oddly resigned.

I hesitate, making certain I heard him right. "And if he says yes?"

"If he says yes, we'll make a plan together." Our gazes meet briefly, knowingly.

"He won't want you there," I hedge.

"I don't really care what he wants. I'll be there."

6

TRISTAN

Fried seafood and the sounds of kids laughing down near Rick's Fish House float through the air as the docks come into view.

Isabel swings our linked hands absently. "It's so pretty down here at sunset. I can't wait for summer."

I don't voice my disagreement out loud. If I could make time stand still, I might. Summer means changes. I like this rhythm we've fallen into and would do almost anything to preserve it for as long as possible.

I take her down to this seafood shack on the river every time I scrounge up enough extra cash. Things are getting more serious. I've never felt this way about anyone. Isabel's stitched herself into my life. Hell, she's singlehandedly holding it together since my mom died. I'm starting to wonder what forever could look like. Forever with someone like Isabel comes with different pressures. She deserves something stable. Right now I'm just pretending to have it together. Maybe one day I really will.

"Come on. Let's feed the fish first," she says with an infectious kind of enthusiasm.

I grin and let her lead us to the rickety fish-food dispenser. I put a few quarters in it, and we fill our hands with little pellets. The kids at the end of the dock come barreling toward us, screaming and laughing as they chase each other.

"Whoa!" I jump back to let the little tornadoes speed by.

Isabel laughs and starts walking to the end where they just were. We sit on the edge. Our feet dangle just above the water, and our faces wave in the reflection. She tosses a pellet a few feet out and we wait. Seconds later, a fish claims it at the surface and disappears again in the murky depths.

"Do you think you'll ever want kids?" She tosses another out casually.

I pretend to focus on what the fish are doing when I'm really scrambling for a decent answer. "I haven't thought a lot about it. What about you?"

She's quiet for a while. "I think I do."

I chuckle. "You hesitated."

She smiles. "I don't know. I guess I worry about what kind of mom I would be."

Isabel is the most kind, giving, and thoughtful person I've ever known. There are no doubts in my mind. "I think you'd be a really good mom."

"Thanks." She smiles again, but it doesn't reach her eyes.

I wonder if she's thinking about her sister, whose death seemed to cast a dark cloud over her own childhood in so many ways.

I figure most of the upper-middle-class kids in Alexandria have hyper parents like hers, but lately I'm starting to think it's worse for Isabel. I've never known anyone to be so damn good and stifled at the same time.

"Do you think things would have been a lot different for you if Mariana hadn't gotten sick?"

She tilts her head to the side thoughtfully. "Having a parent who's terrified every time you leave the house isn't exactly normal."

I toss another pellet out. "You know better than to put your kids through that."

The band at Rick's starts warming up, and the sky gets darker. We can barely see the fish anymore, but I can tell she's not in a rush to leave. For Isabel's sake, I force myself to dig deeper. If she's being honest and baring her feelings and vulnerabilities, I owe it to her to do the same. As her friend and her lover… As the man who wants to earn a lifetime of her love.

I sprinkle the last of my pellets into the water and think about how to start. "My parents met when my mom was in nursing school."

She gazes up at me, curiosity plain in her eyes. I've never talked about my dad, always sidestepped the subject, and was grateful when she never pressed me.

"As soon as she finished, he moved out west. She never told him she was pregnant. She said she knew it would be better if it was just us. I wish I could blame him for being a deadbeat, you know? But I can't blame my mom for making the call she did either. It sucks growing up with half a family, but it is what it is. I hope I'd make the right choice if it were me."

She leans her head on my shoulder. "I think you would."

Something warms inside me. It starts in my stomach and reaches all the way to the tips of my fingers. It's more than a fleeting vision of what it might be like to have a family with her. It's that she thinks I could be capable of getting it right, with her or anyone. No one's ever had that kind of faith in me. Not since Mom left. Even then, she was so busy making ends meet, it's not like we had time to talk much about what my life might look like. What kind of man I might become.

The band gets going for real, so we head over. We eat and laugh. The Christmas lights strung around the deck make Isabel's skin glow. I touch her every chance I can, addicted to the contact and the reciprocation of affection that I only get from her.

For a long moment, all I can do is stare at her in awe and disbelief. I can't believe she's real. I can't believe she's mine. Right now she really is. God, maybe she could be forever.

Her eyes twinkle when she catches me staring. "What?"

That warm feeling hits me again. Warmth and energy. Hope. Isabel.

"Do you think you could ever marry someone like me?"

Her smile softens, but her eyes don't change. They're beautiful and steady. I should be terrified. I should make a joke so she won't think I'm dead serious. But all I can do is wait for her to answer me.

Her lips curl up again. "Yeah. I really think I could."

My eyes flash open. I take a few quick breaths, swallow hard, and blink rapidly into consciousness. Eager to jar myself out of the dream, I check the clock on the table. We slept in. Well, I did. Isabel's side of the bed is empty, which is almost a relief. Right now I'm not me. At least I'm not the

Tristan she's used to waking up to. Until the dream recedes, I'm eighteen and lovesick. Deeply, hopelessly in love.

Yeah, that's not you at all, Casanova.

I rub the heels of my hands against my eyes with a groan because my wheels are already spinning too fast.

I haven't had a flashback in a while. The drugs Townsend gave me are long out of my system. This wasn't one of my usual dreams either. This vision was new. Rich and vivid and already threatening to inspire an emotional excavation I'm nowhere ready for. I don't have to wonder if it was real. I know it was. My sparse memories of Isabel have taken on a texture that make them different from the twisted fiction in my nightmares.

Maybe seeing Mushenko yesterday triggered it. Some subconscious need to know more, to hold on to memories Isabel would want me to have—memories like spring nights on the river in Baltimore, dreaming about what kind of life we could have together one day.

If we weren't so committed to this new path, going to war with the Company and anyone else behind this sordid plan, I think I'd find a way to take her away from it all. Maybe they'd let us disappear and we could find some remote patch of earth to call our own. We could have a life. Maybe not what she envisioned all those years ago, but something a lot better than this.

I'm sending a lamb into the lion's den. Again.

Mere hours from Isabel's request, Kolt arranged for her

to visit the Boswell family's sprawling estate in Manchester-by-the-Sea, a small but affluent town. With my support, she took up the invitation and put the plan in motion.

I must be deranged. But it's worked before. I've taken advantage of her allure to bait the enemy. I've trusted in her natural abilities. I've let her go, begrudgingly…willingly. More often unwillingly. And I swear every time has felt like a death-defying leap into the dark and terrifying unknown. I can't lose her. But if the risk gets us closer to keeping her safe forever, I'm willing to leap once more.

Of course I wouldn't have minded breaking in, guns blazing, but that isn't the plan this time. Once more, I'll have to trust Isabel to hold her own. I'm not about to let Kolt alone with her without eyes or ears on the situation, though.

"You'll be able to hear everything with this?"

Isabel's voice is soft and tentative, solidifying my already ramped-up commitment to keep her safe going into this.

I reach across the car console and take the tiny audio transmitter she's holding. I part her jacket, slip my fingers under the edge of her shirt, and clip the device low on her bra strap. I make a silent vow that if Kolt gets anywhere close to the wire, we'll have bigger problems than whether or not I can hear them. I clench my teeth and try to force those scenarios out of my head for the time being. He behaved last time. He better fucking behave this time.

"If the house is empty like he says it will be, there shouldn't be any background noise. The signal should be clear. And if it's not, I won't be far away."

Isabel lets out a nervous exhale. "It'll be fine."

I withdraw the Glock from the inside of my jacket and hand it to her. "You remember how to use this?"

She reaches for it, slowly and carefully. I don't miss her faint grimace once it's in her hands.

"Yeah."

"Let's go over it one more time."

She shakes her head. "No, I've got it. I mean, hopefully I don't need to use it, but I can."

"All right. Good."

We don't talk about how she couldn't pull the trigger on Boswell the night he beat the hell out of her. And we don't talk about the tiny blades she used to slice through Bones, ending his menacing life. We don't say any of it, but I can tell it's filling up her thoughts.

"Keep it casual. You know how to work him to get what you need. You did fine last time."

She blinks up at me and her lips part. "You think so?"

I force a tight smile. She defied me and put herself in unnecessary danger to meet with Kolt. I don't exactly want to encourage more of that kind of behavior, but all things considered, she handled him well.

"You gave him just enough hope to tell you everything he did. But not so much that he felt like he could put his hands on you. At least from where I was standing, it looked like a pretty good play."

She smiles a little. "Thanks."

"Just stick to the plan. Find out what else he knows. Then try to get access to Kristopher's office. Take photos of anything that looks like it can be helpful. Then get the hell out of there."

"Easy enough," she says with a lightness that feels forced but hopeful.

I scan the landscape from our vantage point down the long, winding driveway. The house is lit up like a work of art, but there hasn't been any noticeable movement since we arrived. "You're sure the place is empty?"

"Kolt said his mother was out of town for work."

"Where?"

"Paris."

I nod. "What about Kristopher?"

She hesitates. When our gazes meet again, I catch a hint of worry there.

"He didn't say. He just said we'd have the place to ourselves."

The lack of detail gives me pause. I don't expect Kolt wants to share his time with Isabel with family members who want her dead. But the fact remains that they *do* want her dead, and she's about to show up on the family doorstep.

"Gut check. Do you still feel good about this?"

She takes a deep breath. "Yeah. I'm good."

The digital clock on the dash reads eight o'clock. Time's up. I wrap the earpiece around my ear and turn it up until I can hear faint static.

"Give me a head start. I'll be close. If you need me to come to you, just give me a signal. Don't hesitate."

"Got it."

Her voice echoes in my ear, loud and clear. With that, I step out of the car and head up the drive. Unlike Isabel, I'm not going to be knocking on the front door, so I veer off the path and creep along the periphery, keeping to the shadows of the woodlands that line the edge of the property. I hurry past the carriage house, my steps nearly silent as I cross the cobblestone drive. Ocean waves crash in the distance.

I press the earpiece tighter against my ear to make sure I can still hear Isabel. Just the steady sound of her breathing. She's walking.

I pause when I get to a side door. A flood light switches on, illuminating the whole area and me. I flatten against the side of the house and wait. Kolt won't be checking the cameras that I'm certain cover every entrance.

"Ringing the doorbell," she says calmly.

Quickly I insert a pick in the lock, working it back and forth until it finally releases. A second later, I can hear the security system disarming beep on the other side of the door. I'm in.

As I step inside the dark entryway, a crystal-clear layout of the house projects onto my brain. When we were killing time waiting for the meetup, I was able to track down city records with the blueprints from the original construction. The bad news is there are plenty of places to get lost in the thirteen thousand square feet of oceanside mansion. The good news is I've got the whole map memorized.

Just as I start to speculate where Kolt will take her first, I realize Isabel isn't saying anything. Did I lose her? I push the earpiece tighter into my ear.

My stomach knots with unease.

She sucks in a sharp breath.

"Hi," she finally says. A long pause. "I… I'm here to see Kolt."

Shit.

I whip out my gun and am already halfway out the door when the sound of Kolt's rushed words fill my ear.

"Eliza, thanks. I've got it. You heading home now?"

"Yes, sir. Unless you need me for anything else."

"No, we're good. Have a good night." A long pause and the sound of a door shutting. "Sorry about that. Eliza helps around the house. She was supposed to leave earlier, but something came up."

"It's okay. Just startled me a little."

The relief in Isabel's voice works its way through me. If I were a praying man, I might send up a few words of thanks right now. Instead, I slip back inside, and the door clasps shut just as the system arms again with a faint beep. No one else gets in or out until this is over.

I make my way slowly and silently through the hallways that will bring me closer to the center of the house. Then Kolt's voice is in my ear again, louder this time.

"Isabel…"

He's too close to her. I don't have eyes on her yet, but somehow I just know it.

Then the abrasive sound of clothing brushing roughly against the mic. Movement. Isabel's voice, fast and muffled, but I swear I can make out the words.

"Kolt. No."

ISABEL

I was already on edge before the housekeeper answered the

door. I'm not ready for Kolt's arms around me. His desperate embrace. His breath in my hair. His hands grasping me tighter to him. I keep my arms wrapped around my torso, terrified he'll feel the gun that's tucked into my jacket. My panic climbs, but I try hard to tamp it down.

My brain convinces my body to relax and pretend for Kolt the way I intended to tonight. He seems to pick up on it, pressing his nose against my neck and inhaling.

"I've wanted to hold you this way for so long. So long. Jesus, Isabel, do you have any idea how agonizing this has been?"

"I missed you too," I lie, even though there was a time long ago when I did miss him. I missed his easy friendship and the simpler lives we had. That was before I knew the truth.

I count the seconds we stay this way, wondering how much more I can stand. He was always a gentleman. Too eager at times, sure. But he never crossed the line. He never made me feel threatened. But things are different now. Maybe he's different too. All I know is I don't want his hands on me a minute more.

Finally he pulls away, gradually, one agonizing inch at a time until I can finally breathe again. I worry he can read the unease.

He licks his lips nervously. "Sorry. I just missed you so damn much. I'm sorry..."

"It's okay. I get it. But being here... This isn't easy for me."

His features pinch with understanding, as if he's just

remembered the life-and-death circumstances that have come between us since the last time he held me that way.

He takes my hand. "Come on. The coast is clear, I promise. You're safe here."

I follow him deeper into the house. Our footsteps along the marble floors echo off the walls and impossibly high ceilings. I can't help but marvel at the opulence of the house, which matches the grand elegance of its exterior. DC has its fair share of sprawling estates, but I didn't have many occasions to grace their halls.

Kolt leads me straight back to a large open room with wall-to-wall windows that overlook an enormous deck and a sandy beach just beyond.

"Wow."

I move closer to the glass and peer out at the dark waves crashing loudly against the shore. Kolt switches on a couple of lamps, illuminating more of the room. The ceilings are vaulted, and the woodwork is whitewashed. Muted watercolors decorate the walls. Everything is light and airy, designed for comfort, but probably cost a small fortune.

He moves to the bar casually, like he's completely comfortable in this space. This is his world. The one he secretly hoped I could have been a part of—as his girlfriend but maybe one day something more. The prospect seems beyond ridiculous now.

"Wine?" He lifts a bottle of red up by its neck.

I don't answer right away. I want to get what I need and get out of here. The house may be empty, but I was telling Kolt the truth before. Being here is uncomfortable and not without risk, despite his assurances. Then I remember Tristan's advice. Play the game.

"Sure," I say with a small smile. I shrug out of my jacket and drape it carefully over an expensive wingback chair, resigning myself to stay awhile.

Kolt pours us two glasses and glides confidently to the middle of the room. He hands me the delicate glass. We have nothing to toast to, so we drink quietly. He watches me over the rim of his glass. When he lowers it again, his eyes are thoughtful. I hold my breath, worried he may try to touch me again, but he's perfectly still.

"It's strange to have you here," he utters softly. "I don't know why. I pictured it plenty of times. Always wondered if you'd be impressed by all this."

"It's kind of hard not to be."

His smirk is filled with arrogant pride. "Come on. Let's sit down."

I'd rather get on with asking him where his grandfather's office is, but I follow him toward the velvety gray sectional and sit out of arm's length. The distance gives me little relief. His gaze never leaves me. His longing seems to fill the room. I need to stay in control.

I clear my throat. "Thanks for meeting with me."

"I'm really glad you reached out. Last time was hardly a reunion."

This isn't a reunion. At least not the way he wants it to be. I decide now is the time to change the subject and move right on to business.

"Have you heard anything more about Felix?"

His easy expression hardens. The change is subtle, but I notice.

"Not really. Mom's been pretty distracted. My uncle's still missing. She won't call the police and risk bad press, though. As soon as they know he's gone, they'll issue a missing person's report, and you can kiss the headlines she really wants goodbye."

I do my best to play along. "Do you still think your family could have had something to do with it?"

"I don't think so. They hired a private investigator in Miami to retrace his steps while he was there. The last time anyone saw him, he was partying on a friend's yacht. Then nothing. No trace of him. That was the last report we got."

I drink my wine, hoping to buy time without responding.

"I heard about what he did to you, Isabel."

I look down, refusing to meet his eyes, hoping he can't read the truth in mine.

"He told me how you fought back and how Tristan left him there in the hotel. You humiliated him, you know. It made everything worse."

The room seems to grow too warm. I hate that Kolt knows what Vince did. I hate everything about that night. The hesitation that could have gotten me killed. The murder in Tristan's eyes when he intervened. Then the gut-wrenching disappointment when he finally saw what Vince had done to me.

"Do you know where he is?" Kolt presses.

A frightening pang of guilty fear hits me, like maybe he

knows the truth. But he can't know.

"No." I wince like I'm stung by the implication.

"I figured you might want your pound of flesh after that."

His gaze is steady and assessing, making my skin hot and my palms sweat.

"Trust me, I've had my hands full with other matters. Is that why you wanted to bring me here? To interrogate me about your uncle?"

"No. I wanted to see you. Be with you."

I set my wine down and pace toward the windows, needing more distance. I keep my back to him, cursing inwardly when I hear him rise and take slow steps toward me. He hovers inches away. *Back off. Stop pushing me.*

He touches my shoulder. I break the contact as I turn.

"This isn't a date. I'm running for my life. People are going to die if we don't do something. Don't you get that?"

"I get it, but I thought tonight was about us."

I rear back a step. "*Us?*"

He sighs heavily. "Isabel, damn, just give me a chance. Haven't we been through enough? Why do you keep fighting it?"

My jaw falls. "A chance?"

"I told you I loved you, and you said 'make me believe it.' Well, that's what I'm doing. Maybe I wasn't the greatest boyfriend back in Rio. Everything that's happened since then has only solidified how I feel about you, though. I know what I want now, and I know what I can offer you."

"You said you would help me—"

"And you knew I'd want more." His pleading quickly turns into something else—something entitled.

I swallow hard and cross my arms. "You're not asking for a chance."

"A night with you. A chance to trust you again. You want me to give you the keys to the castle so you can tear my family apart? I'll throw it all away for you, but not unless I know you're *with* me."

"You reached out to *me*. Don't twist this like I'm manipulating you for my own selfish needs."

"But you are, aren't you?"

"I…"

The lies I should tell him die in my throat. He's right. I'm here to use him for one reason, and I don't know how to convince him otherwise. I'm losing ground.

I try to gain more distance between us, but he crowds me until my back hits the glass. He's close. Too close. I recognize the hunger in his eyes. That edge where his self-control becomes thin.

"Kolt… You said you'd take whatever I could give you."

"I lied," he says, bringing his lips to mine too quickly for me to react.

I make a sound of protest that's muffled between our mouths. He kisses me with bruising force, pressing his body against me so I can feel the entire length of him. When I try to push him away, he circles my wrists and pins them to the glass with a thud.

My instincts are rioting. Everything Noam taught me is itching to release. But something holds me back. If I fight

Kolt off, I'll be making an enemy out of him when I need an ally. Someone on the inside…

I force myself to relax and reach for a time when I could have felt something other than panic with his mouth on me. As I do, he softens his grip and glides his touch down my arms. Before I can stop him, he's palming my chest possessively. He tears his lips from mine. His gaze falls to where he holds a handful of my shirt in his fist. His breathing picks up rapidly.

"You're wearing a fucking wire?"

All traces of lust and longing have vanished. His eyes are round with alarm. "Who are you working for? Did your mom put you up to this?" He tears the device off and throws it across the room, baring his teeth as he does.

I rush to think of what to say that will turn this around, but everything is happening so fast. Nothing about Kolt has been measured since I walked in the door—not his passion nor his patience. I worry his temper won't be either.

"That's not it. Kolt, please—"

"Did you think you could walk in here, take what you wanted, and then betray me?" When he reaches for me again, I flinch away, but he's too close to evade. He cups his hand behind my neck, moving me so our faces are inches apart. Our ragged breaths mingle. "I would have given you everything," he rasps. "Just go. Get the fuck out of my house."

I don't know if it's too late to ride out the storm with him and still get what I came for. I could tell him the truth, but explaining the wire means explaining that Tristan's still solidly in my life, which isn't bound to earn me any more favor.

As I ready myself to say goodbye to him for the last time, a shadowy figure moves in my periphery. That quickly, it's gone. Kolt's imposing posture doesn't match his words. His body still towers over mine, blocking my view, as if he's waiting for me to change his mind.

We don't have time for that because the next thing I hear is Tristan's voice.

"Don't move."

7

TRISTAN

Eliminating him would be so easy. A heady rush of relief. Too bad Isabel is on the other side of his skull.

He has her pushed against the windows the same way he had her pushed against her apartment building in Rio the night I was supposed to kill her. If she'd given in to him then, they'd both be dead. There's no doubt about it.

He stiffens when the cold metal of my gun touches the back of his neck. The fine hairs stand up there. I can smell his fear. Part of me comes alive—the part I'm not sure I'll ever be able to truly bury, no matter how many days I spend with Isabel, no matter how much light she shines on my darkness.

"Back away. Slowly," I say.

After a prolonged moment, he does, creating enough

space for Isabel to escape the cage of his arms. Her lips are pink and her clothes are disheveled from Kolt pawing at her. My nostrils flare.

"Turn around," I growl.

The second I meet his eyes, I pistol whip him across the face. He cries out loudly and doubles over, pressing against the red gash the strike drew across his cheek.

When he pulls his hand back, his fingertips are stained with blood. "Shit. I'm bleeding."

If he only realized how little satisfaction that gives me. This small punishment barely takes the edge off my rage.

"If I had my way, you'd be bleeding out. Look at me."

He awkwardly straightens his crouch enough to look me in the eye. I've never liked him. I haven't even been able to muster the faintest empathy for him through all this. Now I know why. I think back to his posturing when we were first introduced at Isabel's parents' house. He had no idea who he was dealing with, and I had no idea how truly pathetic he could be.

"Now you're going to take me to your grandfather's office."

He swallows hard and parts his lips to speak. "I… He doesn't really—"

I grab him by the collar and yank him toward me. My face is squarely in his, the muzzle of my gun pressed into the hollow of his cheek. He makes a whimpering sound that makes me hate him even more.

I can see Isabel in the corner of my eye. If Kolt does what he's told, I may let him live. But I'm done fucking around. The second he put his hands on her, he changed the plan.

My next words are deep and deliberate so he has no excuse not to fully absorb or heed them.

"From this point forward, I'm not going to ask you anything twice. I ask you once, you comply, or the conversation is over. Do you understand what I'm telling you?"

He starts breathing harder. If I were more capable of compassion, I might even feel sorry for the way I'm humiliating him right now. It's just not possible. I hate him too thoroughly.

"It's upstairs. I can show you."

I release my hold and shove him away with the tip of the gun. "That's more like it."

He starts walking quickly. Isabel and I follow him up a grand staircase and down a long hallway. The walls are lined with family portraits and expensive art.

He slows in front of a closed door, his hand still pressed against his cheek. "This is it."

"Open it," I order.

"I can't. It's locked. I already tried to get in here before."

Annoyed, I tuck my gun away and jimmy the lock in a matter of seconds. The door springs open.

The sound of someone's rough coughing echoes down the hall. No one moves. The coughing goes on and finally fades into silence.

I pin my stare on Kolt. "Who else is here?"

He goes pale when I lift my gun to his forehead,

threatening him to make me ask him again.

His voice quivers when he answers. "My grandfather."

Isabel gasps. "Kristopher?"

He flashes a worried look her way. If he thought she was betraying him, the tables have officially turned. Even better, the plan has officially shifted into my area of expertise.

"I guess you'd better introduce us," I say, more than ready to make sure Company Eleven is down a man before I leave.

Kolt lifts his hands pleadingly. "No. Please. He's really sick."

"Isabel, stay here. See if you can find anything." I motion Kolt down the hall with my gun. "Let's go."

Isabel slips past me without a word and goes right for the filing cabinets. I'm relieved when she doesn't question me. Something like giddy anticipation bubbles through me as Kolt starts walking down the hall toward his grandfather's room. I haven't thought about the ledger in a long time, but suddenly I'm more than ready to scratch Kristopher Boswell's name in it right under Vince's. I shouldn't be keeping a record, and I shouldn't savor the idea of taking a life. That chapter of my life is over. But some part of me has relished the last few entries more than any of the rest. Unlike the others, they have meaning.

The door is ajar when we arrive at it. I can hear faint wheezing inside. Kolt pushes the door wide, trembling as he does. The glow from the outdoor lights filters in through the curtains, illuminating a man's figure in the center of a large bed, his body covered by a thin quilt. The fabric folds softly around the outline of his frail body. I step closer. An oxygen tank chugs rhythmically by his side, feeding into the long tubes wound over his ears and into his nostrils. His eyes are closed and his head is turned to the side in sleep. This is my target.

"Please."

Kolt's worried whisper distracts me from the impact of this discovery. I turn and gesture toward the man. "That's Kristopher Boswell?"

He nods, his expression pained. "He's been sick for a while. I know you think he's mixed up in all of this, and at some point he probably was, but I promise you, this isn't his fight anymore."

Fucking hell. I jerk my head, motioning us out of the room.

"You told Isabel the house would be empty. Why did you lie?"

"My grandfather's nurse usually stays over when my mom's out of town. I gave Eliza the night off when I knew Isabel was coming. It was the only way to bring her here without anyone finding out."

I glance through the doorway again at the unmoving man. "How long has he been this way?"

"He's been bedridden for a few months."

"Cancer?"

"Hereditary emphysema. He didn't get symptoms until recently. Then he ignored them until he collapsed in the office one day. It's been a fast decline since we found out. His liver is shot. It's one thing after another. They don't think he has a lot of time."

"Who knows about this?"

Kolt pauses. "Only the people who need to know. With everything that's been going on, they couldn't risk the bad—"

"The bad press. Of course."

Isabel pops out of the office with a manila folder pressed to her chest. "Is everything okay?"

I walk briskly in her direction. "It's fine. I'll explain later. Let's get out of here."

Isabel doesn't wait for goodbyes. She starts down the stairs like we're running out of time. Kolt eyes me warily. His color has returned, perhaps now that I've decided to spare his ailing grandfather. I revel in setting off one more flash of alarm while he wonders if I'm going to change my mind and put a bullet in his brain. I could threaten him—really scare him—but there's no point. I don't plan on ever seeing him again. Something tells me he won't risk inviting Isabel back into his life after this, even if his heart still longs for a relationship they'll never have. This is the end of the road.

I tuck my gun away and follow Isabel downstairs. She's pulling her coat on as she hurries to the front of the house.

"Wait." Kolt's rapid footsteps echo off the walls. Then he comes into view. "The alarm."

Quickly he passes us and punches in the code to disarm the alarm system. I open the door. Isabel doesn't move. For all her rushing, something has her planted firmly in place.

Her attention is fixed on Kolt.

"Goodbye," she finally says, her tone somber but resolute.

When she says it, I know it's for the last time.

He stares at the floor, avoiding her gaze. "Bye."

"That didn't exactly go as planned," I say.

We're speeding out of town. We should be at least a little relieved, but Isabel's whole body is tense.

"No shit."

I swallow over the latent rage coursing through me. I heard the whole thing. Being spared the visuals only sets my imagination wild as I try to fill in the moments before I saw Kolt come at her like a passion-crazed lover. I should have known he'd take a second meeting in private as the perfect opportunity to try to sleep with her. Losing my mind over it is exactly what Isabel would expect me to do, so I try to harness some self-control.

"I came for you as soon as I heard you walk through the door."

When I look away from the road, her features are painted with regret.

"I'm sorry, Tristan. I didn't realize he was going to be like that."

I shrug and look ahead, even though I feel anything but casual about it. "I should have known he would go too far."

"We had to risk it," she says without much force.

Was finding out that Boswell is on his deathbed worth the permanent visual of Kolt pressed against her? I sure as hell hope so.

"You could have flattened him, you know? You held your own against Vince just fine. Kolt's a puppy next to him." Seething, I shake my head. "Christ, he was all over you. You didn't even try to stop him."

"Yes, I did." Her words have bite now. "I tried to push him away and he came on stronger, so I hesitated. It was a matter of fighting back and turning him against me or waiting it out so I could get to Kristopher's office. It's not like I was enjoying myself."

I work my jaw, letting my frustration simmer. "Sorry. It was hard to listen to. Harder to watch."

"Try experiencing it. Don't forget, I was the bait in there, not you."

My jealousy takes a sharp turn into guilt. Granted, I would have preferred a different approach, but this was the plan we agreed to. Together.

"You're right. I'm sorry."

I hear her sigh. Something inside me releases too. The adrenaline is tapering off, and all I've done is make her feel awful for what played out over a matter of seconds. She made a call, and I have to learn to be okay with that.

"I'm used to reacting to bad situations differently and with a lot less empathy," I say. "I know you're not like me, and I'm glad for that. I just really fucking hate that guy."

She takes my free hand in hers. I can't deny the relief it gives me. I don't want to fight with her. Kolt's not worth it.

"Well, we never have to see him again. It's over," she says.

I acknowledge that with a tight nod, grateful at least one chapter of this nightmare is closed. Doesn't help us with the others much, unfortunately.

I glance at the folder in her lap. "What's in there? I thought you were going to take pictures."

She opens it, revealing a stack of photographs among some other papers. "I found the file he kept on me. Didn't figure they'd miss it." She sifts through the pictures, studying each one closely. "These are from Rio." She sets them aside and starts looking through the rest of the contents. "They had a private investigator following me. That must be how they found my apartment."

"Is there anything else?"

She shakes her head. "Just some canceled checks from the payments to the PI."

"Nothing on Felix?"

"Nothing obvious, otherwise I would have grabbed it."

"If Kristopher Boswell was behind this plan with Felix at one point, it doesn't matter anymore anyway. He's knocking on death's door. The emphysema is going to kill him so I won't have to. I guess karma took care of that one for us."

"I'm not sure how to feel about that," she says after a moment.

"Me neither."

Kristopher's condition is a break in the chain we thought linked Chalys to the Company.

"Why did Jay tell us Kristopher was offered a seat with Company Eleven, then? Was she lying?"

"I don't know. Maybe it happened before he got sick." It certainly wasn't above Jay to lie, regardless of how vulnerable she'd been when she confessed about the existence of the Company. But why lie about something like that? I glance over to the opened file. "Who signed the checks?"

Isabel thumbs through them, one after the next. She's quiet for too long.

"That doesn't make sense," she says, barely loud enough for me to hear.

Tired of being held in suspense, I swipe one from the stack to see for myself.

"Jesus," I mutter under my breath and hand it back.

"I don't get it. Vince knew Kolt could have been killed when you came for me. His mother couldn't have known. That's her son."

"If Gillian Mirchoff signed those checks, that means she knew damn well about the next job. Which means she knew Kolt could have gotten caught in the crossfire."

She sifts through them again. "All of them. My God, Tristan, something's really wrong." I know she's talking about Kolt's safety. The prick who doesn't know what "no" means was born into this mess. That's not my problem.

The bigger problem is the player who was never on our radar.

"With Vince dead and Kristopher incapacitated, Gillian is calling the shots now. Hell, maybe she has been this whole time and no one ever knew it."

Before we can ruminate any more on that possibility, Isabel's phone vibrates. She answers it and urgently presses it to her ear.

"Hello?...Yes, of course." She scribbles down an address on the front of the folder. "I'll be there."

"Who was that?" I ask after she hangs up.

"Landon. He wants to meet."

"When?"

"Right now."

ISABEL

My thoughts are whizzing by faster than I can keep up with them. The call with Landon was brief but promising. As much as I want to hear what he has to say, I can't stop thinking about Kolt's mother. His *mother*. I knew Vince was a monster. Kristopher too.

If what my mother and grandfather believe is true— that Kristopher Boswell orchestrated the untimely end of my sister's life—I have no reason to give his daughter the benefit of the doubt. Kolt and I said our last goodbye. Of that, I'm certain. Still, I can't deny the urge to at least warn him. Even if I did, I'm not sure it would be enough to make him leave. And if he left, they'd probably find him. Oddly, the safest place for him might be right where he is.

Landon's house in Marblehead is only slightly off the route that would bring us back to the apartment in the city. When the GPS announces our next turn, I force my thoughts away from Kolt and hope that Landon can give us some insights that we haven't unearthed yet ourselves.

When we pull up, I wait for Tristan to do his usual surveillance and ready his weapon, which I doubt we'll be needing. Nothing about my meeting with Landon set off alarms. He didn't give me what I wanted, but I never once thought he'd do me harm.

When we make our way up the stone path to the front door, Tristan keeps a step ahead of me. Always my shield, always my protector.

After we ring the bell, Landon's wife answers the door. "Oh." She looks Tristan up and down, her hesitation obvious.

I don't miss the way his gaze lands on her swollen belly before darting away.

I step forward. "Hi, I'm Isabel. This is Tristan. He's with me."

Her apprehension softens. "Right. Blake's expecting you. I'm Erica, by the way. I remember seeing you at the office the other day. Come on in."

She opens the door, and we step inside.

"I'm sorry for bothering you this late," I offer guiltily.

She waves me off. "No worries. Blake keeps odd hours sometimes. It's normal for us."

She motions for us to follow her through the house, so we do. When we get to what looks like the home office, we find Blake parked on a couch, his forearms resting on his knees. His attention is glued to the opposite wall, where various papers and photos are pinned up.

"Blake, Isabel is here. This is her friend, Tristan."

He turns his head, appraising Tristan a moment before rising to his feet. "Have a seat. We have a lot to go over." He walks to the wall and stares at it a moment longer before giving us his attention again. His arms are crossed, his expression stoic. "I promised myself I wasn't ever going to go down this road again. But this is personal."

Erica leans against the wall, worrying her lip.

"Pope?" I say.

"No, although I'm going to enjoy ruining him with all this. Davis Knight is another matter entirely. As soon as you said his name, I knew I couldn't walk away from this. Anything he touches is dirty. If he's involved, you can bet it's a shady operation."

I frown. "How do you know him?"

"We had a little run-in when I was younger. A few friends and I figured out he was running a Ponzi scheme, taking people's money with big promises, dumping most of it into his account, then robbing Peter to pay Paul. He was getting away with it until I hacked into his bank and started redistributing funds. He wasn't the only one involved, but because I was young and far too idealistic, I didn't realize that what I did only became a convenient distraction from the actual crime. He got away with it." He shrugs. "Ultimately so did I. But sometimes the repercussions aren't always what you expect them to be."

The extended pause and his defensive posture aren't inviting me to dig deeper on that topic, but my guess is this is what got him into trouble all those years ago.

"Do you think Knight is linked to this plan to release Felix?"

"I do." He starts slowly pacing back and forth in front

of the cluttered wall. "I started with the accounting records like you suggested. Of course nothing's ever in plain sight, but it put me on the right track. The Chalys records, at least from a cursory review, are unremarkable. So I moved on to the Boswells' personal private banking accounts. They have several accounts in the name of the family trust. They're all flush, of course, but they don't have a lot of activity, which made one particularly significant transaction stand out."

He rips a piece of paper from its pin on the wall and hands it to me.

"A twenty-million-dollar transfer to Oberon Enterprises. Who are they, you're probably wondering. They are a shell corporation, registered in Delaware, naturally, which wasn't enough to keep me from finding out who the shareholders were."

I glance over the transfer statement and back up to Landon.

"Let me guess. Davis Knight is one of them."

"Bingo." He takes it from me and pins it back to the wall.

"Can you find out where the funds are going?" Tristan asks.

"That's where it gets interesting. Davis has been busy. A couple of months ago he was in Houston. I'm guessing to coordinate with Pope, among other things. Then a quick trip to San Diego. Another stop in Los Angeles. Then a couple of weeks ago he was in Miami."

Tristan and I share a look. If Davis was in Miami two weeks ago, chances are high he was on Simon's yacht too.

"So what's the connection?" Landon asks, a grin playing at his lips, like he expects us to guess the answer he already knows.

I'm ready to tell him to spill it when Tristan speaks.

"Ports."

Landon's face splits with a winning smile. "You got it. And if they're wanting to flood the market, San Ysidro's the place to get people to look the other way on incoming shipments. It's the largest land border crossing between San Diego and Tijuana and probably a really good place to drop some cash for bribes." He turns, rips another paper down, and hands it to Tristan. "Significant cash withdrawals were made prior to each stop. Fifty thousand. Hundred thousand at a time. They're probably spreading it around between border agents and the powers that be at the different port authorities."

"That would make sense. They're already connected to the higher-ups at the Port of Miami," I say.

"What about the East Coast?" Tristan leans in. "They want this to be a national crisis. It'll take weeks for drugs to make it from the border to here and filter down to smaller towns where the abuse is rampant."

"Davis is based in New York, so he wouldn't need to travel. But I checked his debit card. He's been spending a lot of time in New Jersey lately. He likes a particular place called Luca's. Happens to be a well-known haunt of the Generazzo crime family. The balance went down pretty significantly around that same time. More than usual. Their people have been linked to port theft on more than one occasion. Criminal or not, that's their turf, so he'd have to pay the toll to set up any kind of operation there."

"Shit." Tristan pinches the bridge of his nose.

Landon narrows his eyes a fraction. "Friends of yours?"

Then it hits me.

"Crow."

"Yeah. Fucking Crow," Tristan mutters. "Idiot. Definitely *not* a friend."

I don't care as much about Crow as how far along the plan has already progressed. "If Davis has already paid out all these bribes, that means the shipments might already be through."

Landon nods. "It's very possible. I get that they want to line this up with their new launch, but this isn't corporate America. They're not going to be able to get the product overwhelming the street market on any kind of organized timetable. Nothing's that precise. But the ripples could very well have already started."

I push my hands through my hair with a groan. "This is starting to feel like a runaway train. We have no idea how many shipments there are, where they're coming from or when. There's no way we can stop this." Not unless we can figure out how to be a thousand places at once.

The room falls quiet. I could cry for all my frustration. We can't let them win, but what choice do we have?

"Maybe you can't stop this from unfolding completely, but you can try to slow it down," Erica says. "There's no way they've paid off everyone who cares about a huge influx of illicit drugs into the country. Tip off the authorities. Let them do the jobs they're already paid to do."

"She's right," Tristan says after a moment. "It's better than nothing. Letting them know to expect an incoming wave could help them stay ahead of it or put some heat on the usual players. Does your father have any friends at the DEA?"

I meet his cool stare. "I'm guessing he might."

Landon doesn't seem satisfied. His brow wrinkles with a deep frown. "I can keep digging. I'll see if I can find any more specifics."

He looks to Erica. She answers with a nearly imperceptible nod. Permission. To help us and expand their own risk. He crosses his arms tightly and casts his gaze to the ground.

"You should know that Knight isn't the only reason I'm helping you. I'd love to see him really pay one of these days for being a serial dirtbag. But what they're doing hits home." He pauses a beat. "I spent a long time, a lot of money, and plenty of sleepless nights trying to get my brother back on track after he got mixed up with drugs. Time we won't get back, time that neither of us are especially better having spent. Maybe these guys really have figured out a cure, and that's great if it's true. But if launching it comes with more drugs flooding the streets, more people dying…" His jaw ticks with tension. "You have my full support. I'll be a resource."

In that moment, I feel his frustration and his resolve. They echo my own but stem from his own pain and experience, the extent of which I can't know. Whatever cause motivates him, I'm fortified knowing he and Erica are on our side and willing to help as much as they can.

"Do you think there are any more stops on Knight's bribery tour?" Tristan asks.

Landon moves to a desk in the room and begins tapping on the keys of his computer. "Next stop is Paris. Actually, he's due to land in the morning."

Paris.

I look to Tristan.

"I guess Knight and Gillian Mirchoff are about to have company," he says.

8

TRISTAN

"Has Simon reached out to you?"

"Nothing yet. Why?" The connection isn't great, but Mateus's voice through the phone is a welcome sound.

"We think the Company might be meeting in Paris in the next day or two. Maybe not everyone, but a few key players at least. Kristopher Boswell's daughter and their money guy, Davis Knight. Not sure who else."

"I'll contact Simon for an update. I can be there in a few hours if he extends the invitation," he says.

I hesitate. If Mateus is in Europe already, he's the perfect choice to collect intel and clue us in to their next move. He's a member of the Company now, after all, though I suspect he hasn't been fully introduced to all they do. I still don't relish the idea of involving him further, but knowing it's an option is the reason I called.

"Isabel and I are going to catch a flight tonight, but it's a matter of timing. They're a day ahead of us."

"Keep the flight, and I'll make the call. It's time they heard from me anyway. We can convene after."

I sense Mateus's determination hasn't waned since we parted ways in Miami. "Knight is staying at La Réserve. We've booked a place nearby."

"Perfect. Let me know when you get into town."

"Will do."

I hang up and join Isabel in the living room. She's in her usual perch in the window seat. She pulls her knees up to make room for me to sit beside her.

"What did he say?"

"He's going to try to get a meeting with them. He's already close," I say.

She rests her temple against the glass and looks out wistfully.

"What are you looking at over here all the time?"

She shrugs. "I guess I've taken an odd fascination with watching strangers live in the world I used to know."

I take her hand in mine. The physical connection does little to ease the guilt weaving itself into these barriers around us. Isabel's life will never be the same. She'll never experience the world the way she did when things were simpler. I'm not the only one to blame, but I was the one who introduced her to all this darkness.

"We're getting close," I say, hoping to sound reassuring.

It's not necessarily the truth, but maybe she needs the

comfort of a little lie.

"Are we?"

"I think so. I hope so."

She stares down at our intertwined fingers. "Why Paris?"

"I'm not sure. Stateside, Knight and Mirchoff are a train ride away from each other. They must be meeting with someone while they're there."

"Someone important enough to pull them away from the Felix rollout here."

"Right."

"Well, at least it's Paris," she says with a sigh.

"Exactly. Could be worse places to chase the bad guys." I lift her hand to my lips and smile, which inspires one of her own, a small consolation.

There's a loud rapping at the door. I know it's Townsend before I rise and recognize him through the peephole.

"Miss me?" He's wearing a smug smile when he enters the room.

"Not exactly," I say. "Where were you?"

"Doing a little research. Making some new friends. How about you?" He drops onto the couch and props his feet up as he has a habit of doing. "Find anything good?"

"Kristopher Boswell is on his deathbed. Kolt's mother, Gillian Mirchoff, has been running the show. At least we suspect she is."

"Vince isn't exactly up for the job these days," he says with a raspy snicker.

"We think she's meeting up with someone else from

the Company. We're hoping to intercept them if we can get there in time."

"Where?"

"Paris."

He runs his tongue along his teeth, his eyes taking on a wicked glimmer. "That is *interesting*."

Isabel's stare is fixed on him. "Why is that interesting?"

"I had a chat with Jay this morning."

We wait expectantly.

"Lorenzo Generazzo was taken into custody just outside Berlin by German *Polizei* a couple of days ago. He was trying to blackmail one of the foreign ministers."

"Generazzo," Isabel repeats.

"Goes by the name Crow in some circles. Ever heard of him?" Townsend takes a cigarette and wedges it between his lips before lighting it. "If I were a betting man, I'd say the Company's sending its best men to come collect their newest problem."

"Now I know why you're in such a good mood," I say.

He laughs. "It's a good news day, for certain."

"The Company must have connections to the German government. People willing to turn him over," Isabel says, her voice more concerned than relieved.

Townsend lifts an eyebrow. "Would that surprise you?"

"He asked Jay about a job he did over there a while back," I say.

My thoughts return to the remote field in New Jersey where I found Jay and made her give Crow everything he wanted to save her own life. I knew he'd make a mess of whatever information she gave him. It was only a matter of time.

"Anita Eschweiler," I continue. "Her uncle was running against the sitting Chancellor and positioned to win. He wouldn't take bribes to back down."

"Until they popped his niece, I'm guessing," Townsend says.

"That means whoever beat him is behind the hit," Isabel says. "And they probably didn't appreciate him circling back to collect an extra payment."

Townsend blows a plume of smoke into the air. "Probably didn't appreciate the Company letting a rogue hitman track down a client either. I don't know what's in Paris, but I'm guessing they'll be paying a visit to whoever has Crow while they're in the neighborhood. With someone at that level, they'll want to smooth things over."

Isabel rises and folds her arms over her chest. "Good thing we booked our tickets."

In the silence lies a question she doesn't dare ask. Will Townsend come? Has his obsession with finding and killing Crow finally come to an end now that he's in someone else's custody? Or will he complicate this even more by making sure the job is done to his satisfaction?

Townsend smirks. "If taking care of Crow is important enough to abandon Felix for a few days, I'm guessing they're not going to go easy on him. I used to work for them, you know. Not exactly the merciful type."

Isabel's shoulders relax, a subtle change that maybe only I notice. "This is goodbye, then."

I don't miss the hopefulness in her tone.

He reaches into his pocket, his cigarette dangling from his lips. He pulls out a thumb drive and tosses it her way.

She catches it. "What is this?"

"A parting gift," he says. "Mush said he found what you were looking for. Some of it anyway."

My mouth goes dry. I know there's not a serum on that disk, but the mention of Mushenko is a jarring reminder of what else is due. Even though Isabel has made her position clear, I'm no closer to knowing what I'd do if and when he delivers an antidote. I don't know if the craving for more of my memories will ever wane or if I'm even capable of resisting the temptation of having it all back.

"Did he give you anything else?"

Our gazes clash.

He shakes his head. "No, mate. Not yet."

THE RED LEDGER

LEDGER

part 8

1

MATEUS

Paris, France

The way of a fool is right in his own eyes. Simon Pelletier. The fool named for a king. He may have the reverence of the others in his secret society, but he'll never have mine. I've lived through enough to recognize conceit as a marker for malice, and the man they call Soloman is drenched in it.

His arrogance is the worst kind—unchecked and bolstered by the delusional world he's built around himself. I could have killed him. I had the chance. But now I'm salivating over the opportunity to best him at his own game. The satisfaction would be greater than any success I'd ever dreamed of as a poor boy from the favela.

My friendships are few, my trust rarely given. The

moment Tristan brought Karina to me, he earned a lifetime of both. God help me, I never knew taking the assignment would push him into a life of murder and darkness. I'll live with the guilt until the day I die. But it was Simon who set the stage and robbed Tristan of his past. Knowing this makes me want to do more than kill Simon.

Death is easy. Failure is painful.

For Simon, I want both.

Dressed in a black suit tailored to his tall, lithe frame, he strides into La Réserve's salon.

I rise casually and greet him. "Soloman. We meet again."

His smile is stiff, his posture the same. I suspect he doesn't like me calling him that, which gives me a sliver of joy as he folds himself into one of the green tufted chairs around the table I chose for our meeting, far from the entrance and other patrons.

"I apologize for the delay. I would have reached out to you sooner, but things have been"—he pushes his black-rimmed glasses up his narrow nose—"a little hectic."

"I wasn't overly concerned."

He waves his hand dismissively. "You needn't be. It's done. No complications."

On the other side of the salon, the musical sound of ice cubes dropping into an empty tumbler reaches my ears. A siren wails outside and quickly fades away. I lift the glass of liquor I've been nursing for a half hour to my lips and let the rest slide down my throat. Decades of wishing for the ultimate revenge on Barcelos give me no other choice than to hold a moment to quietly celebrate this news.

"*Boa viagem*. Or as you'd say, good riddance."

The lift of his lips seems genuine now. "I'm delighted to be of service."

I've waited too long to savor this news, but I didn't meet Simon here to celebrate. I clear my throat and spin my glass on the slick lacquered surface of the table between us.

"Now that it's done, where do we go from here? You denied my offer of payment."

For the past couple of weeks, I've pondered what of mine could be of interest to Simon. With wealth comes an abundance of people trying to latch on to some piece of it. But I never thought it was money he was after.

"Money is nice, but it's certainly not everything," he says.

"Then name your price."

He folds his arms across his lap. "I would very much like the opportunity to do more business with you."

"What kind of business? I'm not sure our specialties intersect. Textiles and—" I turn my palm up, searching for the best word. "Favors."

"The fact that they don't is precisely why I need you. I have a venture that I've been quietly working on. It's off to a very promising start, but I'm sure you can appreciate that sometimes an influx of good fortune can attract unwanted attention. The other investors and I need to create some distance from the revenue."

"Having more money than you know what to do with sounds like an excellent problem to have."

"Thankfully I know exactly what to do with it. I need

it cleaned by a reputable company—ideally an international one such as yours with no ties to ours—and redeposited into an account from which I can make distributions to legitimate entities."

I know exactly what he's asking me for.

"You want me to launder money for you."

He pauses. "You would receive a handsome commission for your troubles. Three percent straight off the top."

I frown, because even if I truly wanted to get mixed up in Simon's scheme, I'm not sure that what he's offering would tempt me. "How much money are we talking about?"

"Drug money represents nearly five percent of the world's financial transactions. You do the math."

"I'm listening," I say, eager to hear more.

"Over the next few months, there will be a significant uptick in illicit drug sales in the States. We have an exclusive arrangement with the top-level distributors to ensure they're on the receiving end of incoming shipments. We're charging a sizable finder's fee for letting them in on the opportunity."

I don't have to do the math to understand the scale of what he's proposing. Our countries aren't far apart when it comes to the thriving underground economy fueled by a vast network of traffickers and criminal organizations that together make the drug trade an unstoppable force. There's more than enough money to be made at any level of the operation.

"That could be a lot of money to move and make it look legitimate."

He tilts his head slightly. "You can be creative. We're

layering on our end. I'd fully expect you to as well for your own protection."

The buzz of his earlier news has worn off. All I'm thinking about is strategy now. How to get the information I need with the least amount of commitment. What Simon's asking me to do is absolutely possible, but saying yes and jeopardizing my business—or pretending I'm willing to—won't do anyone any good.

Simon seems to sense my hesitation. "I understand this is a significant request. Helping us with this would be an important gesture to the group. A show of trust and commitment."

His invitation to solidify my place in the group is more enticing than he realizes, but my reluctance at this point is real. Taking on that amount of risk for a staggering windfall is a poor man's bet—one I'd never make.

"I wish I could help you, Simon. As you said, money is nice, but it isn't everything. I have my reputation to consider."

His nostrils flare slightly as he inhales a deep breath. "How might I entice you, then? Surely there's something you want that you haven't managed to acquire already."

I consider his request. Simon's connections and resources are a veritable buffet of possibilities. But what I really want are the details he's not giving me. He's gambling on me being a well-behaved cog in his operation, which isn't going to be enough.

"When we first met, you asked for context," I begin. "You said it was important to you before you would accept my request. So I gave you more information than I would have given anyone else. Then we had a deal. I'm too impressed by you to believe the scope of this venture is limited to the collection of fees. There must be more to it."

"Of course there is," he says flatly.

I shrug. "Entice me, then."

He waves over the server and orders a Negroni, which she promptly delivers. Every second of silence between us is heavy with anticipation. I have no idea how or if Simon's venture ties into his interest in Tristan, but using it as a vehicle to ruin the Company is just as good.

He takes a drink of the reddish cocktail and wipes the moisture off his lips with the table napkin. "Do you believe in the inherent goodness of people?"

I'm wholly unprepared for the question, which seems worlds away from the proposal he's given me. Unsure if lying might change the course of the conversation or what he might be willing to share, I opt for the truth.

"Generally, yes."

He nods, which could be agreement or simple acknowledgment. I can't be sure until he speaks again.

"I believe in the inherent weakness of people." He punctuates the statement with a tight clasp of his hands on his lap.

"Those two qualities don't necessarily run in opposition to one another," I say.

"They don't. But I believe in man's feeble will more than almost anything else. I can't even attribute it to the grip of addiction. No, we are living in an era where human beings crave real adversity. Perhaps it's a primal instinct for survival in a world that's already solved so many of its most devastating problems. I don't pretend to know the answer. All I know is that the weak, whether you believe they're inherently good or not, will perish, and it'll be by a poison of their own design. Drug abuse is pandemic—a genocide carried out and perpetuated by its own victims. I refuse to entertain a crisis of conscience and ignore the financial opportunities inside this ecosystem that shows no signs of decline."

"I wasn't challenging your motives." Even if his impassioned speech hadn't confirmed it, I already knew Simon was a terrible person. "But you haven't given me a good enough reason to risk my business for this."

"It's true that what I'm asking of you is only one piece of a much larger initiative. Drugs are already flowing into the country, with or without our help. We're simply widening the artery so they flow to the right people."

"And then?"

"Society has created a problem without a solution. We've been developing the solution. Within the year, we'll have acquired at least a hundred treatment centers, armed with a line of revolutionary pharmaceuticals to meet the overwhelming demand."

"Demand that you're accelerating."

He shrugs. "The demand already existed. We're simply guiding its course. Gaining better control over it."

"Seems like investing in people's weakness is a more profitable venture than having faith in their goodness."

He answers with a crooked grin. "Precisely. And if you can deliver this one piece for us, I would be willing to bring you in on the rest. There's plenty to go around."

If what he's saying is true and if this plan is already in motion, they stand to make billions. Unfortunately for him, it'll never be enough to lure me into their world.

I suspect Simon's told me more than he should have, but I can't give him the answer he wants. Not yet. Tristan will be on the ground in the morning. I let my instincts guide me last time. I don't regret it, but I can't cut him out again.

"I'd like a few days to consider your proposal."

"Very well. My offer stands." Simon pushes up his sleeve, revealing an understated but sleek black leather Patek Philippe. The timepiece probably cost more than my penthouse in Ipanema. "And if you can tolerate Paris for another day, I'd like you to meet some of my associates. Unfortunately, I have a rather urgent business matter I must attend to in Berlin. Otherwise I'd join you."

"I'll be in the city for a few days."

I plan to stay as long as it takes to get to the bottom of this.

I stand as Simon does. He extends his hand, his shake confident and firm, as if he's closed our deal. His confidence feeds my own. If he thinks he's already convinced me, it could be the open door I need.

"I look forward to our next meeting," I say, giving him even more hope.

"As do I. Until then, you can expect to hear from a

man named Davis Knight. You could say he's the treasurer of our little group. I think you'll like what he has to say."

2

ISABEL

I'm sprawled out across the crisp white bedspread, doing my best to fight off the desire to sleep. I had hoped the thrill of landing in one of the most beautiful and decadent cities in the world would give me the adrenaline rush I need to get through the day.

If we were here under any other circumstances, I'd be falling in love with every detail and racing through the city to take it all in. Even here, our room at Le Bristol overlooking the gardens is beyond charming, bathed in shades of cream and periwinkle, its walls framed with ornate molding. Crystals from the chandelier above our bed catch the light beaming in from the floor-to-ceiling windows. If a place could get into someone's blood, Paris already seems to be in mine.

The sound of the shower ceases, and a few minutes later, Tristan emerges from the bathroom, a towel knotted at his hip. He rubs a hand towel briskly over his damp hair before slicking his fingers through the dark strands. I recognize that even in that short time apart, I missed him.

He's dark and damaged and beautiful against this new backdrop. Long gone is the sweet, broken boy I fell in love with all those years ago. All man now, Tristan wears the six years between us in his scars and the lean bands of muscle beneath them. The scars don't pain me as much as they used to. They've become reminders that no matter what he went through, he survived. Against all odds, *we* survived.

He catches me looking at him and comes toward me. "Are you going to get some sleep?"

I glance at the clock on the side table. "Not much point. It's already ten in the morning. I'll just stay up."

The bed dips under his weight when he sits beside me. I refocus on the laptop screen in front of me, trying to ignore the sting in my tired eyes.

"Find anything good?"

"I don't know. My French is already a lot better than my chemistry, I guess," I say. "I have no idea what half of this means."

I spent the seven-hour stretch across the Atlantic jamming as much of the local language into my brain as I could and then trying to make some sense of the trials and test results that Mushenko passed on to Townsend in Boston. Felix will be hitting the market any day now, and we still aren't sure how dangerous it may be to the people who are about to flock to it. The window to do anything about it is quickly closing.

"I never thought I'd say it, but I almost wish Townsend was here to help me translate some of this." I sigh, partly in frustration but mostly from the nagging fatigue. "They've been developing this drug for years, but this only goes back two years. Maybe that's when they broke it off from Elysium Dream."

"Maybe." He massages his palm across my back and shoulders, gently kneading the muscles still stiff from the flight.

I moan and let my eyes drift closed. "If you keep doing that, you're going to put me to sleep." The sound of Tristan's laptop clicking closed draws them open again. "I'm not done with that."

"It can wait," he says, sliding it to the floor and rolling me onto my back.

He follows me down and brackets his arms on either side of my head. He brushes the tip of his nose along mine and kisses the corner of my mouth and down my neck.

I laugh as tiny droplets of water roll off his shoulders onto my chest. "You're getting me wet."

"Oh really? You've never complained about it before." His voice is low and playful as he slides his thigh between mine.

I pretend to push him away, but I can already tell by the look in his eyes that he's not deterred. Lying back feels too good, so I entertain his teasing caresses and let them melt my resolve.

He catches my thigh and anchors it over his hip. I revel in the weight of him. The silent demand in that extra pressure. It's protective and possessive, and I'll never get tired of it.

"What's gotten into you all of a sudden?"

"I want to make love to you in Paris. Is that so wrong?"

"No, except we're meeting with Mateus in a few hours. And I still have to make sense of those documents."

"Work, work, work," he mutters before sweeping down for a searing kiss that quickly drains my thoughts of anything but the way he makes me feel.

With the skill of a lover who's come to know every button to push when it comes to my body, he works me over until I'm moaning against his lips, writhing under his touch, and aching for all of him. When he starts tugging at my clothes, I help him until they're scattered on the floor with his towel and there's nothing more between us. I grasp at his waist to coax him close, but he evades me, instead carefully inching his way down my body. His hot kisses and worshiping fingers don't stop when he settles between my thighs.

I clutch my lower lip between my teeth to keep from crying out loudly at the intimate contact. With my fingers twined in his damp hair, I fall into the sensations. I gasp as colors dance behind my eyes, his ministrations bringing me to the edge of relief. The cool, white sheets twist in my grasp when the orgasm rolls over me, leaving me vibrating with the sweet, sharp aftershocks.

I release a weak whimper as he climbs over me. He

kisses me again, the taste of me still on his lips.

"I love that you're mine," he whispers.

Hearing his truth, I melt a little more. I've always been his. Nothing could ever break us apart. Nothing but death.

Slowly I draw my hand over the place where I can feel his heart beating, fast and firm against my fingertips. "I'll always be yours."

He covers my mouth with his, swallowing my moans with a breathless kiss as he claims the deepest part of me. Then we're heat and desire and love, our souls seeking, our bodies climbing.

I'll never stop fighting for a lifetime of this. Just Tristan. Just us.

TRISTAN

I draw the drapes closed, shutting out the daylight and shrouding Isabel's sleeping figure in darkness. When my eyes adjust, I go to her, my steps muffled by the carpeted floor. Her chest rises and falls under the sheet with her silent breaths. Mateus is waiting for me, but for now, I can't seem to move.

I'm gripped by the instinct to keep Isabel close. It hasn't let up since I stole her away from Rio, but this is more. This borders on desperation—a gnawing kind of dedication to make a life with her. A better life. The more I tell myself there's hope on the other side of this nightmare with the Company, the more I need it.

I can't pretend like this morning doesn't make me want it all the more. If we weren't here to crash Knight's rendezvous and investigate whatever shitstorm Crow's gotten himself into, our days here would look very different. We'd be making love every afternoon, wasting time in cafés, doing romantic things that everyone dreams of doing here. What would it be like to go someplace new and see wonder in her eyes instead of fear, to watch her smile and hear her laugh without the burden of this latest quest for justice? What a gift it would be if we could be ignorant of the diabolical plans underway now.

As she rests unaware of this tumult inside me, I trace a featherlight touch along her bare arm. Exhausted from our journey, she doesn't stir. Already I miss her lips, her taste. After years of death and blood and survival, I'm sure I don't have a romantic bone in my body. Every inclination I have to be a better man is directly tied to Isabel—the way she sees me, the way she loves me, the language of hope and sadness I can read in her eyes. But it seems like the closer we get to the truth, the more I can envision the man I could be. A man she deserves.

Until this is over, I won't pretend to ignore the rest. Isabel has awakened empathy in me that didn't exist before, but when it comes to the Company and anyone tied to it, I have none. That will never change.

With that thought, I force myself away and leave the suite as quietly as I can.

Once outside, I walk down the street to the end of the block, making my turn at a palatial government office building set on the corner. Its guarded black gates open slowly so an SUV with tinted windows can gain entrance to the inner courtyard.

I travel farther down Avenue de Marigny and spot Mateus in the gardens. The greens are uncrowded. A few tourists and workers on their lunch break linger, but no one seems to pay much mind to the dark-haired man gazing upon the old, bronze fountain, its water spilling over the edge of one basin to fill another in an endless flow.

"You're a long way from home."

Mateus turns, his eyes lighting up. "So are you, friend."

"Wherever home is, I guess, I'm probably pretty far from it." I spot the brawny man with a blond crew cut standing on the opposite side of the garden, watching us. "I see you brought Ford."

"He proved useful in Miami. And discreet, seeing as we got into a bit of trouble and he wasn't fazed. He was in the market for a new assignment, so here we are." His expression softens slightly. "How is Isabel?"

"Tired. I left her at the hotel to sleep off the jet lag. She wanted to come."

He nods. "So did Karina. I convinced her she would see you another time. I have no idea how long we'll need to stay."

I hesitate. "She's with you?"

He answers with a reluctant sigh. "Not at the hotel. She's with a friend here in the city. She wouldn't accept another trip alone, no matter how I tried to dissuade her. I imagine you know the feeling."

"I know it well. But she has to understand this is dangerous."

"Tristan, we grew up in Rocinha. She's seen death. Hell, she shot a man back in Petrópolis who had his sights set on you. I want her safe more than you do, but she walks her own path. It's not up to me to hold her back."

I can relate to all of that more than he probably realizes. I learned a long time ago that holding Isabel back only spelled more trouble for the two of us. She's taken her place in all of this. While I don't always agree with how things play out, I trust her to measure the dangers and act accordingly.

Mateus must read the concern on my features. "Don't worry, Tristan. I won't be parading her around while I'm here. For all they know, I've come to Paris alone with Ford for security. I don't get the feeling they'll be welcoming outsiders to our next meeting anyway."

"You met already?"

He lifts his brow. "Soloman himself."

Soloman. Simon is in Paris. It shouldn't surprise me, but somehow it does. Simon is close. I didn't realize how thrilling that would be, but the possibility of getting him in my clutches again is so tempting, my palms prickle with anticipation.

"What's so important that he needs to be here?"

"I don't know yet, but I hope to find out. I'm getting closer. I'll be meeting with one of them before I leave Paris. Davis Knight. The one you told me about."

Knight—the one man Blake Landon might loathe more than Michael Pope. I have a feeling he won't let either of their sins go unpunished by the time this is all said and done.

"Anyone who's running their finances is integral to all of this."

"I would imagine. I expect him to reach out to me through the hotel soon. Then I'll get whatever information I can out of him."

Mateus getting closer to the Company's operation is both good news and bad. He has a legitimate livelihood to protect—not to mention his life and Karina's, both of which are expendable to anyone in the Company who suspects his deceit. But when I asked him to do this for me, I also asked him to see it through, which is exactly what he'll do, no matter what I say.

"What did Simon have to say?"

He shakes his head as if in disbelief, which only piques my curiosity. If only I could have listened in on their conversation the way I had on Simon's obscene yacht. Then again, I wouldn't have let him out of my sight a second time without killing him.

"I haven't made any commitments, but at least I know what they want me to do. To be honest, his proposal was a little underwhelming, which made it easy to stall," Mateus says. "They want me to siphon money through my companies in Brazil. Any one of a hundred companies could do the same thing, but I suspect mine is a safer bet than most. I'm not embroiled in any scandals that would bring unwelcome attention to my affairs, or theirs. Whatever ties I have to unsavory enterprises aren't widely known."

"If I don't know about them, I don't suspect many would."

He chuckles softly. "I'm not a saint."

"I don't think we could be friends if you were. But outside of wanting Barcelos dead, you haven't given Simon any reason to think you have skeletons in your closet that would cause problems for him. Did he say where the money is coming from?"

"Drug money. Good luck tracing it, though. I imagine they'll be channeling it through several accounts before it ever gets to mine. Somehow they're controlling the drug flow into the US, then imposing a hefty tax on the dealers at the top of the food chain. The amount must be significant enough that they need someone like me to clean it. From where I stand, it's a weak offer, but if I do it, Simon's agreed to bring me in on something bigger."

That intoxicating anticipation ripples through me again. "Did he elaborate?"

"With some gentle persuasion. I don't get the impression he'll be taking no for an answer now that he's told me, though."

"Taking a cut on the incoming drug shipments makes sense, but this is only one piece of the puzzle. The drug money is a perk, but the Boswells' pharmaceutical company is about to launch a new drug that's supposed to revolutionize opioid addiction treatment. It's going to be a billion-dollar win for them, and the more drugs that hit the streets, the more they feed the demand for it."

Mateus stares into the bubbling fountain. "Round and round it goes."

"Simon's pulling all these strings, but the Boswells are getting the windfall. I'm just trying to figure out where his cut comes in."

"Rehabilitation." He meets my eyes, his own thoughtful. "Simon is capitalizing on the life cycle of an addict. A human being who succumbs to addiction is an opportunity for him, not a beating heart. He sees them as little mice working their way through a maze of tunnels that he's designed with the help of human nature. It's both brilliant and unthinkable. His total lack of regard for humanity…" He shakes his head as if searching for the right word.

"It knows no bounds," I finish for him, trusting this to be true. Everything I know about Simon, from the murders he facilitated to orchestrating this vast scheme, points to him being one of the most soulless people I've ever known. And I haven't kept great company the past few years.

"I believe that, truly," Mateus says. "I suppose in the traditional sense, if you want to develop a drug, you create something that will meet a demand, and then you do your best to control the distribution. He's going a step further by enhancing the demand and owning the distribution. They're investing in rehabilitation centers. At least a hundred of them this year alone. God knows what other cottage industries he'll expand into if he hasn't already. He said there would be plenty to go around, and I have little doubt."

Simon's plan is more than appalling. It's frighteningly well thought out. And he's arrogant enough to believe he can pull it off, or that he already has.

"There was a time when I thought taking Simon out

of the picture would solve everything. Even if it won't, I'm beginning to realize it still needs to happen. He masterminded this, and so much is already in motion. When does it stop?"

Mateus tenses his jaw. "It won't, Tristan. Nothing will ever be enough for a man like Simon."

A part of me wishes Mateus had killed Simon that night on the yacht, but if he had, we wouldn't know the scope of this plan—a plan I'm determined to upend. But he has to be taken care of, and right now I'm certain there's no one better for the job than me.

"When do you meet again?"

"Simon's in Berlin, but Knight should reach out soon. Once he does, they'll expect me to be impressed enough by the numbers to accept the proposal. I'm not sure if I'll see Simon again until he needs something else from me."

I curse inwardly. I was hoping he'd be at the hotel with the others. No such luck. I'd bet good money that Simon's probably mopping up Crow's mess in Berlin, making nice with the client Crow tried to twist for an extra payment. Wherever his next stop is, at least a meeting with Knight could lead us in the right direction.

If Mateus is concerned about walking deeper into this world, he doesn't show it. I should give him a chance to get away and take Karina with him, but we're too close, too entrenched in this to turn around and pretend like this might solve itself.

After a moment, I ask, "How far are you willing to take this?"

Mateus slides his hands into his pockets and answers first with a small grin. "Like you, Tristan, survival is the game I play best. When I can't stall anymore, I'll give them the answer they want. Once I do, the clock starts ticking."

We share a look full of solemn understanding. Simon must be stopped before Mateus has to become one of them. If his name or bank account is linked to theirs, he'll be risking too much. I worry he already has.

3

ISABEL

What if Felix really is a cure?

Alone in the hotel room, I'm recharged but no more enlightened following an afternoon immersing myself in the development of CH-958, the name given to the early version of felixedrine. I'm questioning Townsend's suspicious theories around the drug and my own ability to weigh its potential harm on the millions of people who are about to have access to it.

No doubt, the experimental version they injected Tristan with was a true failure, but what if they were able to correct the mistake? Thousands of pages and dozens of clinical trials confirm the efficacy of Felix. Billions of dollars went toward research and development of the drug, which would give Chalys at least a billion reasons to push it through and cover up any hints of problematic side effects, but what if it got this far on its own merits?

I'm programmed to distrust anyone or anything linked to Chalys, but the truth remains, Chalys has been developing and manufacturing new drugs for years. If all they did was churn out poisons disguised as cures, they'd have been put out of business long ago, no matter how dedicated they may have been to covering up their failures. I have to consider that, with all the unthinkable acts taking place around its launch, Felix itself could be legitimate.

The sound of the door unlocking interrupts my tumbling thoughts. Tristan joins me in the hotel room, a backpack slung heavily over his shoulder.

"What's that?"

He drops it in front of an accent chair before sitting. "Supplies."

I frown. "Supplies?"

"You didn't think I was going to smuggle guns and ammo on the plane, did you?"

"Oh." In the rush of traveling, it didn't occur to me that we'd arrive in Paris unarmed. Generally, I prefer not to be, but that's not Tristan's style. "Where did you get it?"

He shrugs out of his jacket and tosses it aside. "Some people can score drugs in any city, whether they know people or not. I can find guns and people willing to help me do unsavory things for the right price."

I decide I don't want to know more. Tracking down illegal firearms can remain one of Tristan's life skills that I don't need to share.

"Any luck?" He nods toward the laptop as he unzips the bag.

I push it aside with an unsatisfied sound. "I know more than I used to but not enough to find any discrepancies in the test results. If there was a failure, no one seemed to think it was alarming enough to include it in the summaries, which honestly are the only pieces of this that make any sense to me. From what I could find about it online, the side effects aren't anything close to what you've experienced."

"Your grandfather exposed them twenty years ago for skewing data. What makes you think anything's changed?"

"Believe me, I take nothing for granted. If there are adverse effects that Chalys has been trying to hide, they won't be able to hide them forever. People will find out. But I think we have to consider that if they've come this far with it, Felix could actually help people."

His brows crunch as he looks down, riffling through the bag in silence. I don't blame him. If the drug that robbed him of his memories weren't linked to Felix, he may be less skeptical about it. For now he seems committed to believe the worst.

"I'm sorry I missed Mateus. How is he?"

"Determined as ever. He met with Simon. It appears he's thought of everything. From bribing port authorities all the way to investing in drug treatment facilities that will shell out Felix like candy. And of course skimming a little off the top from his go-to dealers. Combined, you're talking about serious money, a lot of which is going to need to be cleaned. That's where Mateus comes in."

A knot begins to form in my belly. It was only a matter of time before Simon asked for repayment. He wouldn't kill a man for nothing if he could ask for something valuable in return. According to Jay, that philosophy was the driving force behind Company Eleven's league of assassins, eliminating people for leverage over money in most cases.

"Did he agree?"

"Not yet. But he will." He pulls out a gun that looks like the one he favors.

I straighten in the bed. "If he does what Simon wants, Mateus will be implicating himself. He can't do that."

"I know that, Isabel. That's why I'm going to make sure Simon stops breathing before it comes to that."

I swallow hard. "That's not going to fix this."

He tilts his head to the side, his attention fixed on the gun he's holding like he intends to use it sooner rather than later. "I think it'll help."

I can't deny he could be right. Simon's hand in this has been critical. Without him, the operation could carry on, but I suspect no one can pull strings like he can. I haven't endured so much that I relish the idea of Tristan killing again, but something tells me now isn't the time to question his instincts. If anyone's name belongs in the ledger, it's Simon's.

When Tristan's phone rings, he pulls it from his pocket. "It's Mateus," he says, putting him on speaker. "Isabel is here too."

"Davis wants to meet tonight." Mateus's familiar voice echoes through the room. "He just called."

Tristan stays silent. He seems deep in thought, furrowing his brows.

"Tristan?" Mateus says after a moment.

"We'll be there."

I widen my eyes. "We will?"

"We need to find out why they're still in Paris if Simon already left," Tristan says. "Davis is our only lead, and I'm not letting him out of my sight. Isabel doesn't need to be on your arm, but she can be close enough to have eyes and ears on you. And I won't be far. Until we figure out what the hell they're up to, we go where he goes."

"If that's what you think is best. I plan to be at the bar at seven," Mateus says. "It should be busy enough for Isabel to go unnoticed. If not, we'll improvise."

Bloodred curtains frame the threshold of La Réserve. Night has fallen, but the street is busy with traffic and pedestrians. All the activity has my attention pinging everywhere. My heart rate has gone up a few notches at the prospect of being recognized, even though I've been able to pull this off so many times before.

Tristan takes my hand, halting our forward movement toward the entrance. "I'm going to wait out here," he says, his voice low enough that the doorman ahead can't hear us. "Stay out of Knight's line of sight, and text me if anyone moves."

I shake out my free hand, attempting to steady my nerves.

His gaze travels the length of me. When our eyes meet, he gives one of the curls from my wig a little pull, letting it spring back into place a second later.

"Do I look okay?" Unlike nearly every other time I've gone into a situation like this, I'm aiming for understated, which means a simple black sweater over black pants and a wig I hope does more to obscure my face than bring attention to it.

"You look good," he says with a confidence that manages to soothe me. "Keep me posted every step of the way, all right?"

I nod and head toward the doorman, who greets me and gestures for me to proceed inside.

The reception area is gleaming and glittery with slick marble and ornate lamps. Hoping not to attract any attention, I pretend like nothing here is new to me and meander farther inside until I find the bar.

My heart takes residence in my throat as I quickly scan the room. Mateus is at the far end on a long red couch that faces the rest of the room, one leg crossed over the other, his posture relaxed and friendly. He's not alone. Another man sits adjacent, his body turned away from me as he speaks to Mateus. All I can see is the back of his reddish-blond hair and his navy suit straining around his thick body. I pray he doesn't bother looking my way and that I don't garner attention from either man. I do my best to appear casual on my journey, relieved when Mateus doesn't make eye contact.

I move closer and take a nearby chair, my back to them, and then pull out my phone and shoot off a text to Tristan.

I'm in. They're here.

"I'm sorry Simon couldn't make it," Mateus says. "I've enjoyed getting to know him. He's…very unique. I'm not sure I've ever met anyone quite like him."

Knight laughs loudly. "And you never will. No one really knows Simon. I'm not sure I've ever seen him with his guard down. But he's a good person to have on your team."

"I can see that. Few men are better connected, or influential, than he seems to be."

Knight clears his throat. "He said you were in Miami for the cruise a few weeks ago. I must have missed you."

"There were a lot of new faces. An enjoyable night."

"You must have made an impression on Simon for him to want to cut you in on what we've been working on."

Mateus's silence makes me wish I could see his face. There's a hint of defensiveness in Knight's tone, like he may not be completely convinced of Mateus's worthiness.

"No one was more surprised than me," Mateus answers calmly. "He's very persuasive, though. I'm always looking to diversify when it makes sense."

"We've been working on this for a long time. We're talking about years of planning. You're lucky getting to come in on the tail end of it all."

"Sounds like it's the beginning, not the end."

Knight pauses. "Right. Well, Simon has discriminating tastes. He demands the best of everything. Never settles. So if you're good in Simon's book, I suppose you're good in mine." I hear his chair squeak with movement. "So, is this a go? If there's one thing Simon isn't, it's patient."

"He assured me I'd have a few days to consider."

"We'll be out of here in a few days. I was hoping we could nail this down tonight."

Knight sounds like he's the impatient one. He talks fast, like he's already thinking about the next place he has to be. I'm holding my breath, waiting for Mateus's answer, when I hear the crinkling of paper.

"Here's the deal," Knight continues. "We'll start small and scale up once we know things are going well. Hundred-thousand-dollar increments give or take. You let me know the account to wire it into, hold three percent for yourself, and wire the rest into this account in the Cayman Islands. Rinse and repeat."

"That part is simple enough. What about the rest? If you've been working on this for years, I can't deny I'm apprehensive to understand the scope of it."

Knight sighs, a loud exaggerated sound. "Anyone ever tell you you're a hard sell?"

"In so many words."

"Why am I not surprised?"

Mateus laughs softly. "I was born in a town near the border of the states of São Paulo and Rio de Janeiro. Before my parents were killed and my sister and I were forced to go to the city, we would go to a nearby river for fun. It was rocky. The water moved fast, and it was refreshing on a hot day. The biggest thrill was jumping off one of the highest rocks into the deepest part of the river. You had to know the exact spot to jump in, or you'd break your leg on the rocks—or worse. My friends would harass me every time we went, taunting me to jump. I wasn't afraid, but I'd seen some people get hurt. I wasn't going to leap in and hope for the best. I wanted to be sure."

"So did you do it?"

"I did eventually. Straight as an arrow, not a scratch."

Knight is quiet for a moment. "You have any plans tonight? Because if you're free, I'd like to show you something."

"What might that be?"

"A piece of the operation. An important one. I could tell you about it, but I think you should see it for yourself. It's not far. About twenty minutes outside the city. It's usually locked down for operations, but security is light tonight because of something else we're working on. It's a good time to give you the tour without any prying eyes." He pauses a moment. "Might make you feel a little better about jumping in."

"Very well," Mateus says. "I'll call my driver."

TRISTAN

I'm pacing down the street, waiting for another update from Isabel, when I hear my name. She's rushing down the front walk toward me.

"Is everything okay? What's going on?"

"They're leaving," she says breathlessly. "Knight wants to show Mateus something. They're taking Mateus's car."

"Do you know where they're going?"

"No idea. He says it's part of the operation. Something

that will help Mateus make up his mind."

After a quick glance toward the door, I swing my gaze toward the street and the passing cars. In the distance, I see a taxi with its sign lit. I grab Isabel's hand and take her with me as I hail down the black sedan. We slide into the back, and only then do I realize I have no instructions to give the driver or language skills with which to do it.

Through the windshield, I see Mateus walking casually toward the curb, Knight beside him. They're smiling and talking, like all of this is perfectly normal. Ford appears, his frame towering over the other two men before guiding them into the SUV.

"*Suivez cette voiture*," Isabel says, pointing ahead to where Mateus's car is pulling away.

Our driver acknowledges her with a dismissive grunt and follows.

Isabel tugs the wig off her head and runs her hands through her flattened hair.

"What happened in there?"

"Mostly small talk. Knight is eager to seal the deal, but Mateus is still holding out. I get the feeling Knight is under instruction to make sure this goes down no matter what. He seemed pretty confident that after tonight, Mateus would be on board."

I worry that Mateus might be testing their patience or causing unnecessary suspicion. He'll have to agree at some point, likely tonight. Coming to Paris was an invitation to move deeper into the Company's world, one we have to take advantage of. Once he accepts, the rest is up to me.

After a few minutes, the taxi speeds up. We merge into a congested roundabout that's loud with motorcycles and car horns. Mateus's SUV is still in sight when we're forced to a near stop behind a group of cars slowing down to catch a close-up view of the Arc de Triomphe.

The taxi driver's curses meet our ears as he slams his hand on the wheel.

"Fucking tourists," I mutter, figuring we have the same frustrations in mind.

Isabel peers out the window, her eyes lifted to the monstrous glowing arch where a dozen boulevards converge. Despite this delay, the landmark is awe-inspiring, breathtaking in its sheer size and design. I'd love to enjoy her wonder and even share in the moment, but Mateus's car is quickly moving out of sight.

"Whatever you do, do not lose that car," I shout in plain English.

This earns me a narrow look from the driver before he hits the gas, cuts someone off, and swerves dangerously around the slower-moving vehicles until we're back where we need to be, thankfully exiting this chaotic cluster.

As we near the outskirts of the city, the journey becomes less crowded.

I take note of every sign along every highway, mentally orienting us but having no idea where Knight could be taking Mateus. They're a couple of cars ahead, but easy enough to follow as we turn down a street lined with glassy corporate buildings.

As if he knows we're not supposed to be seen, the taxi

driver hangs back, braking as the SUV in front of us does.

One of the new, sleek buildings is bigger than the others, with angular lines and turquoise-tinted glass sides. Bright-white letters beam from the top-floor windows.

Chalys France

Isabel's jaw drops. "Chalys... My God, they're everywhere."

"They're a multibillion-dollar company. With everything they're putting into this, they'll want Felix available all over the world, along with anything else they're slinging."

Mateus's car turns into the main entrance, where his driver punches in a code, and they pull through the gates.

"Go around the block," I say.

The driver doesn't acknowledge me but follows my instructions and takes us to the other side of the building.

"Drop us here."

The driver hits the brakes, lurching us forward abruptly. I shove fifty euros into his hand before he can update the fare. I think we've both worn out our welcome with each other. Still, he catches me in the rearview and nods his thanks.

Once we're outside, the taxi speeds off. Isabel watches him leave. I can see the wheels turning in her mind. How will we get back?

Peering up at the building, I'm more concerned with how we're going to get inside. With Knight, Mateus will be able to walk right in. We're not that lucky, but I'm not waiting around for him to come back out.

"Here. Let me help you." I urge her toward the fence, grateful she's wearing one of her more practical outfits so I can hoist her easily over the top. She lands on the other side with a soft thud. I follow her over.

As we cross the parking lot, I spot the loading docks on the south side of the building. All are closed except for the one closest to us, giving us a perfect place to slip inside undetected. We're nearly at the opening when the sound of a man talking stops me in my tracks. I look back to Isabel and press my finger to my lips.

I creep slowly forward, peeking inside the bay of the dock to catch a glimpse of the man. He's leaning against the threshold of a doorway, a lanyard around his neck.

He laughs every once in a while. We don't move, don't make a sound, until finally he pushes off the jamb and disappears farther inside, his voice fading away with him.

It's now or never.

I take Isabel's hand and guide her to follow me. I lift her onto the ledge. She stays crouched in place as I move silently forward. Beside the door, a thin coat is draped over a hook. I dip into the pockets and find a ring of keys. Bingo.

I peer around the edge of the doorway. Not seeing the man, I wave Isabel closer.

We're in.

We move fast then. Down one hall and then another. The building seems to be deserted in the off hours. Wherever Mateus is, he's probably alone with Knight, hopefully gaining intel and nothing worse. Having access to one of the Chalys facilities is an opportunity I wasn't expecting.

Isabel may be holding on to hope the drugs they're pushing can fill an unmet need, but I'm not convinced. If I can find more vulnerabilities, I will, and this is a great place to start.

"This place is huge. They could be anywhere," Isabel says in a hushed voice.

"The surveillance room should be on the ground floor somewhere. Probably close to the front."

"Tristan, here." Isabel grabs my arm, pointing to a sign on the door we nearly passed.

Personnel Autorisé Seulement

"How the hell do you do that?" I mumble, reaching for the keys.

"Latin-based languages are easier than others. Here, let me try."

I hand them to her when a loud slam echoes through the huge open foyer ahead. The echo dies down, leaving an eerie, empty silence.

"What was that?" she whispers.

"Not sure. I'm going to investigate."

"No, you're not." She squeezes my arm, her hazel eyes storming with worry. "We should stay together."

"I'm sure everything is fine," I say in the most even tone I can manage.

"Which is it, Tristan? Is Mateus in danger or not?"

She knows I'm placating her. In my defense, we weren't expecting the night to lead us here. Letting her be in a hotel bar with Knight is a lot different than letting her wander around this huge facility. He could be anywhere.

"Try to get in there and figure out where they are. If I can't find them, you will."

She's about to argue with me again, so I cup the back of her head and seal my lips over hers. The silence around us offers no distractions, so I sacrifice a few more seconds to kiss her until we're both out of breath. What the hell is a life of death and danger if I can't let myself drown in the woman I love in the spaces between?

She blinks up at me, flushed but still holding me with her beautiful gaze. "You think you can kiss me senseless and then get away with whatever you want?"

I grin. "I don't know. Can I?"

"Not a chance," she answers without missing a beat.

I wish I could prove her right, but I don't know what we're getting into. I'm not taking risks…not when it comes to her.

"Don't worry. I can handle Knight."

She softens a fraction. Enough that when I start to walk away, she lets me go.

4

ISABEL

Watching Tristan walk away makes me faintly nauseated. Kissing him was a welcome distraction, but the reality that we're facing danger and uncertainty once more quickly overrode the moment.

Tonight isn't going anything how I thought it would. Mateus was supposed to give Knight the answer he wanted. Because he didn't, we're on a wild goose chase through Chalys's French headquarters. Tristan's right about one thing. With the money flowing through their corporation, they probably have locations all over the globe. I'm not convinced that is the only reason they're in Paris, though.

I try one key after the next, my hands shaking as I do. I swear I've tried nearly every single one on the ring before the lock finally gives. Inside the control room, two walls are lined with screens broadcasting black-and-white video. Each one is streaming surveillance of key areas of the building. I jump when the door latches closed behind me. I take a deep breath and go to the desk, leaning in to get a better look.

Only one of the screens is showing movement.

Knight is walking Mateus through what looks like an empty research lab on the fifth floor. Knight is laughing a lot. His gestures are exaggerated. He must be going for the hard sell at this point. Mateus wears a steady, measured expression. His hands are tucked casually into his pockets, which could mean anything. His calm exterior is one of his greatest assets.

I release a grateful sigh. For now, he's safe. Now I just need to find Tristan, except he's managed to avoid all the cameras, leaving his whereabouts unknown. I should be surprised, but I'm not.

I pull out my phone and text him.

> *Fifth floor. They're just*
> *talking. No problems.*

I wait for him to answer, glancing up to follow Mateus's meandering tour through nearby rooms.

A flicker of movement near the back of the building catches my eye. The man at the loading dock has paced into view. He's still on the phone, which means he's not looking for his keys yet. As badly as we may have wanted to get into Chalys to see what they've been up to, right now I can't wait to get out.

I look down at my phone. Tristan hasn't answered, so I text him again.

Where are you?

I'm cursing him for leaving me now. I recognized that familiar glimmer of determination in his eyes—steel will to keep me safe no matter how much we've endured together.

My phone chimes, offering a shot of relief until I read his reply.

Get out.

I have trouble taking in my next breath.

Get out?

Is he serious?

My heart is beating wildly, hammering in my chest so hard I can hear the blood thrumming in my ears. Panicked, I search the wall of screens for any clues to where Tristan may be. He has to be somewhere. How could he have disappeared that quickly?

Only then do I realize one of the screens in the top corner is blacked out. Beside it, another seems to be pointed down a length of hallway, but the camera is aimed too high to capture anything.

I roll the chair out and sit down at the enormous desk, scrambling to figure out the controls. With trembling fingers, I punch in the code from the screen into the keyboard in front of me and tilt the joystick. The view pans to the right, revealing more of the empty hallway.

"Where the hell are you?" I grit the words out, as frustrated with him as I am fearful for his safety.

Why did he have to leave? We should have stayed together. Instead, he's left me in the dark to worry and wait.

I shift the joystick down until I can see the floor.

Then I freeze.

Someone's unmoving arm reaches out into the hallway, resting in a puddle of blood that seems to be growing.

"Tristan. Oh my God, Tristan, no."

The nausea in the pit of my stomach grows. I jump up from the chair and mold my hands against my temples.

Think. Isabel, think, goddamnit.

Twenty-six years of living a normal life shoves the idea of calling the police to the forefront of my mind. No. The police can't help us now.

Mateus is still here, though. We exchanged numbers back in Miami in case we got separated on Simon's yacht. If I call right now, Knight might suspect something, but I'm running out of options.

I scan the screens once more, hoping to see Mateus again with Knight. But they've disappeared too.

A cold sickness spreads through my whole body.

The helpless panic I'm used to fighting begins to change into something else. Something primal. Something bigger than the emotions ricocheting through me. It fuels me as much as it frightens me.

I look around the control room. In the corner is a desk covered with stacks of paperwork. I go to it and slam open the drawers one by one, finding nothing useful except a long, thin letter opener with a hammered bronze handle. I take it. It won't stop a bullet, but it's better than nothing.

TRISTAN

The man at the bedside is dressed in street clothes, but this is a hospital. Right? He wipes at the crook of my arm with a patch of gauze, then tapes it in place.

My vision is blurry at the edges. Plain white walls. Where am I?

I'm on a metal hospital bed, my arms strapped down tight. I struggle against them, but I'm too weak to fight the restraints. This isn't right. In the corner is a metal chair with the same kinds of straps. No one else is here. Where are the doctors? The other guys?

I squeeze my eyes shut and think about the last place I was.

Gunfire. Sand and dirt and blood and Brennan's face in mine, so scared, telling me to hang on. Help is coming. Who came for me?

The man stands up and reaches over me to secure a plastic mask over my face. I suck in a panicked breath. A metallic taste fills my mouth when he flips some switches on the machine that's beeping at my side.

"What's that? What is all this?"

My voice is muffled by the plastic barrier, but I know he hears me. He pats my leg absently.

"Time to take a little nap. Let the medicine do its work."

The placating rasp of his British accent is the last thing I hear before I plunge into sleep.

I blink rapidly and swallow hard. I don't know how I

know it, but I do.

This was the place. This was the room.

As bare and basic as it is, the memory of it feels more like a shockwave than an echo. I don't have time to piece the rest together. I just killed a man, and things are a long way from being right.

I step over the guy who was guarding the door, with the barrel of my gun aimed at the tall blond woman standing behind Crow.

Tears stream down his face. His dark eyes are swollen, like maybe he's been this way for hours, strapped to a metal chair in the center of the room. If I hadn't heard the faint sounds of his agonized screams through the thick door, I may not have found him. What I'm seeing is so disturbing, I almost wish I hadn't.

"Back away."

I bark the order at her, but she doesn't budge. No introductions are needed. I know she's Kolt's mother. They share the same baby-blue eyes, shadowed with entitlement and spite. I can see Vince in her too and immediately enjoy the satisfaction of knowing I killed him. He was a cold and vicious predator. I'm certain Isabel wasn't the only one to discover what he was truly capable of.

In this moment, though, I'm beginning to wonder if Gillian Mirchoff is worse. Her sleek bob frames the strong set of her jaw. Her chin is high, and her hands rest over Crow's broad shoulders almost affectionately. Except a long, clear bottle, its contents half gone, hangs perilously from her gloved fingertips.

"This isn't your business," she hisses through gritted teeth.

Crow got himself into this mess with a little help from me, but she's not wrong. Their desire to dispose of Crow is Company business. He more than defected. He betrayed them. I shouldn't care, but the puckering acid burns spidering across his chest have my normally ironclad stomach clenching. His tears are warranted. God knows how long she's been torturing him like this.

She shifts her weight, eliciting Crow's desperate whimper.

"Red, please. I'm sorry, man. I'm sorry I shot at you. I'm sorry about Jay. All of it. I was stupid, man."

Gillian's nostrils flare at the mention of Jay. I'm a threat to their operation. Crow is an irritant. But Jay is more—the real treasure trove of damning information they don't want anyone else to have.

"Things are really falling apart here lately, aren't they, Gillian? First me, then Crow. Now Jay and Townsend. Hard to know who you can rely on when the going gets tough."

"You have no idea what you're talking about."

"I'm getting a pretty clear picture these days. Pull strings at the ports and lay out bribes at the border so you can push your poison on to people. You and Simon have it all worked out, huh? All the while Daddy Dearest is laid up in bed waiting to take his last pathetic breath, and no one even knows about it. How long have you been running the show anyway?"

"Long enough to appreciate what's at stake. We'll help

more people than we kill."

I let out a rough laugh. "Yeah? Is that what you said when you had Townsend melt my fucking brain so you could use me to do your dirty work all this time?"

Saying it out loud is like acid on my soul. I'll never show her how much it hurts, but being here now is an ice pick in the wound.

"Is this where you play doctor on people? Mix up your potions and see what works?"

She shakes her head. "You were the first one. The only one. You'd been through severe trauma—"

"I know what I went through!"

She flinches when I raise my voice. I force myself to keep my head. I can't lose control here, but my curiosity is running rampant.

"How long did you keep me here?"

"I don't know," she says quietly. "You weren't really on my radar until you started causing problems."

Until I stopped being a good little soldier and refused to kill Isabel. Until I decided the Company was the real enemy.

"Where's Simon?"

"You'll never find him."

"I found him once. I can find him again."

A faint line forms between her eyebrows. She doesn't know I was close enough to kill him in Miami. As close as I am to her now.

"Why are you in Paris?" I press.

"We just had a little mess to clean up. Isn't that right,

Lorenzo?" She squeezes his shoulder. "And if you don't mind, I'd like to finish cleaning up. If I were you, Tristan, I'd start running. There are cameras all over this facility. The authorities will know your face in a matter of hours. You'll never get out of the country if you don't leave now."

"What makes you think I'd let you live?"

"Because if you kill me, Simon will never stop hunting you down. He *will* find you, and when he does…" She sweeps her turned-up hand over Crow's ghastly wounds.

"He hasn't found me yet. He must not be looking very hard. Or maybe I'm a lot better at this cat-and-mouse game than he realizes."

"We've been a little busy," she utters, her tone hostile. "And quite frankly, it'd be easy enough to forget about you altogether if you would do us the honor of disappearing for good. You served the Company well. Simon knows this. If you agree to leave now, leave gracefully, and we can forget you ever existed."

"That's a tempting proposal, but I doubt you'd honor it. You've been trying to hunt me down since Rio. You haven't let up. You just ran out of leads."

She's too quiet. I know it's true. They thought they had us in DC. Then New Orleans… They almost won.

"What a waste. You had something good with the Company. It's only just beginning, and you gave it all up for her." She laughs weakly. "Better you than my son, I suppose. Her family is a curse. Every last one of them. Every tragedy that's ever fallen upon them, they've brought upon themselves."

The mention of Isabel makes me want to press the trigger before another word can leave this woman's lips.

"Every tragedy that's fallen upon them came at the hands of your family, starting with you killing her sister. What kind of monster kills a sick kid to send a message?"

"Why do you care? How many people have you killed? And for what, money? We were protecting our family. Our legacy!"

I shake my head, pushing down the unpleasant truth. "Doesn't matter. You don't get to talk about her. Ever again."

She tenses a little. "If she means that much to you, disappear with her. Isn't that what you want? Isn't that why you won't give up? You have my word. You can walk away right now with a clean slate."

A clean slate? Funny. That's how I left here last time. Didn't work out so great. The prospect of walking away with Isabel and leaving all of this behind is everything I want right now. Unfortunately I don't believe a word out of Gillian's mouth. Her promises are sweet lies.

She's studying me, trying to unravel my intentions. "Just walk out the door, Tristan. No one's going to stop you."

Crow starts crying again. "Red, no. You can't leave me here. She's going to fucking kill me."

I used to be immune to people begging for their lives. Crow's been nothing but a thorn in my side from the day he barged into Mateus's house, hoping to finish the job I refused to. I shouldn't care about his gory wounds or his desperate pleas, but I do.

Because I hate this woman more than I dislike Crow.

If I shoot her in the head right now, Crow's going to get a lapful of acid, which is the only thing that's kept me from ending her.

"Gillian?" A man's voice echoes from down the hall.

One set of footsteps.

"Sounds like your friend's here to save you," I say lightly, all my senses on high alert.

Her pupils dilate, making her eyes seem bigger and darker. "You have a choice, Tristan. Make the right one."

Then the footsteps stop.

5

ISABEL

I turn the corner and freeze. At the other end of the hallway, Davis Knight stands at the edge of the bloody puddle, his mouth agape with shock.

"Gill—" He looks up and stops. Light from the room illuminates his face.

"Shoot him, you idiot!" a woman screams.

I jolt at the shrill and sudden sound. Knight fumbles under his suit coat.

I don't think.

I run.

I run through fear and the sense of self-preservation that should have led me straight out of the building the second Tristan told me to get out. I run knowing there's a chance Knight could turn and use his weapon on me as soon as he sees me coming. I run because somewhere deep down inside, I believe there's a chance I won't let him.

My footfalls are loud. Cool air whirs over my skin.

He sees me. Surprise and then recognition mark his features. Then a teeth-baring sneer as he twists his body toward me. He swings his arm. I see the gun. A flash of silver meant for me. I measure the seconds I don't have to reach him in time.

A frantic breath fills my lungs. A prayer forms without words. Then an ear-shattering bang corresponds with the sharp jolt of Knight's body against the wall. The gun flies from his grasp and lands with a clatter.

I skid to a stop and pick it up.

"Oh shit," he says. His eyes go round as he brings his hands to his chest, touching the place in the center that's started to seep with dark red. He slides to the floor, leaving a bloody trail behind.

Nothing seems real. Not the corpse on the floor who definitely isn't Tristan. Not the man slowly dying beside me. Not the wild-eyed woman I glimpse through the doorway who looks like she's been melting the skin off the man in front of her.

I'm pretty sure I know her name, but she doesn't need one. I already know she's a monster. She's one of them.

I'm still running on adrenaline. Fearless determination chugs through my veins as I lift the gun, aim, and breathe out.

The force of the gunshot jerks me backward. High-pitched panicked screams penetrate the pulsing of my eardrums.

The man strapped to the chair fights his restraints with vigor. "Not my dick! Red, fucking get it now. Hurry up."

"Stop moving. You're going to spill it." Tristan runs to him but pauses, looking around frantically. He goes to the wall and rips down a handful of surgical gloves that he then uses to carefully wrap around the glass bottle tilted precariously against the other man's groin.

Once it's safely away, Tristan unstraps him from the chair.

The man lets out another painful sound, somewhere between relief and pure anguish. His hands are shaking. More tears pool in his eyes, which are already swollen and red. I can't even begin to comprehend what he's been through.

For a split second, his horror is enough to distract me from what *I've* been through. I just killed Kolt's mother.

And just like with Bones, I didn't think about it. I'm not sure if I would have had time to, but maybe I should have.

Jagged cracks in the window behind her spider out from the hole where the bullet passed through. Her lifeless body rests on the floor in an ugly splatter of blood—her blood. Her limbs are twisted unnaturally.

I did this. She did this.

I'm still shaky and unsteady as I step over the mess in the hall and enter the room. "Are…are you okay?"

He gulps over a swallow, seeming to pull himself together.

"What was that? What did she put on you?"

"Acid. Motherfucking acid." He stares down at his

marred chest. If he weren't such a brute of a man, I'd worry about him passing out.

"We need to get you to a hospital," I say.

"Can't go to a hospital. I'm not even supposed to be in this country. Fuck, I'm not even supposed to be alive." He winces. "I need water. I need to rinse this shit off me before it kills me."

I move closer, even though I can't do much to help him. He's twice my size. "Can you stand up?"

"Yeah." He swallows hard, pinches his mouth tight, and straightens slowly and soundlessly, though I imagine not without great pain.

The three of us maneuver to another room with a sink, but the rinse brings him little relief based on the sounds he's making.

I look to Tristan. "I really think he needs a doctor."

"I'm good," the man says breathlessly. "I don't need a doctor. I need a fucking drink."

"This is Crow, by the way," Tristan says. "And for once, he's right. We can't take him to a hospital if the authorities might be looking for him soon."

Crow. The assassin. Lorenzo Generazzo.

I blink up at him, taking in his dark features. He's much bigger than Tristan, but I'm guessing not as skilled.

He tried to kill us both back in Brazil. He kidnapped Jay and ignited Townsend's hunt for vengeance. Then he turned on the Company with less care than Tristan would have liked.

How do I feel about Crow? I can't begin to unpack it.

All I know is that he's just been through hell.

He catches my stare. "You're Isabel."

I nod.

He offers a pained smile. "Nice shot."

I blink again and realize his fate could have been different if my aim had been a few inches off. I silently thank Tristan for everything he taught me, even though I was barely thinking when I got the shot off. Crow is lucky indeed.

"Mateus is waiting outside with his driver." Tristan looks up from his phone. "Knight ended the tour early when they heard a gunshot."

"What are we going to do about all this?" I gesture to the hallway, where just beyond our view lies all the evidence of tonight's violent bloodbath.

"I'll take care of it," Crow says with finality.

Tristan holds up his hand. "I don't think you're in any condition to take care of anything but yourself."

"Fuck you. I said I'll take care of it. Sweep the building. Make sure there's no one else here. I've got it covered up here."

Tristan's hesitation could mean anything. Distrust, disbelief, or pure curiosity. I get the strong feeling their mutual hostility is normal, though.

"The building is empty," I say. "I checked all the camera feeds. There was just the driver in the back."

"I'll deal with the driver if he's still around. Meet us out front in five minutes," Tristan says.

We leave Crow and take the elevator down. I brace my

hands on the metal wall behind me, hoping to ground myself as quickly as possible. Tristan looks me over, his expression pinched. He doesn't try to touch me. I'm not sure I'd know what to do if he did. I'm wound too tight. Too scared. Too numb.

"Are you okay?"

I swallow over the knot in my throat and focus on the floor. If I lose myself in Tristan's eyes, I'll fall apart. And it's too early to fall apart. This isn't over.

"Probably not."

"You did the right thing," he says gently. "And if you hadn't done it, I would have."

It's probably what I'll tell myself for the rest of my life. That I did the right thing. That maybe it was better to have one less name in Tristan's book.

"Maybe I need my own ledger," I mutter.

It's an ill-timed play at humor, but the second I say it, I'm gripped with a fresh kind of horror that we'll be fighting this war long enough to warrant my own list. My own red ledger…

I close my eyes. *Please, God, no.*

The elevator dings with our arrival, saving me from more of those troubling thoughts.

When I open my eyes, Tristan reaches out his hand. I hesitate a second before taking it, but the contact fills me with a sudden overwhelming relief. Whatever haunts me now…whatever haunts me tomorrow, I know I'm not alone with it. No one will ever understand the way he does.

We walk to the back of the building in silence, searching

for any signs of life. The bay is closed, and there's no sign of the driver.

"He must have left. Coast is clear," he says. "Let's get out of here."

We hurry back to the enormous lobby and reach the doors where Mateus waits just beyond. The elevator opens, and Crow walks through.

The bottom of a white lab coat that's far too small for him billows behind him as he walks briskly toward us. "Let's go. Come on."

"That was fast. Is it all set?" Tristan asks.

Our wounded accomplice passes us and barrels through the double doors with a bang, not answering us.

We don't wait for one as we pile into the vehicle. Mateus turns around in his seat, eyeing Crow. He opens his mouth to speak, when an explosive boom shakes the vehicle.

"Fucking drive!" Crow smacks his hand loudly against the window.

Ford puts the car into gear as another boom louder than the last rattles the windows. I grip the edge of my seat as we whip out of the lot and onto the street.

"What the hell did you do?" Tristan shouts.

"You wanted it taken care of, so I took care of it. It'll take them weeks to find out what happened in there. By then, we'll be long gone."

I twist around to look through the tinted back window and see flames glow from the floor we were just on. A third blast pushes a cloud of smoke into the midnight air, but we're too far to feel it much.

Crow leans back on the headrest with his eyes closed, seemingly oblivious to the vibration and faraway boom. "Where are we going?"

Mateus makes eye contact with Tristan in the rearview mirror, silently asking him the same question.

"We can't take him to the hotel. Not like this," Tristan says, resignation laced in his tone. "Is there someone else we can stay with?"

Mateus doesn't answer right away. He's the one with connections in the city. If he doesn't help us, I don't know what we'll do with Crow in his current state.

I don't blame Mateus for his hesitation, though. Crow isn't a friend. His missteps are the only reason our paths have crossed again, not his loyalty nor his willingness to help. Even if Tristan just saved his life, I doubt he'll ever count Crow as someone who can really be trusted.

Still, leaving him to fend for himself seems cruel after what we've all just been through. One thing Mateus isn't is cruel.

He types into his phone, delaying his answer, the bright screen lighting up his face as we drive through the night. He directs his next words quietly to Ford.

"Take us to Cristóvão's."

TRISTAN

We drive down Sebastopol, past cafés and clothing shops. Most of the restaurants look like they've already closed up. We're miles away from the explosion at Chalys and the carnage we left behind. Crow might be crude and unpredictable, but trying to torch the building at the last minute wasn't necessarily a bad call. The less there is to trace, the better. I don't care if Simon pieces it together. I'd prefer if the authorities don't.

"We're here," Mateus says, pointing ahead to an ornate gated arch built into the strip of connected buildings.

Ford parks at the curb.

"Looks like a dark alley to me," Crow mutters groggily.

"It's a *passage*. One of the last in the city, actually. Cristóvão owns some of the storefronts inside, but he lives in an apartment upstairs," Mateus says.

We leave the vehicle, and Mateus guides us past the locked gate, through the dark alley-like tunnel, and up a set of narrow stairs that brings us to Cristóvão's apartment.

"How do you know this guy?" I ask as we wait.

"He's a designer from Brazil. He's made Paris his home now. Before he moved, our paths crossed, and Karina took to him right away. We've remained friends." He looks to Crow. "I've asked him to call a private physician to see you. He assures me he'll be discreet."

"Thanks," Crow answers gruffly.

The man who answers the door is shirtless with black leather pants and a bright-orange scarf cinched around his head, a vibrant bolt of color against his dark features.

He brings the bottle of red wine he's holding by the neck to his lips and swallows. "You bringing trouble to my door, da Silva?"

"Friends," Mateus says in a reassuring tone, giving Cristóvão's bare shoulder a friendly squeeze. "We're all friends here."

Cristóvão moves aside, and we file into his living room.

Karina jumps up from a weathered chaise across the room and comes toward me. "Tristan!"

She captures me in a tight embrace I don't deserve. Isabel smiles, at Karina's unexpected affection or my awkwardness or maybe both. I hug her back, wishing she were somewhere else, someplace safer. Her being here is a sharp reminder that I've done nothing but put Mateus in danger since I landed on his doorstep in Petrópolis.

Karina pulls back and hugs Isabel too. "It's good to see you. Both of you."

She has no idea what we've been through tonight, except when she finally notices Crow—the ogre in the room—her enthusiasm noticeably dims.

"What happened to him?" she asks.

Cristóvão looks him up and down, his upper lip curled with disgust. He extends the bottle. "Here. I think you need this more than me."

"Thanks, man." Crow takes it and finishes the bottle in a few gulps. "Keep it coming," he says before going farther into the apartment and claiming the longest couch, which barely contains his frame. His feet hang off the arm.

"That's Crow, by the way," I say, half apology, half introduction.

"I'll get Mr. Crow something to drink. And that outfit has got to go." Cristóvão says on his way to the nearby kitchen, wiggling his fingertips in Crow's general direction.

I follow Crow inside the apartment. Everyone else crowds in, taking every available seat.

No one expected a meeting with Knight to go this far off course. Now two more people from the Company are dead, we've incinerated one of their facilities, and we've inherited a new problem. Crow.

"I thought the police arrested you in Berlin," I say.

He doesn't open his eyes as he speaks. "They did. They interrogated me, slapped me around a little, and threw me in a van. Next thing I knew, that bitch was coming at me with her questions. Wanting to know everything I knew."

"What did you tell her?"

He answers first with a sneer. "Let's just say when the acid came out, I started getting really gabby. Doesn't fucking matter anyway. They're toast now."

"It matters if she talked to the Company first."

He squints an eye. "Pretty sure she was having too much fun using me as her own personal science experiment. I seriously doubt she stopped long enough to tell anyone about it."

Cristóvão returns with a full bottle. "Been saving this one for some fancy friends, but you look like you need a good vintage."

Crow doesn't bother checking what's in the uncorked bottle before slugging back a few big gulps, following it with an audible sigh. I can't imagine what it'll take for a guy his size to start to feel numb, but he seems determined to get there.

"As soon as they nabbed me in Berlin, they knew Jay turned on them anyway," he says, rubbing the back of his hand over his lips. "I don't think anything else was big news after that."

He has a point. The important thing was apprehending him and putting a stop to any more trouble he could create for them.

"Did you connect with any of the other people who paid for hits?"

"Nah. I figured this one would be the best payoff."

Of course Crow would focus on the money first, the risk later. He went after someone with enough reach to take him down the second they smelled trouble. Hopefully Gillian turning his chest into pizza is enough to change his course.

"While you were trying to blackmail Soloman's clients, we were getting deeper into his circle and figuring out their plan."

"I don't want to know," he grumbles, and under the pain and the inherent sarcasm, I hear the truth. He really doesn't want to know. He's been through enough.

"You giving up on chasing the rest of Jay's leads, then?"

He sighs again. "Yeah. Might be time for an early retirement. I probably should have stuck to the family business. Sure was fun for a while. Money was nice too."

I tense. He doesn't know what we know. The family business isn't a safe place for him anymore.

"You can't go back home, you know."

He narrows his eyes at me. "Why the fuck not?"

"How many people did you tell what you were doing?"

He opens his mouth, but nothing comes out for a few seconds. "Just a few people. People I could trust."

I shake my head and try to think of good reasons I saved his life. The Generazzo family wouldn't have missed him. Of that much I'm sure.

"The Company has been spending a lot of time at Luca's. Some big cash withdrawals came out of their accounts around the same time."

He stills, seeming to process this bomb of a realization. Then he tries pulling himself up. I shoot up and push him back down by the shoulder.

"What the hell are you doing? The doctor is going to be here any minute. Do you really think you're going to find out who sold you out tonight?"

He drops back with a grunt, his teeth grinding as he does. "Mother*fuckers*. Someone's going to pay."

"It's probably going to be you if you go running back there right now. They're the least of your problems. As soon as Simon finds out you weren't in the building, you can guarantee you're going to be on every watch list from here to the States. Your best bet is to go off the grid for a while."

He doesn't look convinced. "I've got people back there. I can't just disappear. I'm not like you."

"The Company wants you dead. Your family figures you're as good as dead. Townsend does too, and if he finds out otherwise, you're going to have that lunatic on your tail."

"What the hell does Townsend have to do with this?"

"He's with Jay," Isabel offers quietly.

He frowns. "Like *with* her?"

I nod. "Seems that way. I never thought she'd get that close to any of us. But apparently they had enough of a connection that as soon as I took her off your hands, Townsend tracked us down."

I decide to skip the part about Townsend being the one responsible for wiping my memories and nearly killing Isabel, because Crow doesn't care. He only needs to know enough to disentangle himself from this nightmare and disappear for a while.

"Anyway, Jay's with him now. And as soon as he found out what happened with your cousin, he's been obsessed with hunting you down."

Crow takes another drink. "Townsend's always been a pissant. Taught me everything I know about mixing chemicals into explosives, though. Really came in handy tonight. I guess I'll never get a chance to thank him now."

The resignation in his voice gives me hope that maybe he won't go back to New York after all. I'd rather not have saved his life for him to immediately get himself killed. I've never had to deal with the Generazzos, but I've never known a crime family that was above taking out one of their own for the good of the whole or the selfishness of one.

"Do you need help getting out of the country?" I ask.

If the German government let Simon smuggle Crow into France to settle the score, I'm guessing they didn't bring his passport with him.

"I don't know. I'll probably figure something out."

"I can arrange a private flight," Mateus says. "New identification if you need it. Depending on where you want to go, if you arrive on a private jet, you're not likely to get flagged by customs. You'll have to clean yourself up, though."

"Thanks, man. I owe you one." Crow closes his eyes again. He clenches his hand around the neck of the bottle. His forehead wrinkles. "Red, if you can manage it, I need you to do me a favor when you get back."

Crow's parting wishes aren't high on my list of priorities, but we've come this far, so I can at least hear them out.

"I can't make any guarantees."

"I know. But if you're in the neighborhood one of these days, there's a girl back home. I made some promises that I'm not going to be able to keep. If I'm not coming back, she's going to think the worst."

I share a look with Isabel. I never expected Crow to care about anyone but himself. I'm in no position to chide him for having romantic ties when his life is on the line. Never seeing him again will be nothing short of a blessing for me, but no one knows the pitfalls of disappearing out of someone's life forever better than I do.

"Who is she?" Isabel finally asks.

"She goes by Dusty. Red knows the club. Just tell her I couldn't come back. She'll understand."

6

ISABEL

It's well past midnight. We've all been through enough in one night to last a lifetime. The doctor's shot Crow up with some morphine for the pain, and we're all ready for a rest. Thankfully his burns aren't life threatening, though once he manages to smuggle himself out of France, he'll need more treatment and probably skin grafts to repair his marred flesh.

I don't know where he'll go. He and Mateus will have to work it out. And maybe after all this is over, we can find the girl he's leaving behind to give her some closure.

At the door, Mateus holds me in a tight hug that seems to communicate more than a simple goodbye.

"You are his miracle, Isabel. Never forget that," he whispers before letting me go.

His sentiment presses down on me like a physical

thing. After tonight, I'm not feeling like a miracle. I feel like someone who's losing her humanity one devastating moment at a time. I don't recognize the person I've become, yet I've become her. Life will change me again, but I'll never be the Isabel who existed before Tristan found me. I have to come to terms with that somehow. I'm not sure it'll happen tonight.

Mateus pulls a piece of paper out of his pocket and hands it to Tristan. "This is the account number Knight gave me to deposit the funds into. Maybe it'll help."

Tristan folds it before putting it into his pocket and meeting Mateus's eyes once more. "You've done more for me than I had the right to ask for. Thank you."

"Friends worth having ask only for what they truly need and answer with all they can give. You have to know I was never keeping score."

Tristan doesn't answer but surrenders himself to Mateus's embrace. In their silent exchange, I can sense the gratitude and the commitment between them.

After a last goodbye, Tristan and I descend to the quiet boulevard. The streets are damp from a light rain. The scent of wet earth permeates the air. Tristan's hand is warm in mine as we linger there. We're miles from the hotel, but nothing is drawing me back. I should rest and try to wash the events of today off me, but I can't.

Once upon a time, when life got scary, I'd want to run to the place that felt most like home. Now I just want to run. If I keep moving, maybe I won't have to think about everything that's happened. Maybe we'll never stop running…

"Do you want to walk for a while? I'm not ready to go back yet."

Tristan looks at me thoughtfully a moment. "Where do you want to go?"

Nowhere. Anywhere.

"I don't care."

With that, we cross the street and walk through a little park. We turn down narrow winding streets that carry us again to wider boulevards. Step by step, we wander through a labyrinth of history stacked upon itself.

Without the commotion of people and cars, I see more. The way the light glimmers off the Seine as we pass over it. The quiet majesty of the churches and old buildings in the darkness, their intricacies taking on new dimensions in the shadows. Restaurants with stacked furniture waiting for the bustle of morning customers.

The walk is calming. I wonder if it's the silence or the darkness. I would never have thought I'd be safer in the dark, but tonight, with murder on my hands and sadness heavy in my heart, I know this is where I belong for now.

We meander around the Left Bank until we find ourselves in front of an old church with uneven towers. We've hardly stopped a moment, but my feet won't carry me forward.

"What is it?"

"I kind of wish I could go inside," I say after a moment.

Tristan purses his lips as he studies the facade. "Wait here a minute, okay?"

He unclasps our hands.

I tense at the break in contact. "Where are you going?"

"I'll be right back," he calls back as he jogs around the side of the church.

I take a seat on the edge of the grand fountain that sits in front. A handful of pigeons coo casually around me, interested in what I can offer but cautiously keeping their distance. They're dirty little creatures but fascinating all the same, especially in the otherwise quiet night.

A groaning creak draws my attention up to where Tristan is standing in the doorway of the church. I should be worried about us getting caught, but all I can do is laugh. When I do, he smiles and waves me forward.

I climb the steps and pass through the church's columns to meet him. "You can't stay out of trouble, can you?"

He grins. "I guess security's not too tight in God's house."

As he says it, I question being here. We could have admired the church and moved along. Tristan's made his aversion to this kind of place known before. Maybe the fact that I'm still shell-shocked makes it possible for him to overlook his reservations for now.

We walk inside, our footsteps echoing off the walls and beautiful arched ceiling. This place is designed to awe and to humble. I feel both acutely.

Tristan walks ahead of me and begins lighting the candles sitting on a tiered stand behind the pews.

"It's five cents to light a candle," I tease, pointing to the laminated sign taped to the stand.

He reaches into his wallet and stuffs a hundred-dollar

bill into the little metal box for donations. "There. Absolved."

I lean my cheek against his shoulder, watching the flames flicker. The burning wicks mix with the smell of old wood and must. It's cold, and for all the reasons why I shouldn't want to be here, I'm grateful I am.

"Thank you," I whisper, not taking my eyes off the rows of lit candles meant for prayers. "I guess I needed some peace."

He strokes his thumb rhythmically across my skin where our hands are grasped again. "You're still good, Isabel. You have to believe that."

I shake my head against him. I'm not good, and I'm no one's miracle. Not anymore.

"How am I supposed to feel good about what I did today?" I can't hide the tremor in my voice.

"Sometimes you have to fight a war to have peace." He squeezes my hand before bringing it to his lips for a gentle kiss. "And to win a war, you have to be ruthless. It's the only way."

I close my eyes, fighting the sting behind them. Tristan speaks a hard truth. My mother may have raised me to be a thoughtful, careful child, but this war has forced me to peel back my skin to see what I'm truly made of. My ruthless insides, a teeth-baring will to survive and protect, a determination to walk a path paved in blood if it gives us our lives back.

Surviving this will leave me in scars. Today will be a scar. Tristan wears his with a hardened kind of grace. They're ugly and true, like his words. I have to find it in me to accept all of it.

"Come on," he whispers, guiding me away from the flickering lights and my sadness.

We walk around, our soft words echoing lightly through the huge empty space. Set back from the aisles of the church, Saint Paul with his staff stands in stone against the backdrop of a stained-glass window. I trace the thin chain that hangs around my neck until I reach the molded pendant and hold it between my fingers.

Centuries of prayer cling to these old walls. In the stillness, I send off one of my own. A prayer for forgiveness and a vow that once this war is won, we'll do better. We'll *be* better.

Our forbidden tour brings us to the back of the church, where we leave the way Tristan broke in. The sky has gone from midnight to a dusty shade of blue that promises dawn.

"Where to next?" Tristan says. "We have Paris to ourselves for a little while longer."

I'm tempted, but the weight of the day and walking the worry off my mind have me wishing for our soft bed at Le Bristol.

"I think the hotel is our safest bet before you get us arrested."

He smirks. "They'd have to catch us first."

TRISTAN

Gunshots ring out, a distant sound that penetrates the thin walls of our tent. Someone's probably going to die tonight. Maybe one of them. Maybe one of us.

I can't remember what day of the week it is. It never matters here. All I know is I can hardly remember what home feels like. The house is gone. Mom's gone. Home doesn't even really exist for me anymore.

I roll onto my back and stare into the darkness. I should pop a few of the sleeping pills all the guys have been relying on to get through the nights and knock myself out. Even if there weren't a war going on outside, thoughts of Isabel make it impossible to rest.

I got another letter from her today. I read it in private so no one would give me shit about it. I even tried to catch her scent on the lined paper. What I would give to have a day with her. Hell, an hour.

The distance between us is agony. She feels it too. She tries to sound upbeat, but I can read her sadness between the lines. Her truth. How many days of missing me can she endure? How many can I? Once this tour is over, they'll station me somewhere for a while. Maybe California, maybe somewhere she'll never want to live. I try to imagine her being part of this life, but I can't. I really thought one day we'd get married, maybe have a family. But the stories the guys tell, tales of betrayal and people growing apart, are a constant reminder of all the ways this can go wrong.

Things change. People change. We're both rolling the dice that this can last or that I'll even live through this sprawling war that has no end in sight. If I don't, how much time will she have wasted waiting for me to come home?

It's never going to work.

I can't stop saying it in my head. The more I say it, the more I believe it.

I sit up, sneak out of the tent, and head for the main tent. A couple of people on the B shift are hanging around watching TV, not caring what I do. I swipe a notepad from one of the desks and sit down to write Isabel a letter.

It'll be the last letter she gets from me. I promise myself this as I search for the right words. The best words. I won't drag this out. I won't make her wonder if we can find a way to work it out. For her sake, she needs to believe it's really over.

Even as I figure out how I'm going to destroy any lingering hope she carries for our future together, I cling to some of my own. Maybe when I'm out of the military, I'll be in a better place. Financially, emotionally. Maybe we can try again if she hasn't fallen in love with someone else.

The mere thought of someone else having her love makes me hurt everywhere. God, I miss her so much. I can't make myself forget the way she smiles, the way she tastes, the way her body gives under me. I press the heels of my hands against my eyes, refusing to allow an emotional outburst.

It's never going to work. I have to give her up.

Finally, I pick up the pen with shaky hands and start to write.

Isabel—

There isn't much to do here but think about my life. Being over here has changed a lot for me. I thought enlisting would buy us a better future, but I realize now that I was wrong. Sometimes I wonder if I left because deep down I knew things weren't going to work between us. Our lives have always been too far apart. It's only going to get worse.

I swallow hard in disbelief that I'm really doing this. I'm ending it. I can't end it here, though. More needs to be said. This is the part where I wish I could tell her what she's meant to me. How she held me together during the darkest time of my life. I should tell her how much I love her—that I'll never love anyone the way I've loved her. That would be the truth, but now I have to lie. For her sake, I need to lie.

I feel sick. I should rip the sheet off and throw it into the trash. I should be stronger than the voice in my head that keeps reminding me we're doomed to fail. Instead, I keep writing.

I'm sorry it took so long for me to tell you this. I guess I wasted a lot of time pretending we could be anything more, but I think this is the best thing for both of us.

They're moving us to another base in a couple of weeks, so if you write me again, I won't get it. I'm sorry I couldn't do this face-to-face. You deserve more. I'm sorry.

—Tristan

I reread it over and over again. I fold it up, resolve to read it once more after a shitty night's sleep, and will send it off knowing that in a few weeks, she'll know what I know. That we're over.

I suck in a ragged breath and jolt upright.

Sweat cools on my skin as I relive the vivid dream that feels more like a nightmare.

The letter. The camp. The ache of missing Isabel, then losing her for her good. The last goodbye that wasn't even a goodbye I wanted.

Why did I do it? *How* could I do it?

Tearing Isabel out of my life now would rip me to shreds after everything we've been through. I couldn't even do it to save her from this horror show of hunting down the Company. I couldn't let her go…and I never will.

The door unlocks, and she slips inside our room soundlessly until she notices I'm awake.

"I thought you were still sleeping."

I swallow over the knot in my throat, forcing myself to let go of what's already gone. But one look at Isabel compounds my guilt, because now I know what I put her through. For six years, she kept me in her heart when I gave her every reason to forget me and the pain I inflicted.

"Is everything okay?" She walks over to the bed and sits beside me. "Was it another dream?"

Her voice washes over me like the sweetest salve. Her presence is water in the desert. My own personal Eden. I'll never deserve her, but I'll never make the mistake I made all those years ago.

I shake my head. I don't know how to communicate any of this to her. It's all too much.

"I'm sorry," is all I can manage.

"Why? What happened?"

I take her hand, needing the physical connection between us. "You know, I kept your picture with me all the time."

She blinks a few times. "My picture?"

"When we were back in DC, I met with an old army friend. He was the only one who made it out of that last mission alive besides me. I wanted to know what really happened so I could piece more of it together. Afterward, he asked about you. Totally threw me off, because last he knew, we were over. He didn't seem to think we really were, though. He said I'd try writing you a letter every week and set it on fire before I gave in and sent it to you. I kept your picture pinned on the wall until the very end. Until it all went black, I guess."

Her eyes glisten with tears. Two glittering pools of understanding. My heart's in my throat again. I'll never be able to show her how sorry I am. For all of it. Every shred of unhappiness I've ever caused her.

"It's okay." Her voice is a watery whisper. "I held on to you too. Every day."

"I broke your heart."

"It was worth it." She smiles sadly. "We've been through hell, and I'd walk through it all over again to be with you."

I bring her into my arms and hold her. I breathe her in. I have her now. The past is gone. Maybe one day I can make up for all this hurt.

When I let her go and pull away, I'm far enough from the torment of sleep to notice the laptop under the newspaper in her hand.

"What is this?"

"Oh, it's Knight's laptop."

"You're kidding. How the hell did you get your hands on that?"

Her lips quirk up with a mischievous little smile. "I called Landon to find out what room Knight was staying in at La Réserve. You were sleeping so soundly, so I walked over and swiped a master key from one of the cleaning carts. Pretty easy, actually."

"Look at you. My little assassin is all grown up." I never thought I'd have a literal partner in crime, but in this moment, I don't even feel bad about it.

She preens a little. "I was careful, don't worry." She sets the newspaper flat on the bedspread. "The fire at Chalys made front-page news, but I don't think anyone has a clue that Knight is missing yet. It'll probably take a while for Simon to figure it out. But when he does, we should probably be a long way from here."

"I'm guessing that's not the press they were wanting."

"It'll definitely push back the Felix launch in Europe. Whatever Crow did in there caused enough damage that they'll be shut down for a long time." She pushes the laptop to the side. "Unfortunately the computer is password protected, but Landon is going to do his thing and try to find something useful on it."

"Did you tell him what happened?"

"No, but when he finds out Knight's out of the picture, I don't think he's going to be too heartbroken about it."

7

ISABEL

I'm reading *Le Monde*, trying to make sense of some of the other articles with my limited French, while Tristan puts a dent in our massive room-service order.

"So where to?"

I shift the paper to see him just as he clears one of his plates. "Huh?"

"You were right," he says. "We should get out of Paris. As soon as Simon figures out we're behind this, he'll be trying to track us down again. So… Where to?"

I contemplate his question. In truth, I've been contemplating it since before we boarded the plane to Paris. I razor my teeth along my bottom lip, unsure how Tristan will feel about what I have to say.

His stare is unflinching. "What's on your mind?"

I take a deep breath and set the paper down. "I think we should go back to DC."

He pauses a moment. "Any particular reason?"

"I know the plan was to reach out to my dad so he could tip off the right people about the incoming drug shipments."

"And…"

I chew on the corner of my nail. "And the more I thought about it, the more I doubted whether it would do any good. The information we have is so spotty. I mean, we know the ports, but the volume of goods going in and out of these places is probably massive. Even if they stepped up their inspections, the chance of them catching anything is still extremely small. So I was waiting until we knew more and I could give him a better picture of what's happening."

"Okay. That makes sense. Why do you seem so apprehensive about that, though?"

I stare down at my lap and trace the seam of my jeans back and forth. My dad's part in Tristan's enlistment has been haunting me since I found out about it. Unless my mother told my father about the letter I found, he has no idea I've been digging this invisible chasm between us. A space filled with a betrayal too painful to revisit until I absolutely had to.

"I've been nervous about reaching out to him at all," I admit. "Even connecting with my mom about the Halo files was difficult. But my dad…"

"You still haven't forgiven him."

I shake my head. "No, but I want to. When this is over, I need to let it go. I have to. I'm carrying so much of this shit around with me as it is. I can't change what he did, and neither can he."

"Then forgive him. Let it go. Then we can ask for his help."

"There's something else that's been weighing on me. It's not something we really have time to deal with right now. I don't know how to ask my father for help when he doesn't even understand what we're truly up against."

He's quiet for a moment. "You want to tell him everything."

"And that means telling him the truth about Mariana."

Tristan leans back and tosses his napkin on the table. "You really don't think Lucia's told him already?"

"I think it's something she'd take to the grave if I let her. I mean, she couldn't even tell me until she had to arrange a fake funeral for me. She's held this grudge on her own all these years. Not to mention she's done things that would compromise my father's career if anyone ever found out."

"She let him believe a lie that saved him the pain and anguish she's carried around for the both of them."

"You're right, but I don't know if he'll see it like that. At least not right away. This is... It's not an infidelity. It's almost worse. I don't want to be the one to destroy what they have together, but I can't hang on to this lie with her for the rest of my life."

"You shouldn't need to."

"Well... That means telling him or convincing my mother she needs to."

"Then we'll go to DC and regroup. Maybe you can

talk some sense into Lucia, and we'll cross our fingers that Morgan doesn't go nuclear when he finds out. In the meantime, we'll get Landon scouring Knight's laptop for more information. Hopefully he can track the account number Mateus was given to a name."

"Then what do we do?"

"Follow every sign that points to Simon."

There's no lightness to Tristan's voice when he says it. The end of this journey is the end of Simon. We both know it.

"We can probably get a flight to Dulles tomorrow."

"Let's book it." He reaches for a croissant and breaks the flaky heaven in half. "In the meantime, I say we eat our way through this city."

The airport is teeming with travelers on a Saturday afternoon. Every culture and language seem to be represented as we go through the motions of checking in and advancing through the long security line. Through it all, I'm sweating, not only because we're late being stuck in this rush, but the effort to look innocently calm takes more energy than I would have ever guessed. Ever since Tristan sent me home from Brazil with a fake passport—one that could have landed me in custody—I've appreciated not having to fly again. Until Paris.

I hold my breath through the full-body security scanner, releasing it when the TSA agent waves me through. Tristan grabs our bags off the belt, and together we navigate the small terminal and hurry toward our gate.

I check the time on my phone against the boarding time on the paper ticket in my hand. "We have five minutes." The impact of running into Tristan's back momentarily stuns me. "Tristan, what the—"

He's an unmoving wall. "You've got to be kidding me." His voice takes on a sobering tone that makes the hair on my hand stand up.

I follow his gaze to a TV broadcasting the news from one of the gate's sitting areas. I can feel the blood drain from my face as I recognize another flashed across the screen.

"Crow," I whisper.

I walk closer to the TV to pick up the sound, doing my best to translate snippets of what the newscaster is saying. The mug shot of the man they're referring to as Lorenzo Generazzo slides to the left half of the screen, making room for video of the charred Chalys building. It's still standing in daylight, but the damage is significant enough that I'm shocked to see them replace Crow's photo with Gillian Mirchoff's corporate headshot.

They know she was in the building.

I'm not breathing again. If I move a muscle, I'm certain everyone in the terminal is going to know how guilty I am. They'll know what I did. The segment plays out a little longer, listing out Crow's height and build. The smallest amount of relief hits me when I realize they don't have him in custody. They must have taken the photo in Berlin or God knows where else. I have a feeling this wasn't Crow's first brush with the law.

I think the segment is about to end, but then they start playing a dark, highly pixelated video once at regular speed, then again in slow motion. Surveillance taken outside the building.

I grip Tristan's arm when he stands beside me again. Now I'm breathing so hard, I worry I might pass out. Because we're in the video. Again and again, I watch as all three of us rush out of the front of the Chalys building and into Mateus's waiting vehicle. I know it's us, but the darkness and distance of the camera picking it up hide any detail that would clearly define our faces.

Tristan turns away from the TV, pulls his phone out, and presses it firmly to his ear. "Mateus, are you out of Paris?" he says after a moment. "And Crow?" A pause. "Good. His face is all over the news. You'd all better lie low until we figure out what they know." After a few more seconds, he hangs up. "Shit. This better not come back on Mateus."

"Did they get out?"

"They flew out this morning. Already landed."

"Where did he go?"

"Probably the most obvious place Crow could think to go. Italy. Like they won't find him there." He rubs his fingers over the lines in his forehead vigorously. "I seriously don't know why I care. He's like one of those throwaway fish you win at the fair, except I'm that kid determined to keep the fucker alive. I swear he needs his own bodyguard just to talk him out of making the worst possible decisions."

"How do the police even know it was Crow? You can't see anything from that grainy video."

"That's the problem. They wouldn't know unless someone told them. If they had decent footage, our faces would be up there too. Simon's behind this. He knew they were holding Crow there."

"They didn't mention Knight."

"He rode to the building with Mateus. Even if they can't identify bodies right now, Gillian probably had her car in the lot. It doesn't matter. They'll find out about Knight eventually. We just need to get to DC before they do."

Tristan takes my hand, and we rush toward our gate at the end of the terminal. My thoughts are still flying as we join the growing line to board.

"Do you think Simon knew it was us on the video?" I keep my voice low enough that the other people in the line can't hear me.

Tristan's jaw is tense. "I don't know. I really don't know."

I breathe deep, but my nerves are rioting. "If he can splash Crow's face across the national news here, what's stopping him from doing the same with us?"

"For starters, Isabel Foster is already dead. And Tristan Stone has been missing for three years. Both of those are a can of worms Simon probably doesn't want to open. Even if he did, he might know our faces, but he has no idea what aliases we travel under."

"Jay never knew?"

He frowns. "Hell no. I'd never trust her to know that."

I force his reassurances to override the sudden panic that we'll be found out. I never thought I'd be so terrified of the police, but two months on the run with Tristan has changed all that. If anyone knew about us and what we've done to protect ourselves, we'd never see the light of day again. The authorities wouldn't care if we were saving each other or ourselves. They wouldn't care if the people who died were the worst kind of people. Murder is murder.

I file my worries somewhere else, at least for a few minutes, as I get closer to the agent scanning passports ahead of us. I think of Alexandria and my parents' pretty yellow house with the red door on Midday Lane. I think back to a time when I didn't know all the things I do now.

I hover in that imaginary place—the place I can never be again—as the agent holds her hand out for my passport. I give it to her and point my face into the camera taking my picture. The scanner beeps green, triggering a plastic smile from the agent.

"Have a good flight, Miss Santos."

TRISTAN

All that's left of the day is a sliver of fire streaking across the horizon. Deep purples and oranges dominate the rest of the sky above the clouds. We're chasing the sunset. Losing time. Going backward.

It doesn't really feel that way, though. We'll find answers in DC. We'll find Simon. I have no idea how I know. How does a panther know where to hunt its prey? When to go for the kill?

I've circled around Company Eleven for long enough,

unraveling who they really are, dismantling them piece by piece. With Gillian Mirchoff and Davis Knight gone, there's only one thing left to do, and nothing can keep me from it.

Being shorthanded, Simon won't stay in Europe long. If he thought Berlin was a fire he had to put out, he's facing an inferno now. I'm not going away with a meeting or a bribe or a promise.

I'm not going away until this is over.

The plane bumps through the air as we hit a patch of mild turbulence. Miraculously, Isabel doesn't stir. She's been so on edge…since Mushenko gave us the Felix files…since she blew a hole through her ex-lover's mother before the bitch could do any more damage, to Crow or to me. I'm not sure what Gillian's ultimate plan was. I'm sure it didn't involve me showing up and interrupting her torture session. The irony that someone so evil could be charged with developing drugs designed to cure people is not lost on me.

Maybe Isabel is right and Felix will fulfill all its promises. If it does, at least there's one less monster in the mix to enjoy the profits. Soon enough, Kristopher will pass. Unless other arrangements were made, the company will be left to Kolt. He'll inherit more than an empire. He'll inherit all the dirty laundry Gillian and Vince aren't around to cover up anymore.

The plane bumps again, and the seat-belt sign goes on with a *bing*. But a couple of tiny bottles of the airline's cheap wine seem to have given Isabel at least a temporary break from the emotional roller coaster she's been on.

Taking advantage of her nap, I find my phone and

bring up the text conversation I had with Townsend this morning—one I decided not to share with her yet.

I have a care package from
Mushenko for you.

Where should I send it?

                    You aren't going to hand deliver it?

Believe it or not, my schedule doesn't
revolve around your shitty life.
An address should suffice.

I smirk to myself. Townsend is maddening, but at his best, he's at least entertaining. Doesn't change the very sobering situation I'm now faced with, though. The care package is the antidote. There's nothing else it could be. The mere mention of it has my stomach twisting uncomfortably. The possibility of getting my memories back is still scary as hell, a dangerous cocktail of hope and desperation.

I scroll farther down to where I directed him to Makanga's post office box in Arlington. I need to touch base with Makanga anyway. Taking care of Devon Aguilera on short notice was a favor, but he typically likes to get paid for them. I connect to the airplane Wi-Fi and shoot off a text to Makanga now that it's a decent hour in the States.

                    I have mail coming your way.

Are you in town?

What kind of mail?

Actual mail.

Good. Otherwise I was thinking of setting up my own witness protection program and raising my rates. By the way, you owe me.

When can you meet?

Call me tomorrow.

I power off my phone and glance out the window again. Contemplating what I'll do with the antidote when I get it in my hands quickly consumes me. I should tell Isabel about it. I know I won't. We promised transparency, but I'm a liar and a killer and I'm having enough trouble sorting through my own emotions when it comes to the demands I made on Mushenko. I'm not sure I can add hers to the mix and trust the outcome. Maybe the decision should be ours since she shares so much of my past—at least the moments that mattered the most—but in the end, it'll have to be mine.

I rest my head back and close my eyes. The dreams that hit me these days are random and uninvited, but they feel so incredibly real. The memories live on my skin and stay wrapped around me long after I've woken up. Sometimes I wonder if my mind shows me pieces of my past when I need them. The important things. The moments that try the hardest to break through the invisible barrier of these two lives I've lived.

But I can't know what I don't know. Will opening up the floodgates of memories make anything better? Will I love Isabel the same? Will I be so different than I am now? Isabel once said that I was guarded before the mission and Jay's lies turned me into someone else. Something tells me it wasn't this bad.

Isabel has made me feel things I never knew how to before my past went dark. It's a journey I'm not sure will ever end as long as I'm with her. But is it enough? Bursts of remembrance? A disappointing but quiet acceptance that some things will always be lost?

The thinning yellow thread of the sun finally ducks under the clouds, outrunning us but leaving us with a view so magical, it doesn't seem real from this vantage. In Ipanema, I witnessed hundreds of sunsets melt behind the jagged mountains. No matter what brand of hell I was coming home from or running into, I could understand in those moments why people believed in heaven.

8

ISABEL

We're home. DC was the closest place to home either of us ever really had. I register an unexpected relief being surrounded by signs I can easily read and people I can understand. Maybe it's grogginess from the long flight, but routing into the line for US citizens is a small thrill.

We move through the long line until an available customs agent calls us to the kiosk. As I hand over my passport, I glimpse at the man's name tag. An unexpected smile forms as I recognize his face too. Officer LeBaron. His expression is the same as I remember, void of emotion. His severe haircut hasn't changed either. He'd be more intimidating if I didn't remember the smile he finally gave up last time he welcomed me home after I fed him a lie about my vacation in Panama.

He slides my passport over the scanner, his bored stare aimed at the tinted computer screen.

"How long were you in France?"

"Just a few days."

"Short trip," he says flatly.

"We were there for a friend's wedding," Tristan adds.

LeBaron doesn't acknowledge this and proceeds to scan Tristan's passport. "Where did you stay while you were there?"

"The hotel Le Bristol in Paris," I answer, trying to sound confident and normal, whatever that sounds like.

The fatigue quickly dissipates as little pulses of worry hit me. What if I don't end up getting LeBaron's welcome-home smile because he's figuring out we're frauds right now? Seconds pass. He flips through Tristan's passport pages casually, studying all the stamps.

"What do you do, Mr. Gallo? Looks like you're a heavy traveler."

"I'm a consultant for a pharmaceutical company." Tristan delivers the answer like he's given it a thousand times before.

I rub my slick palms against my jeans.

"What's the company?" LeBaron swings his focus back to the computer screen.

"Chalys Pharmaceuticals. Have you heard of them?"

If I could get away with kicking Tristan, I would. Judging by the subtle grin on his face, he thinks this is funny. He probably gives customs agents a different story every time and they buy it.

And LeBaron must be buying it, because a few seconds later, he's stamping our passports loudly and gesturing us to pass through. No smile.

I shoot Tristan a glare. "Really?" I hiss quietly.

"What? I had to come up with something."

"Like you don't have a dozen other answers at the ready for when they grill you like that. Are you trying to give me a heart attack? Like I need more anxiety in my life."

I expect another snarky response, when his smile begins to fade. He looks straight ahead to where a young man in a light-gray suit stands between us and the escalators that will take us to baggage claim and the exits. He's flanked by two police officers. All three of them are staring right at us.

I look down. Swallowing over the sudden tightness in my throat, I pretend to be distracted before taking Tristan's hand. He squeezes it. Reassurance maybe. More likely an unspoken confirmation that he's thinking what I'm thinking.

What if they're here for us?

We don't slow down or make eye contact as we get closer to them. Hopefully they'll let us slide right by. Maybe they're just here to make people uncomfortable.

We're a few paces away when the man in the suit takes a step forward and holds his hand up.

"Hold up. Can I see your passports, please?"

We both make an abrupt stop and put on our best confused faces.

My heart is jackhammering in my chest now. I hand over mine, furious at the way my hands shake as I do. He accepts Tristan's a second later and glances at them so briefly,

I wonder how he's read anything.

"Is there a problem?" Tristan asks.

"I need you to come with us," the man says.

Tristan's grip tightens. "What's this about?"

"You were randomly flagged for security checks."

"You're not with airport security," Tristan says, pointing to the two hovering cops.

Both outsize Tristan, and sure enough, their badges identify them as Metropolitan Washington Police, not airport security. The smaller of the two already has his hand resting on his gun.

Tristan eyes the man in the suit. "Who exactly are you?"

The big cop folds his thick arms across his chest. "Are we going to have a problem?"

Tristan holds his ground and levels a steely look at the man. "If this guy doesn't tell me who the hell he is, we might."

"It's fine," I interject, my voice high with worry. "They just want to check our bags. It's no big deal."

I glance hopefully to the other men. Their expressions aren't promising. Tristan and I only have our carry-ons. We're not stupid enough to travel with items that would set off security. Something must have tripped them about us. Or maybe it's random, like they said.

We should just let them paw through our bags and then we can go. What other choice do we have? Resisting will just cause more problems for us, and we don't want them looking any closer.

But Tristan doesn't seem like he's going to move

without an answer.

The man in the suit finally peels back his jacket to retrieve a leather badge and flips it open casually. "Special Agent Jax Rivero. FBI."

He tucks the badge back into his jacket and spins on his heel, waving for us to follow.

With my jaw locked tight, I follow him, keeping Tristan beside me. The cops circle behind, effectively corralling us past a large silvery window and through an unmarked door beside it.

It's going to be fine. They're just going to check our bags. We haven't done anything wrong. Nothing that they know about anyway.

I keep my self-assurances on a constant loop as we step into a long corridor. We pass by open doors where various airport staff are talking. Some are security. Some are dressed professionally with lanyards around their necks. Everything seems normal enough, except that we're here and we shouldn't be.

Tristan disconnects roughly from our grasp at the same time Rivero places his hand on my back to guide me forward a few more paces. I stop and look back when I hear Tristan's voice.

"Where's she going?"

They've stopped him in front of one of the rooms I've already passed.

"Travelers are searched separately. Standard procedure," the cop answers brusquely.

I can barely see him past the two officers who don't

look like they're going to take no for an answer. Why are they both with him? Why are they separating us?

"This way," Rivero says, impatiently coaxing me farther away from Tristan and toward the next empty room.

When the door shuts behind me, all I can do is scream inside.

TRISTAN

The smaller of the two cops gives me a shove forward. I bite down on the instinct to spin around and break his fucking neck. There are different rules here that I have to follow if I'm going to get us out of here.

"Have a seat," he says, taking my bag from me and dropping it beside the door.

I sit in one of the cheap chairs set around a round table. The room is small. Hardly an intimidating interrogation room. Already I'm taking in details that may help me get out. No windows, but there's a drop ceiling. Unfortunately the cops don't look like rookies. Disarming them is possible, but I'm not sure I want to go there yet. Not with Isabel in another room.

My gut tells me we're not here for a random drug search, but for the time being, I'll play along. The cops are standing guard by the door, never taking their eyes off me.

"Are you going to search my bag?"

"Rivero can do that when he gets here," the big one answers.

I nod like that doesn't sound like a total bullshit answer. "How long is this going to take?"

"As long as it takes."

I'm about to compliment him on how helpful he's being when someone knocks on the door. They move to the side as Rivero enters. He jerks a thumb behind him, a silent order that sends the smaller cop out of the room.

Thinning out the company doesn't make me feel much better. The other cop is still glaring at me like I'm a walking weapon. I worry he may know who I am. Rivero doesn't seem entirely at ease either. He takes the seat across from me after dropping our passports onto the table.

He lets out an exaggerated sigh like he's been on his feet all day. I'm waiting for him to get to it, but he's just looking at me, tapping his thumb on the edge of the table.

"You going to search my bag or what?"

He purses his lips a little. "Let's talk about Paris a little bit first."

Great. This should be fun. Internally I roll out the red carpet for the wave of dread I've been holding back since they stopped us.

"How was the trip?" Rivero begins, his voice mockingly friendly.

I reach for patience I don't have. "Romantic."

"Which part?"

I lift my eyebrows. "You want details?"

He chuckles. "Not really."

"I'm not sure what you want me to say. I took my girlfriend to Paris. We had a great time."

"Where'd you go while you were there?"

"We stayed at a hotel near the *Champs-Élysées* and walked around the city a lot."

"Did you ever go outside the city?"

"No."

"No? No road trips?"

His sarcastic tone keeps the lie trapped behind my lips. I'm done playing this game with him. He must sense this, because he takes a four-by-six glossy photograph from his jacket and puts it in front of me.

"Know him?"

I glance down at the photo of Crow. It's the same photo they're plastering all over the news.

"I just saw him on the news this morning. I don't speak French, so I don't know why."

"Let me enlighten you, then. This is Lorenzo Generazzo, and the French government is pretty sure he blew up a building north of the city this week. He had a few friends with him."

"Why are you telling me this?"

"Thought maybe I'd jog your memory."

"Sorry to disappoint you, but I don't have anything to do with this guy."

We stare at each other for a while, a long, awkward standoff.

If he's found a legitimate way to link me to the Chalys explosion, we wouldn't be having a conversation about it. I'd be in handcuffs. Unfortunately for Rivero, I'm not going to be confessing and neither will Isabel. I hate to think of the anxiety she's going through right now, but she's not stupid. She knows what's at stake.

Finally Rivero picks up the top passport and flips it open to the photo page. "Isa Santos." He tosses it back down like it's trash. "How'd you two meet?"

"We met at a bar a couple months ago."

"And you're already jetting off to Paris together? Sounds like a real whirlwind romance."

I shrug. He drums his fingers on the table, a steady rhythm that starts to wear on my nerves after a few seconds. For once, I'm grateful when he pauses to talk.

"Did she tell you about the trouble she's in?"

I frown. What the hell does he know?

"I have no idea what you're talking about."

"Her real name is Isabel Foster. Did she tell you her real name?"

Fuck.

"Did she ever talk about her dad? He's CIA, by the way."

Fuck fuck fuck.

"I've been tracking her for the past two weeks," he continues. "Whatever shit she's got you mixed up in, Gallo, trust me, it's not good. I suggest you tell me what you know before she pins all this on you."

I maintain my game face, but confusion is ripping through me. *I'm* trouble. *I'm* the guy with the checkered past who Rivero should be pinning every suspected act on, not Isabel. Rivero's preoccupation with her is totally throwing me. I'm so curious how he's drawn these conclusions about her that I've momentarily suspended my plan to knock him out on the surface of the table, deal with the cop, and steal out of here with Isabel.

"It might be easier to help you out if I knew what you were after."

His dark eyes light up with a hungry glimmer. He leans in closer, resting his arms on the table. This would be an ideal time to reach for him, but I rein in the instinct.

"Listen, you seem like a smart guy. If you want to work with us, we can figure something out," he says.

"You're offering me protection."

"Yeah, but you have to talk. I want details. Names, dates, everything. And I want to know exactly what happened in Paris. Don't even try to tell me you weren't involved with this." He stabs his finger onto Crow's picture.

I tilt my head slightly. His proposal is genuinely fascinating. If only we could turn the tables and I could offer him the same deal. Protection in exchange for all the information he knows. As it is, his fate is perilous at best.

"How did you track her down?" I ask.

"It hasn't been easy. I'll be honest, everything around this girl is a giant clusterfuck. I don't know how her father is involved yet, but I'm guessing I'll find out as soon as he realizes we brought her in."

"She hasn't had contact with him in weeks," I clarify, just to see what he'll do with the tidbit.

He leans back in the chair again. "How do you know?"

"I know."

He nods. "All right. Then I'm guessing you know Isabel

Foster officially died in Rio de Janeiro two months ago."

I don't need to answer because we both know it's true. Lucia and Morgan Foster buried their daughter's name days after she left DC to keep her safe.

"Faking her own death wasn't even how we found out about her. She came onto our radar when one of our informants was found dead in New Orleans a couple weeks ago. Shot in the head in her own church. She ran a safehouse in the neighborhood. Turns out Isabel was her last guest."

9

ISABEL

Rivero told me to sit down, but I'm alone now, so I'm pacing the room. Instinctively I search for anything I can use as a weapon. Then I remind myself I'm being held captive by the authorities, not mercenaries. I'm not going to kill a cop. I have to get out of here, though.

With each passing minute, I worry we've turned onto a path with no chance of return. Unless my idealistic notions and Rivero's unconvincing promises are actually true and we're only here for a random search, we're on our way out of the underground world we've been living in.

I wonder what they're doing with Tristan. What they're asking him. His fuse was too short with Rivero before. I don't trust that whatever they're talking about is going well. I'm not looking forward to facing Rivero myself either. I'm a mess. I'm decent at lying when I'm prepared to, but I'm not here on my terms. Already it feels like Rivero could know more than he should about us. I don't know how to act or who to be.

My throat is painfully tight. I would almost prefer imminent danger than the possibility of discovery. I trust my ability to protect myself more than my ability to say the right things if pressed.

I halt my pacing when male voices carry down the hall. I strain to hear them. The sounds are muffled but contentious. Then someone's yelling. Is it Rivero?

I walk to the door and mold my ear against it.

"I don't care who you take your orders from," a man shouts angrily. "You're going to tell me where she is."

I freeze. It's a familiar voice. Not Tristan's, but one I used to trust.

"I'm not supposed to let anyone in or out. As soon as Agent Rivero is done—"

A dull thud of someone getting shoved against the wall vibrates the door.

"You listen to me right now. That's my fucking daughter he has in custody, and unless you want the deputy director of the CIA breathing down your neck over this, you'd better stand down and tell me where she is."

Dad.

He's here. He came for me...

Desperate now, I grab the knob, turn, and yank the door open.

He's snarling at the cop, murder in his eyes. I've never

seen him like this, but I've never been happier to see him either.

"Dad," I sob. Emotions I've been holding back for too long surface in a deluge at the sight of him. Anger and resentment and regret and weeks on top of weeks feeling fear like I've never known.

He forgets the cop and takes long strides to reach me. Even before he manages to get his arms around me, I'm crying—desperate sobs that produce hot, unstoppable tears. He hushes me, but nothing can calm me down. I can't bury myself any deeper into his embrace, though I wish I could.

"Dad…" I keep saying his name, and every time feels like an apology. For what, I don't know. I didn't create this hell, but I'm so sorry for this place I've found myself in that I can't help but feel like it's my fault. All the lies and all the evil that have driven us apart. Suddenly it's so much more overwhelming than I ever let myself believe.

"It's okay. It's going to be okay now," he says in a hushed, soothing voice that seems to pull me down even deeper, reminding me of home and that sense of security I'd always taken for granted.

Even though it's exactly what I want to hear, I don't believe him. He doesn't know who I've become. There's so much he doesn't know…

"Come on. Let's sit you down." He guides us into the room and leads me to the chair I abandoned earlier.

He hunts down a box of tissues and places it in front of me, pulling his chair close beside mine. I hiccup over the tears that have slowed but won't seem to stop. He brushes his thumbs over the apples of my cheeks, stopping each new one. His eyes are kind and sad at once. The lines around them are deep with worry.

"I'm sorry," I whisper. Another tear falls.

"Me too, sweetheart. I should have never let you go."

I close my eyes. "This isn't Tristan's fault."

"He promised to keep you safe. He promised me he would."

"It's not always up to him." I blow my nose and try to collect myself. "How did you know I was coming back?"

"I have a contact at Homeland Security who's been pinging me every time there's a search for you in the shared databases. Someone at the FBI started digging, so I started watching. Your mother told me about your other alias, so when no one could tell me where you were, I made sure I'd find out if you got in the air. I didn't have time to follow you to Paris, but I was sure as hell going to meet you back here the second I saw you book a flight." His lips tighten. "Unfortunately the FBI beat me to you, but we're going to figure this out."

"What do you think they want?"

"I don't know yet." He closes his eyes before speaking again. "Isabel, what the hell has been going on? Your mother convinced me that letting the world think you were dead was the right thing to do after Brienne died. I believed her then, but then you cut us out. Now the FBI is looking for you. It's getting hard to help when you've left me in the dark."

The way he says it compounds my regret. He could

have helped us, but I never let him. Somewhere deep down, I convinced myself that my straight-and-narrow, follow-the-rules father wouldn't believe me when I told him the truth. That his distrust of Tristan would hinder his willingness to use his resources to get us out of this together. More than anything, I kept telling myself that him finding out about Mariana would hurt more than it would help anything.

"I want to tell you everything. It's time. But…" I stumble, not trusting myself to say anything with grace. "Bringing you deeper into all of this will have serious consequences."

He winces. "Do you think I'm worried about my job, Isabel? I'm your father. You're the most important thing in my life."

I believe him. Telling the truth could cost him his job, but it could also cost him his marriage. Life as he knows it.

I think back to the day Tristan left me at the hotel so he could find Jay, trusting my mother would keep me emotionally grounded in the wake of Brienne's death. I remember my mother's intensity then. This nervous, panicked energy that didn't make sense until she finally told me the truth. She had to. Nothing else could have made me sign away my name and my life.

"I've been dreading this day since I left DC. I guess I thought maybe after everything that's happened, I wouldn't have to be the one to tell you. I just don't think Mom ever will."

TRISTAN

"Isabel's grandfather and her mother were really tight-lipped when I questioned them. As soon as I figured out about Isabel's supposed death, I got suspicious that there was more going on. And of course I was right. I interviewed a couple of the girls staying at the safehouse." He grins. "One of them slipped up and mentioned another girl. Isabel."

I'm not the betting type, but I'd put my money on Skye. Whether she led them to Isabel on purpose or not, we'll probably never know. One mention of Isabel was blood in the water after that, though.

"As soon as we figured out she might be involved, we decided we needed to bring her in," Rivero continues. "We couldn't figure out what name she'd be traveling under, though, so we used her last DMV photo and plugged it into the system to scan CCTV footage for a match. We got a hit in Boston, more in Paris. As soon as we knew she was on a plane, we were ready to welcome her home."

Someone bangs on the door, interrupting his excited retelling of how he finally tracked us down.

Rivero glares at the door. "What?"

I'm almost as frustrated, because somehow I've managed to get him to tell me more than he should have. I don't want him to stop.

Martine's power lust and questionable ethics definitely make more sense. Selectively feeding information to the FBI would have given her a degree of immunity against her more questionable ventures. Securing a place of trust in the Company would have been the ultimate coup—as an informant and as someone who was helping herself along the way.

Rivero doesn't realize any of this, though. All he cares about are the two dead bodies at St. Joan of Arc and the family who was poised to take over everything Martine left behind. And of course Isabel.

A little part of me wants to give Rivero credit for sniffing out at least some of the truth with so little to work from. We've been so focused on evading the Company, it never occurred to me that the legitimate authorities would make this much progress.

Of course, none of this is really good news. Even if Rivero is largely wrong about Isabel's motives, he's still onto us, and our chances of getting out of here without a scene are getting slimmer.

The cop inside opens the door so the other can peek his head in. "Agent Rivero, there's someone here. He's with the CIA. He says he's her father."

"Damn it."

Rivero slams his hand on the table and pushes up. That quickly, his mood has shifted from arrogant delight to totally pissed off. Any progress he thinks he's made is about to hit a brick wall. That wall is Morgan Foster.

He's only here for one reason—to protect his daughter. Unfortunately I don't think Rivero is going to let him open up the back door and let us slip away.

Over the next few seconds, I figure how it'll all play out. Rivero and Morgan are going to clash. They'll both try to claim jurisdiction. More people are going to show up. My guess is Morgan will land on top because of his time with the agency. Rivero is definitely outranked. Smart, but maybe a little too green to realize how this works.

Either way, as soon as anyone finds out I'm more than an accomplice boyfriend, they won't be holding me in a tiny interrogation room. The jail cell I've been trying to avoid since Jay adopted me into the Company is looking imminent. Rivero may have his sights set on Isabel, but my gut tells me Morgan isn't going to let that happen. I doubt he's going to start advocating for me.

Rivero steps out. I can already hear him arguing with Morgan down the hall.

"You're interfering with a federal investigation."

"Are you trying to tell me my missing daughter is a federal investigation?"

"When she's traveling with fake identification, it is. You need to back off and let us do our jobs," Rivero says, his tone authoritative enough that even from here I can tell it's going to send Morgan over the edge.

I can't wait any longer to see who wins. The cop who should be keeping an eye on me isn't. As soon as he disappears into the hallway, I take the window. Soundlessly I get up, grab my bag, and jump onto a filing cabinet in the corner. Pushing up a tile in the ceiling, I spot a thick water pipe and hoist myself up onto it. The yelling in the hallway hasn't stopped, but I can't understand any of it now. I replace the tile and drag myself along the pipe until I reach a beam that will hold my weight and take me farther away.

Their voices are nothing but angry muffles now. I can't worry about any of it. I need to get out of here. I may have only seconds before they figure out I got away. Maybe a few more until they realize how.

I'm crouched but trying to move fast. The space above the ceiling is too warm. Perspiration lines my forehead.

Unfortunately I don't have a map of Dulles in my head, so I have no idea where I am. I follow the water pipes and stop at a juncture where they go below. Another large grid of ceiling tiles spreads around it. I lower and lift one up. The sound of kids yelling and toilets flushing filters through the small opening.

Women's bathroom. There's a long line.

I manage to get a good enough look to orient myself. I move down the tiles and lift another one up carefully. It's an empty stall, which isn't likely to stay empty for long. I shift the tile and let myself drop. The force of my body shoves the door closed just as someone on the other side tries pushing it open.

Time to make a scene.

I sling my bag over my shoulder and open the door. A young woman on the other side screams.

"Sorry," I offer quickly.

I don't waste any more time with apologies. I speed past the line of outraged women and into a busy terminal. Security will start looking for me soon, so I move fast. Thankfully a man running through the airport isn't cause for alarm. Following the signs to the exit, I pass the baggage belts and drag in a ragged breath once I get outside.

I swing my gaze up and down. The line for the taxi stand is too long, so I walk past it and bang on the door of a taxi farther down.

"Sir! Sir, you have to wait in the line. The line starts here," the airport employee managing the taxi stand shouts.

The taxi driver rolls down the window. "What's up, man?"

"Three hundred bucks to get me out of this line and take me to Arlington?"

"You got it." He snaps his seat belt on and grins. "Better get in before this guy has a hernia."

"Make it fast," I add, slamming the door behind me.

"You got it." With that, he peels out of the line and we speed away, rapidly putting the airport behind us.

My heart is hammering from the race to get out. But I made it. I got out.

I'd be celebrating more if I hadn't left Isabel behind.

I drag my fingers through my hair roughly, looking back at the jetways as they get smaller and smaller.

She'll be safe with Morgan. I force myself to believe it.

Hell, she's probably safer with him even with the FBI's half-baked theories than anywhere with me. She'd never accept that as true, of course. She's thrown herself in danger to find a way to be with me. She can't do it if she doesn't know where I am, though.

I curse inwardly, replaying it all. Trying to take her with me would have ended badly and might not have been successful. I did what I had to do. I did the only thing I could do short of letting them cart me away in cuffs and lock me in a metal box. The last thing Isabel needs to worry about is whether or not I'll have to face the music for any of my many crimes.

I take out my phone and contemplate sending her a message, just to let her know I'm okay. That I'll find her. But someone will probably intercept it.

I dial Makanga's number instead. He picks up on the fourth ring.

"Red. You back in town?"

I decide to cut right to it. "Are you home?"

"Yeah. Why? What's up?"

"I'll be there in half an hour."

I hang up and turn the phone off for the last time. I can't call her. I can't make contact. Not yet.

As the miles between Isabel and me grow, so does the ache of not knowing when I'll see her again. All I know is that I will. When all of this is over, I'll find her.

10

ISABEL

I twist the tissue in my hands over and over as tight as it'll go. It's no longer something to dry my endless tears. It's become a stress-management tool as I sit and wait in my father's empty office.

I've never been here before. I never knew he looked at an old picture of my mother, Mariana, and me every day he came to work. The photo of all of us is grainier than the others beside it—me at my graduation and more recent family portraits. But I can't take my eyes off that particular one. It's a looming memory that will soon take on a new dimension for my father.

The prospect of telling him the truth seemed overwhelming until Rivero barged in with his threats and accusations. Meeting here so he could finish his interrogation under my father's supervision was the compromise they struck moments before everyone realized Tristan had vanished.

I twist the napkin impossibly tighter.

He's gone. He had every reason to get out as soon as he had a chance, and I'm glad he did. If Rivero knows who I am, what does he know about Tristan? If he had any idea about his past, Tristan had no choice but to run.

The second I saw my father at the airport, I wanted to spill every truth to him, but now I don't know what to do. Rivero seems like he's determined to nail us to the wall.

I nearly jump out of my chair when the office door opens abruptly. My father walks in, Rivero and another man behind him. My father circles around his desk and sits calmly in his chair. Rivero doesn't seem so at ease when he takes a seat beside me. The other man, holding a notebook under his arm, leans against the wall beside my father's desk.

"Isabel, Agent Rivero, this is Agent Damon Parish. He works under me. I'd like an impartial witness here for this."

Rivero lets out a caustic laugh. "Impartial?"

My father levels a cold look at him. "Don't question my team's integrity."

"I call it like I see it," he snaps back. He slides his gaze to me. "Let's get this over with. As soon as we knock this out, I have another suspect to track down, and then we can start writing down confessions."

Rivero has no clue where Tristan is. My heart does a little leap at this realization. If he slipped past security at the airport, he'll be impossible to find now. Rivero's lost his chance.

"Gallo said you two haven't been in contact for a while. If that's true, what's changed?"

I share a look with my father. Rivero is still referring to Tristan by his alias, which means my father hasn't corrected him yet. He's protecting him. Thank God.

"For the sake of her safety, our communications have been very limited," my father says.

"Why don't you let her answer the questions?" Rivero says.

"Why don't you get to the fucking point? You think she hasn't been through enough? You've got ten minutes. Then I'm shutting this down. If you want to embarrass yourself and hold her on having falsified documents, you can explain it to the same people who created them to protect her."

I rear back a little at my father's venom toward the other man. Parish seems to lean back a fraction, like he's not used to seeing it either.

"There's a lot more to this than a fake ID," Rivero argues. "I've got two unexplained homicides in New Orleans. One of them was Martine Benoit. Probably doesn't matter much to you, but she was an informant for us for over a decade. Now I've got a building explosion in Paris and three more bodies, all tied to a company that my informant was collecting a file on." He bends over to withdraw a laptop from his suitcase and drops it onto my father's desk. "I've got a laptop registered to Davis Knight that your daughter's been traveling with. He's been missing since the explosion, and the last ping on his phone was in Paris. Want to explain that?" He lifts his hands into the air. "I mean, I've got more.

Do you want a full report, or should we start filling in the blanks?"

I can read the concern in my father's eyes. Rivero knows too much. He certainly knows enough to make it impossible for me to walk away. Dancing around the truth isn't going to satisfy him.

I twist the tissue anxiously, replaying everything he said. "Martine was an informant?"

"Yeah. A good one too. She had dirt on everyone, and if she didn't, she knew how to get it. A few days after she was murdered, someone sent us a file. Her death must have triggered it. Looks like she had a lot more than she ever shared with us. Unfortunately I've been too busy trying to figure out how you're involved in all this to start weeding through all the intel."

"If she really had dirt on everyone, that's a hell of a lot of people with motive to kill her," my father says pointedly.

Rivero doesn't seem deterred. "Why were you staying with Martine?"

I look at my father, wishing we could have talked before and worked out a strategy. If I say the wrong thing, I can't take it back. Rivero is out for blood.

"Why were you staying with Martine Benoit?" Rivero repeats the question with emphasis on each word, like I'm hard of hearing.

I close my eyes, wishing I could shut him out. All of it. If I could somehow transport myself out of here and into the safe cocoon of Tristan's arms, everything would be okay.

Everything's going to be okay.

My father promised me. I want so hard to believe it. Except it feels like I'm being torn apart as every world I've ever lived in drives toward a single point of convergence. Tristan's underworld. The old life I ran from. The new life I chose. I've been fractured between them all—holding on to the broken pieces, mourning the painful past, fighting for an impossible future, never knowing who I truly am or where this path is taking me. I've been doing it all as a girl without a name.

"Isabel..."

I open my eyes to catch my father's gaze. Something in it seems to say, *Tell the truth.*

Even if it's going to break his heart.

I look Rivero in the eyes.

"I was staying with Martine because she was friends with my mother. She thought I'd be safe there. It was her idea for me to start over. She was scared for me. Really scared."

"So scared you had to fake your death? Why?"

I have to keep going. I have to tell him.

"Because the same people who are trying to kill me are the ones who killed my sister."

Rivero blinks a few times. Then takes a quick scan over my father's desk. His gaze lands on the same photo that's been haunting me since I arrived. Every ounce of antagonism seems to have drained from him as we both watch my father's reaction.

His expression is unreadable. "Mariana was very sick," he says, his voice deceivingly calm, resolute, like this is the truth he's told himself for the past twenty-three years.

Hot tears burn behind my eyes. "And the Boswells stole whatever time she had left. The experimental treatment wasn't what they promised it would be. It was so much worse. Killing her was their revenge on Papa for trying to expose them all those years ago."

"Why are you saying this?"

"Mom knew. She didn't want to hurt you, so she and Papa kept it to themselves. I think she was scared you'd blame her for it and you'd never forgive her."

He shakes his head. "This is a theory. There were doctors involved. Paperwork. She can't really think they'd kill a sick little girl."

"I've met these people. I know what they're capable of. So did Mom. So after Mariana died, she became friends with Martine. They started working together to try to hit back against the Boswells. Nothing they did was enough to cripple a company that was growing so fast, but they were persistent." I stare into my lap. "Too persistent, I guess."

A long silence. The way he's looking at me, I can tell he's putting it together why Tristan came back into my life, the man who was hired to kill me but wouldn't.

"They came for you too," he finally says.

I acknowledge with a small nod. A long silence. Everyone seems to be waiting for him to say something. To react. To freak out and scream. Anything.

Red creeps up his neck as he drags his fingers through his silvering hair. "I need a minute," he says, his voice gravelly with emotion.

Rivero stands up.

My father pins his stare on him. His eyes are a little wild. "Don't even think about looping anyone else in. No one makes a move until you and I get to the bottom of this."

"Fine," Rivero says after a short pause.

"I want your word," my father says firmly, leaving no question that there will be consequences if it's broken.

"You've got my word."

TRISTAN

I have the driver drop me a mile away from Makanga's place and walk the rest of the way, stopping at an ATM on my way. The last thing I want is anyone tracing me to his doorstep.

When I arrive, yellow light spills from the windows of his little house onto the little lawn in front. His crappy car is parked in the driveway.

He doesn't do exactly what I do, but somehow he's managed to stay in one spot. It's hard to imagine having that kind of stability again when we've been thrown from place to place for months. All the wishing I've been doing for a better life for Isabel and me seems to have been washed away with the events of the day.

I stride up the walk and knock on the screen door. Makanga answers a few minutes later.

"Hey, man. Come on in. Good to see you."

Inside, everything looks the same. A no-frills bachelor pad. "You didn't say that last time I showed up."

He chuckles and walks lazily to the refrigerator. "Yeah, well. Doesn't seem like you have anyone shooting at you this time around. Want something to drink?"

"Sure." I sink into his old couch, feeling the weight of the day acutely.

He hands me a chilled beer, claims the recliner he seems to love, and takes a swig from his own bottle. "So, how's it going?"

A loaded question.

"I've been better and I've been worse."

"I hear ya. What's up with your girl? I thought she'd be with you."

One mention of Isabel is a swift punch to my gut. I hate not knowing where she is or what she's doing. I have to trust that Morgan has a handle on things. He may hate me, but he loves his daughter.

"You guys still together?" Makanga presses.

"We had to split up. The FBI nabbed us at the airport. I managed to slip away."

"Damn. Sorry."

"It's all right. Her father is involved now. He'll make sure nothing happens to her."

He nods thoughtfully. "Helps to have family in high places."

"Doesn't help me much."

He chuckles. "Let me guess. Her dad's not a big fan of the company she's been keeping."

"Understatement of the year." I unzip my bag, pull out two bricks of cash, and place them on the coffee table between us. "Thanks, by the way. For Aguilera."

His eyebrows lift when he sees the money. "My pleasure."

"Did she decide to go public about the affair?"

He shakes his head. "She was talking about going back to Florida but found out there were some shady characters hanging around her apartment. Whoever wants to take her out doesn't seem to be backing down."

I curse inwardly. Of all the balls Simon has in the air, I didn't think Aguilera would still be a priority. But if she is…

"Who's the senator?"

"The one who knocked her up? Keegan, I think."

"Do you know anything about him?"

He shrugs. "Not really, other than she seems convinced he's not behind this. She really wanted to make contact, but I managed to talk her out of it until the coast is clear."

Back when I accepted the assignment to kill Devon Aguilera under the pretense of luring Jay into a meeting, I figured it was just another random hit. I didn't know what I know now. That every hit had a purpose. That the Company's number-one objective has been to support the plan around the Felix launch and all its offshoot ventures. Chances are high that Aguilera's surprise pregnancy threatened some piece of that plan.

I pull up a search for Senator Keegan on my phone. I get a few news articles and a photo of his perfect family, the one he probably doesn't want to give up for his mistress. Then I navigate to the legislative initiatives he's involved in. Scrolling through dozens of acts on issues across the board, I stop on one that snags my attention over the others.

"Unbelievable," I mutter.

"What is it?"

I read on, ignoring Makanga. Every sentence is worse than the last, but somehow none of it is a jaw-dropping surprise.

"Looks like he's sponsoring a bill that will allocate billions in federal grants to rehabilitation centers. A graduated plan over the next five years."

"What's wrong with that?"

"Everything." I toss the phone aside, my thoughts whirring through the possibilities now that I have this nugget of information. "He's working for the same people who've been after Isabel and me. Or maybe Simon just has him in his pocket for this one piece. One way or the other, he's part of pushing their plan forward."

Makanga tugs at one of the dreads spiking from his head. "Who's Simon?"

"Someone who needs to go away."

He purses his lips and nods. "Sounds like your department."

"We need to draw him out." I lock my gaze with his. "Do you think Aguilera will work with us?"

"Maybe. I think she's still in love with this guy, though. She's not going to do anything if it means putting him in danger."

"I don't want to kill him. I want him to lure Simon out for me. If Keegan knew about the hit on her life, though, that's going to be a little trickier."

"Pretty sure you can get him to set up a meeting with Simon whether he wants to or not," Makanga says with a sly grin. "And if he's going to be a problem, I can keep him quiet for a few days until you do what you need to do."

"Is that too much heat for you?" I challenge. His reluctance to help us after Brienne was shot hasn't been forgotten. I don't blame him for not wanting to get involved in my mess, but he's either in or he's out. There's no middle ground anymore.

"You keep the heat off my doorstep, Red, and we're good. I wouldn't mind a few more stacks of those either." He nods to the cash on the table.

"That can be arranged. First I'll need a few things if we're going to do this right."

"Make a list. I'll get it done."

11

ISABEL

It's been twenty minutes, and we're still congregated around Parish's modest cubicle. Every once in a while, my father's shouting reaches us.

"Is he going to be all right?" Parish shoots a concerned look toward my father's office.

Rivero swirls a stirrer around a Styrofoam cup of steaming coffee. "That's the kind of news a thirty-year career in intelligence prepares you for."

"I highly doubt it," I mutter.

"You have no idea the kinds of things we see."

He's right, but I don't especially care. I'm pretty sure my parents' marriage is ending right now. Unfortunately, telling my father the truth about Mariana is only the beginning. Once the dust settles, I'll have to share more of the ugly truth if I'm going to convince Rivero that his accusations, or most of them, are misplaced. I've been his target since Martine's death. They have to know about Chalys and their plan if we have any hope of putting a stop to it.

My father's door swings open. His skin is ruddy and his hair is mussed. "Isabel, get in here. All of you," he barks.

Just like that, I'm a little girl who's scared to death of stirring her father's ire. I walk briskly to the office. Rivero and Parish follow me, and we take our seats around the desk again. My father drops into his chair loudly.

"All right, Isabel. What the hell is going on? According to your mother, I'm not the only one who's been kept in the dark."

"It's a long story," I say.

There's too much blood and discovery and deceit. I hardly know where to begin.

"Start wherever you want. Let's hear it," Rivero says.

I take a deep breath and start at the beginning for Rivero's sake. My grandfather's troubles with Chalys. My mother's war on the Boswell family. The hit on my life that would have been a distraction from something a lot bigger than a twenty-year-old grudge, though I keep Tristan out of it.

I tell them about Felix and all the moving pieces we've uncovered from Simon's plan. The ports. The drugs. Simon's business plan with the rehabilitation centers. I point to the laptop, where they're likely to find even more to substantiate everything I've told them.

"I know it probably seems like I've been at the wrong

places at the wrong times, but this is why. I've been chasing down the truth so I could protect myself. I never realized I'd find something this…overwhelming."

When I get to a stopping point, Rivero drops his head into his hands. "Holy fuck."

I exhale a sigh of relief. My father's rage seems to have simmered, because his expression is tense, like he's trying to work out a very important, complicated problem.

"Why didn't you come to me about this? We could have had people on this already. Who knows how far along this plan is already."

Because you hurt me. You took Tristan from me. Because I didn't want to watch your heart break over Mariana all over again.

I can't tell him any of that with Rivero in the audience. One day I'll tell him. One day we'll make peace.

"As soon as I started to figure out the scope and scale of this, I planned to tell you. Why do you think I'm here?"

My father softens a little at that. No other reason would have brought me to DC so soon.

Rivero still looks like he's in shock. His hands are steepled over his mouth. "I knew this was big. I don't know how. I just knew it."

Parish speaks up from his post beside my father. "This is an enormous operation they're trying to pull off. One that I'm guessing they've protected pretty strongly. How did you find all this out?"

His question is the one I've been hoping no one would ask. Who are my sources? The answers open the door to another world of trouble that I'm not willing to bring into the light yet—or possibly ever.

"When my mother faked my death, I had to go underground. In the process, I met a lot of people who've been able to point me in the right direction."

"What kind of people?" Rivero asks.

I'm not about to start naming names, even though I'm sure he would love it if I did.

"I found some friends along the way. Some of them were defectors. Simon has a team on the ground who does his dirty work. They're paid to take care of people who get in the way of his plans."

"People like you," he adds.

"People like me. Because he couldn't get to me, it set off a chain reaction inside the organization. For one reason or another, a lot of key players left. They weren't necessarily on my side, but they weren't on Simon's anymore. And if you're not on his side, you're as good as dead, so getting people to help wasn't always so hard because we all want the same thing."

"What's that?" Parish asks.

"To stop Simon. I won't get my life back until he's stopped. I'll never be safe. And no one else who's ever crossed him will be either."

My father rises from his seat and starts pacing behind his desk. "We can get the DEA on this. That's not the problem."

"My team would have a field day looking into this guy's ties," Rivero says.

Parish raises his hand. "I volunteer to scour the laptop."

Rivero scowls. "That's FBI evidence."

"Stop." My father halts his pacing and stares down at all of us like we're his pupils.

No one speaks until he does.

"We're not turning this into a bureaucratic shitshow. We'll waste time we don't have working around all the fucking red tape between your agency and mine. We're not doing that."

Rivero stares at him. "What do you propose we do? I mean, we have to get people on this. Start tapping our resources."

"We will. But we're going to do it our way."

Rivero stands up and starts pacing his own circle. "We can't do this without telling anyone. I'm not losing my job over this so you can chase a grudge."

My father brackets his hands on his desk. "You're worried about losing your job over keeping this quiet?"

Rivero widens his eyes. "Uh, *yeah*."

"We're dealing with bribes at all levels of government. We're dealing with Big Pharma. Banks. Criminals. All of it steered by some of the most powerful people in the country. You think people aren't going to start losing their jobs—hell, their *lives*—as soon as they find out we're sniffing around their operation? If we were stupid enough to publicly launch a full-scale investigation, they'd be throwing everything they could at us to stop it. You'd be the first to go. If you're not squeaky clean, they'll use whatever they can find to ruin you, first chance they get. And because Isabel's right in the middle of this, they're not going to let me anywhere near it." He pauses and straightens. "And that's just not going to work for me."

Rivero shakes his head, more in disbelief than disagreement, I think. "How are we supposed to put a stop to this without an investigation?"

"We get the right people to launch their own investigations in their own jurisdictions. Get them a nice little care package of what leads they'll need to follow. Then there will be fifty investigations to try to shut down. Good luck burying all of them."

"And what about Simon Pelletier?"

My father doesn't answer right away. I'm curious too. How do you begin to take someone like that down? Protected by endless money and the best legal teams, he's likely to get away with everything, and then we're not any closer to giving me my life back.

"Let me worry about him," my father says.

Rivero laughs roughly. "You took an oath, you know. Don't throw away your career over this."

My father circles the desk slowly, stopping when he's right in front of Rivero. Face-to-face, my father's dominance is clear. Rivero might be younger and stronger, but my father has height and something you can't see but can sense—experience, confidence, and determination like I've never seen before.

"I solemnly swore to support and defend the Constitution of the United States against all enemies, foreign and domestic. Are you going to stand there and tell me these people aren't an enemy to our society?"

Rivero taps his foot on the carpet nervously. "No. I'm just… I'm just trying to be the voice of reason here. You're obviously emotionally involved in all this."

"So are you. You've been trying to hunt Isabel down for weeks with a degree of commitment I honestly wish I saw more of out of my own team. Maybe you don't want to see justice as much as I do now, but you still want it."

"I haven't slept for a week," he says with a hint of resignation.

"Then let's be the good guys and shut this shit down. Together."

THE RED LEDGER

LEDGER

part 9

1

ISABEL

Alexandria, Virginia

I catch the scent of my mother's perfume, a weakening trace of her presence. My father shutters himself in his office, leaving me to face the palpable void alone.

The otherwise empty house creates space for a swirl of emotions I'm not ready for. The prospect of facing my mother after revealing the truth about how my sister died has been eating at me for hours. I don't know how I'll sleep after today, even though I feel the exhaustion deep in my bones. My mother will see this as a betrayal, this sudden breaking open of the secret she's held on to for twenty years—a terrible, heartbreaking secret that was born from someone else's sins. I hope my father can see that. Maybe not today, but one day when his anger has cooled. She was only trying to protect his heart.

My stomach rumbles loudly, marking a sudden hunger after this harrowing day. I go to the kitchen, switch on the light, and make myself a sandwich. Everything is the same. The condiments in the refrigerator door. The breadbox on the counter. The kettle on the stove that only my mother ever uses.

The familiarity should give me some comfort, but when it comes to the things that really matter, everything is out of place. My family is fractured. My future with Tristan is uncertain. My freedom is in question. My entire life has become a sea of broken glass. I'm just praying any of the pieces can keep me above the water.

I resist the urge to cry. All my tears today couldn't bring Tristan back to me. They couldn't heal my father's hurt. I'm certain they can't touch mine. So I deny their existence. I go to the kettle, fill it with water from the tap, and light the burner underneath, all the while holding on to the feeble hope that somehow tomorrow will be better.

After a few minutes, I pull out my phone and stare at the blank screen. Calling Tristan again is pointless. Every time sends me immediately to a generic voicemail recording. Knowing the authorities are trying to track him down, he likely trashed his phone the first chance he got, severing the line between us too.

It burns me that he left without me, but I know he didn't have another choice. I had my father there to protect me. Tristan couldn't count on mercy from the man who sent him to the front lines to begin with. He saw an opening and took it.

And he'll find me. I have to trust that. What we have is too strong to walk away from. We've endured the threat of death and dangers beyond anything I could have ever imagined. We weren't expecting the FBI to track me down, but that's not enough to keep us apart. Agent Rivero bending to my father's insistence that we keep all of this under the radar gives me hope. I won't abandon my father's mission, but once he gets what he needs, I have every intention of disappearing again. I'll figure out a way to find Tristan if I have to walk to the ends of the earth to do it.

I can barely hear my father's voice on the other side of the house, but he's talking to someone. Maybe my mother. If he's on the phone, I take it as a sign that he's past wanting solitude. The kettle whistles, and I make two mugs of tea.

He's sitting behind his desk beyond the French doors of his office when I arrive. He sees my hands full and jumps up to open the door.

"Can I come in?"

I brace myself for him to turn me away. He has every right to want space after everything that's happened today. Even if his mood is grim, having his company would be a welcome change. Being alone right now is too painful.

Sadness swims in his eyes as our gazes lock, full of quiet understanding.

"Of course," he says, stepping back so I can enter.

"I made some tea for us." I set his down and hold mine in my lap.

He takes his chair again, eyeing the steaming mug wearily. "I'm a coffee guy. You know that."

"It's too late for coffee. Besides, Mom always says tea makes everything better." I shouldn't be bringing her up when everything is so raw. He doesn't want to talk about this, or maybe even think of her, but I can't keep from trying to mend things however I can. "Do you have any idea where she is?"

"No, I don't." He traces his fingers along the ridge of his desk. "I know it's hard not to worry, but try not to. We're not missing any suitcases. Her toothbrush is still in the cup. I already checked." His smile doesn't reach his eyes. "She probably just needs some time. Same as me."

"And here I am interrupting it. I'm sorry."

"I'm happy you're here. I want to be alone with my thoughts about as much as you do, I'm guessing." He studies me like he can see the past two months written on my skin. "You've been through hell, haven't you?"

My throat tightens painfully. I can barely manage a swallow to hold back the emotion chugging through me, threatening to take over my whole body. I can't answer him. I can't begin to explain all that's happened. I take a sip of my tea and let it scald my tongue. The heat feels good on its journey through my chest.

One day I might be far enough away from the horror of it all that I can heal. I'll never forget, but I'll need to find a way to move on. It's hard to make peace with it on my own. Having Tristan with me has been a grounding force. Without him I'd be reeling. And I'd probably be dead.

"I'm just glad I haven't been alone."

"It's always been easy to place the blame on Tristan," he says. "But the fact that you're sitting here right now probably means he's had a pretty big hand in keeping you safe through all of this."

I've lost count of the number of times Tristan's saved my life. I'd like to believe I saved his a time or two. I can't imagine how I could have endured any of this without him.

"Your mother told me you found the letter," he continues.

I nod, avoiding his eyes. The letter nominating Tristan for a special operations team at my father's wish is one I haven't been able to forget. It's the letter that's kept me from reaching out to him for so long, not knowing if I could ever truly forgive him.

"I know you were trying to protect me, but..." I take in a shaky breath. *But you destroyed us. You broke us.*

"I was, and I still am. That doesn't make it right. If I could change things now, I promise you, I would."

His admission means more than he realizes. After feeding my resentment for so long, I'm not ready for his change of heart. He never approved of the relationship. If he acted like he did, I could always sense his pretense. Defying his wishes for me for so long carried its own weight, compounding the pain of Tristan leaving.

"You have no idea what it means to hear you say that, Dad."

"You probably blamed him for a long time for leaving you," he says, waiting for my answering nod before continuing. "When it came to enlisting, you should know I didn't give him much choice. I manipulated the situation to edge him out of your life. I was blinded by wanting a better life for you than I could imagine him giving you. Lucia kept you safe in her way. This was mine. We both did the things we did out of love, which is probably hard to accept after everything you've been through. All I can tell you is that I'll lie, cheat, and manipulate the hell out of this mess with that same single-minded determination. I'm going to get justice, one way or the other."

When he says justice, it sounds like revenge. For Mariana. For all this pain.

My lips tremble. I want to speak, but I'm afraid of crumbling. I sniff and wipe at the tears already spilling down my cheeks. "Thank you," I manage.

"Thank me when this is over. Until then, I just want you to know, I am sorry. For what it's worth…" He pauses to hand me a tissue. "I figured today was a good day for the truth, all things considered."

I take it, wishing the tears could stop. "Dad… Tristan's changed. He's done things… I've done things. We can't take any of it back, but I don't care. He's still the person I'm supposed to be with. I need you to believe that."

"I do."

I pause. "He's…a criminal."

He tenses slightly but doesn't waver. "I honestly don't care right now."

The weight of his disapproval all these years lifts a little more. At least I won't have to fight this war with my father anymore. Thank God, because there's still the rest of the world to contend with.

"I'll protect you both. As long as I can keep Rivero locked down, we'll be fine. Try not to worry about that right now."

"I have no idea where Tristan is. Even if I knew where to look, I have to worry about leading the FBI right to him."

My father rests his hand on the desktop and captures the tiny tab of paper at the end of the tea bag between his fingertips. "I have a feeling he's going to come for you no matter who's looking for him, don't you?"

God, I hope so. With all of my being…but not if it puts Tristan in danger. I won't put his freedom in jeopardy.

"I want that and I don't."

My father leans forward, holding my gaze steadily. "I'm going to do everything in my power to fix this. I'm going to make it right, Isabel. If it costs me my job, my savings, so be it. I don't care. Mark my words, it's not going to cost me my family."

We stay that way a long time, holding the promise between us, before he slowly reaches for his tea. He brings it to his lips and drinks.

"What kind is this?"

I laugh softly through my tears. "Earl Grey."

He sets it down. "I guess I could get used to that."

Our worlds have been turned upside down. Our lovers have left our sides. We can't know what tomorrow will bring. But in that small moment, in the solitude of the night, I'm grateful we're in this together.

TRISTAN

Makanga and I arrive at the garage before dawn. The sky is metal gray, but it's light enough to make out the lettering on the worn sign for Dion's Body Shop.

"You sure he's here?" I ask.

The neighborhood is deserted at this hour. The birds chirping in the trees are the only sounds.

"Oh yeah. He's an early riser. Likes to do his important business before people start rolling in for repairs and shit."

We get out and stroll up to the main door. Makanga walks right inside, so I follow.

"Dion!" he bellows, no doubt waking up the whole damn neighborhood.

Dion enters suddenly through a doorway toward the back of the building.

"Hey, it's the mailman."

"Postman. Get it right, brother," Makanga shoots back with a grin.

Dion laughs as he takes long, casual strides to meet us. He's lanky. His blue mechanic's coveralls catch on the sharp angles of his shoulders.

"Dion. Nice to meet ya," he says, holding out his hand to me. He gnashes gum on one side of his mouth, which makes for a crooked smile.

"Red." I shake his hand, noticing the hard calluses on his palms and the grease stains on his uniform. He may be the man to go to for everything we need, but my guess is he's no stranger to hard work.

Makanga claps his hands together. "So, what have you got for us?"

Dion pitches his thumb over his shoulder. "How about this for starters?"

Behind him is a red BMW coupe. It's an older model but appears to be in good shape.

I look to Makanga.

He winks. "I got you."

I walk over to feather my fingers along the slick curve of the hood. "You could have lent me a beater, you know?" But I'm not arguing. He knows my weakness for fast cars.

"I figure you're good for it."

"I am. Why don't you let Dion hook you up with some new wheels?"

Makanga shrugs. "I like Betsy. She's got some miles left in her."

"I've tried, trust me," Dion says with a laugh. "Come on. Check out the rest."

We follow him into his office. He takes out his keys and unlocks a closet with a metal door. He pulls out a heavy black duffel bag and deposits it onto his desk with a huff. "Merry Christmas."

I unzip it and start pulling out the contents. "Santa did well."

Dion snickers. "Have fun. Here's a burner too," he says, pulling a flip phone out of his pocket and setting it next to the bag.

There's enough firepower in the bag to support the overthrow of a small government. Handguns, automatic weapons, silencers, small explosives. I'm not sure what Makanga is envisioning for the next mission, but I don't mind shopping from Dion's collection.

As I start setting things aside, Makanga's phone rings. The shrill sound reverberates off the walls of the small room. He glances at it, then up to me.

"It's Aguilera."

Dion has his arms crossed and is leaning against the wall, glancing curiously between the two of us.

"I'll be right back," I say.

Makanga hands me the phone as I walk out of Dion's office. I answer it.

"Hi, Devon."

"Hello?" A woman's tentative voice is on the other end. "Who is this?"

"I'm a friend of Makanga's. Listen, I need to ask you some questions about Senator Keegan."

She's quiet for a few seconds. We're not going to get far if she's already clamming up.

"You understand that someone's trying to kill you, right?"

"I'm still trying to wrap my head around that. But why? Why would someone want me dead?"

Not so long ago, Isabel said those same words with that same innocent disbelief. I hope Devon Aguilera doesn't have to travel the road Isabel's taken to figure out how real the threat is.

"Does Keegan know you're pregnant?"

"Yes."

"Was he happy about it?"

Her voice is softer when she speaks. "He wasn't angry. He was… I don't know…overwhelmed, I guess. We both were. It's complicated. He has a family."

"Did he tell you to get rid of it?"

She's quiet again. "He didn't *tell* me to, but he didn't rule it out as a possibility. He knew it was up to me, though."

"And you didn't want to."

She huffs out a sigh, like she knows what I'm getting at. "Whatever you think you know about him, I'm in love with this man. I didn't want to be the woman to tear his family apart, but that doesn't mean I'm giving up on us. We made some mistakes, but we're not over."

Little does she know, the commitment to her own happily ever after with the senator is exactly why she has a dot on her head.

"Have you reached out to him since you left?"

"I've wanted to, but I'm scared."

I think for a minute, weighing everything she's said. Keegan could have told someone Aguilera was carrying his child, triggering concern about his political reputation and ability to follow through on the legislation that Simon is no doubt counting on getting pushed through. If Keegan was financially involved enough, he could have justified asking for it himself. If he was that heartless, Aguilera doesn't seem to have a clue. Either way, he'll want to see her if she reaches out. To reunite or to get her killed. I'll be ready for both.

"Where do you usually meet?"

"He decided not to move his family up to DC yet, so

he flies home on the weekends. Sometimes we'll see each other at my apartment before he leaves. Sometimes I'll fly to DC to see him."

"Where do you stay in DC? At his place?"

"No. He's worried about people seeing us. We stay at a hotel."

"What's the name of it?"

"Hotel Madera."

"Good. It's Sunday, so he'll be flying home tonight. Give him a call and tell him you need to meet tomorrow night. Eight o'clock at the hotel bar. Don't tell him anything else. I don't care how genuine he sounds. If he knows where you're staying, you're not going to be safe there anymore."

She takes a few anxious breaths. "Am I going to be able to see him?"

"No." I frown, concerned now that Aguilera has missed the whole point of our conversation.

"You're using me to set him up? Then what? What is this really about?"

"This is about figuring out who wants you dead."

"Then don't bother. Whoever is behind this, it's not him."

"If it's not him, it's someone he knows. And I can't get to that person unless I talk to Keegan directly. It has to be unexpected, or things could get complicated."

Several seconds pass in silence. I worry she's going to renege on the deal.

"Fine," she says. "But I have one condition."

I roll my eyes but do my best not to sound as frustrated

as I'm getting. She has no idea what's at stake, and I'm not about to tell her. I just need her to cooperate.

"What's your condition?"

"Once you meet with him, I want to see him."

"Are you trying to get yourself killed?"

"Those are my terms," she says firmly. "You want the meeting, then give me mine."

I pace a circle, mentally mapping out ways to prevent this from turning into a disaster. Bringing her into the mix is a complication I don't need. If every single thing goes right and Keegan proves a friendly resource, having her there could work in my favor. But that's a big if. I need her help, though. I don't have time to follow him around DC and figure out his patterns.

"All right, but if you stray from the plan and fuck this up for me, I can't protect you anymore. Do you understand? You're putting your life on the line, and I have enough people I'm trying to keep alive right now. Got it?"

"I've got it. I understand," she says shakily, like suddenly she's overwhelmed with hope. Like she's so in love with this guy she can barely get the sentence out.

"Set up the meeting. Call this number when it's done."

2

ISABEL

My father is behind the wheel, his jaw set with determination or perhaps fresh worry. I doubt he slept well, if at all. After waking from my own restless night, I quickly realized Mom hadn't come home. Concern for her wellbeing compounds the heavy guilt of having driven her out with yesterday's events. She may still want time, but I'll call her when we get home later if she's still gone. My father may be furious and my mother may be too, but after more than two decades of marriage, they'll have to talk this out at some point.

"Are we going back to your office?"

He shakes his head. "We're meeting at a bar a few miles away."

I lift my eyebrows. "A bar?"

"It's dark and quiet, and the barflies who hang out there

before a respectable drinking hour won't remember a damn thing we say."

"Okay," I say, trusting that when it comes to keeping things under the radar, he knows best.

Twenty minutes later, we arrive at the Widow, an Irish pub set on the corner of an intersection about twenty minutes from our house. We find Jax Rivero and my father's colleague, Damon Parish, at a table in the back. As promised, the bar is dark and quiet, and the two older men at the bar are fixed on the TVs above and pay us no attention.

"Gentlemen." My father pulls out my chair before sitting in his own. "Thanks for meeting here."

"I'm positive no one will find us here," Rivero says with a sarcastic smile.

A night's sleep hasn't warmed me to him since he yanked Tristan and me into the airport security offices. And a night's sleep doesn't seem to have eased his agitation at the predicament we're facing.

Parish, however, seems perkier than the rest of us. He places his laptop on the table, his eyes bright. "I don't know about the rest of you, but I couldn't stop running all this through my head last night. So I hacked my way into Knight's computer. Lots of interesting things to work with."

Rivero leans over to peer at the screen as Parish lifts it open. "Like what?"

"Well…in my experience, just because someone has a lot of money doesn't necessarily mean they're careful with their information. He really must have thought he was above the law to be this careless. Everything is in the cloud.

I mean *everything*. Organized? Yes. His file structure makes finding everything really easy. All the corporate filings, most of which are shells, I'm guessing. Spreadsheets of accounts with balances."

"Too bad he's dead," Rivero snaps. "We could nail him on everything and get him to dime out all his associates for a plea deal. Easy stuff." His lips form a disappointed curve as he looks my way.

I didn't kill him, I say to myself with a strange kind of defensive detachment, like a kid trying to dodge blame. *I just watched him die and walked over his body on my way out of the building before Crow blew it up.* Of course, they can lock me up before I tell Rivero any of that.

"I think we both know it wouldn't be that easy by a long shot," my father says sharply. He focuses on Parish again. "So where do the accounts lead?"

Parish cants his head. "Most are linked up with the shell companies, the majority in Knight's name. Some with Mirchoff, some with Pope. Interestingly I haven't found anything formally associated with Simon Pelletier. There are some international ones I can't access, though. I have no idea whose name those are in."

"Where are the accounts located?" I ask.

"Cayman Islands. A couple overseas," Parish says.

I don't want to say it aloud, but I'm almost certain one of those accounts was the one Mateus was given.

"Can you find out who's on those accounts? Work with the local government or something?"

"There are agreements in place to combat tax evasion,

but they don't really help us in this case. The Cayman banks have to report tax information on accounts owned by US citizens, but it's channeled through the IRS. That's some pretty significant red tape on our end."

"This is why we need an investigation, Foster. We can't subpoena shit without one," Rivero barks, his voice carrying loud enough to reach the bar patrons. Thankfully no one seems to care.

I chew the inside of my lip. Tristan has the account number Mateus gave him. I can't narrow the list down for Parish without it.

"Isabel, do you know anything about this?"

My father's calm request invites the truth. A part of me wants to give it to him, but I can't tie any of this to Tristan or the people who've helped me along the way. But if I don't work with them, we'll never get ahead.

"An account number was given to us through a friend. Someone who was helping us. Simon wanted him to clean the funds through his international businesses before depositing them into an account in Cayman."

Rivero frowns. "So what's the account number?"

"I didn't memorize it. But if you can't link it to the account holder, why do you need it?"

He blows a frustrated breath out through his nose like an angry bull. "What aren't you telling us?"

So much. And he can stomp around all day long and I'll never tell him half of what I know. At the end of the day, he works for a government agency and I've broken more laws than I can count. I don't trust Rivero, and I never will.

"You work above the board, Rivero. I don't. If I'm being evasive, it's because I don't trust you. I have information you want, and I have ways of finding it that probably go against your moral code. But if you want names on the accounts, give me the list. I know someone who can find out."

"Who?"

I pause. "A friend. He's a hacker."

Rivero rolls his eyes. "Right. Some kid living in his mother's basement hacking websites for credit card numbers. That's not what we're talking about here."

"I know exactly what we're talking about. Banking software. He knows it better than anyone."

Parish looks at me like he's discovered the Holy Grail. His jaw falls open slightly. "Oh shit," he says on an awe-filled exhale.

My father stares at him with a bewildered look. "What did I miss?"

The way Parish is looking at me makes me feel like he can read my mind. Or maybe I said something I shouldn't have.

"Blake Landon? Has he been helping you?"

I don't answer and try to school my features, even though I'm freaking out inside. How the hell can he know that?

"You were in Boston," he continues, his words coming fast like a stream of consciousness as he puts it all together. "That's where his offices are. That makes sense. Did you meet with him? Do you think he'll help?"

His questions are coming too fast for me to mask my

reaction to them—the stunned, very obvious way his name resonates.

"Who's Blake Landon?" my father asks.

Parish's next words are excited and rushed. "He's... basically a legend. He's one of the most respected hackers in the world. If anyone can get the job done, it's him."

"If he's so well known, why isn't he behind bars or hanging out in Russia?" Rivero asks.

"Because he got caught when he was still a minor. No one knows the whole story, but he got off the hook, and then he developed Banksoft. Every major bank's software runs off the framework he built. He sold it for billions."

All three men look at me like they're waiting for me to confirm what Parish already seems to know is true. What the hell am I supposed to do now? If I lie, they'll know it.

Thankfully my father doesn't give me a chance to debate it any longer. "You think this hacker friend of yours would be willing to get the account information for us?"

I share a look with him. It's filled with worry and hesitation because Landon has already done more than he should have. He has a life and a family to think about.

"This can't come back to him."

Rivero crosses his arms and leans back in his seat. "Listen, I don't even care who this guy is. I'll probably forget his name tomorrow because there's a lot more to sift through here. Get us the details, and we'll forget how they showed up. Same way I guess we're going to forget how this dead guy's laptop showed up."

I hate Rivero, but I feel like we're matched in an odd

way. Some balance exists between what he's willing to do to get to the truth and what I'm willing to do to protect the people I care about.

"I'll work on it," I promise. "What else? Can we get the DEA involved now?"

"I have a meeting with a contact of mine tomorrow," my father says. "I'll point him toward the ports Knight was targeting."

"The bribes were cash," I say. "It's going to be hard to pinpoint the leaks."

He tilts his head. "I'm hoping they'll take this seriously enough to ramp things up across the board. If they know there are bribes involved, they'll start looking more closely. Once they find one, hopefully they can start connecting the dots."

Then it hits me.

"Javier Medina. You should start with him."

Not wanting to get into how Tristan and Jay led us to Medina or the meeting Mateus and I took with him, I never mentioned him before. If they need a starting place, though, he could be it.

"He works under the director of the Port of Miami," I continue. "He's closely connected to Simon, and I'd be willing to bet Knight met with him when he was in Miami a couple of weeks ago. If Simon gets wind of the DEA poking around that part of the operation, it could be a way to scare them into at least slowing things down."

"I'm on it," says Rivero, scribbling notes onto a small pad he pulled from his pocket.

My father's expression remains tense, but there's an energy between us that feels promising, like we have enough threads to pull to start making a difference.

TRISTAN

The map of DC is spread out on Makanga's coffee table. I memorized it an hour ago, plotting out points of interest—the Hotel Madera, Keegan's condo in the city, and his office at the Capitol. I've gone as far as I can go without a meeting locked in with Simon. I'm edgy and frustrated. I'm ready to work, but all I can do is wait for Devon to follow through with details.

Once I get my hands on Keegan, I'll be one chess move away from Simon. He won't see it coming, which will be the best part. Seeing the devil himself and letting him see me. Recognizing his shock, then his fear. The old Tristan would make it quick. Get it done and get out. I don't know if I'll be able to do it that way. Not this time.

I close my eyes and press my temples hard like it will drive out the dark thoughts that won't quiet. Isabel is a better person than I am, and she doesn't want him alive any more than I do. That doesn't make me feel better. Every step of this journey has made me despise Simon a little more. It's been a runaway train of hatred for the man. And I've never cared this much. I've never been this invested in someone's imminent death.

Holding on to this kind of contempt is about as foreign

to me as love used to be. I can't tell if it makes me more or less human. Either way, it's fucked up. *I'm* fucked up. And the only person who makes me feel the least bit normal isn't here.

Fantasies of ways I could kill Simon are almost better than missing Isabel. I hate not knowing where she is. I can't risk a drive by her parents' house yet, but I console myself by imagining her there. Safe with Morgan. Hopefully he got Rivero to back off. If he did, they'll still want to know what she knows. Unfortunately, so much of it points back to me. The more they know about me, the harder it's going to be to get close to her again.

The front door swings open and Makanga walks through, bringing a blast of cool air and sunlight into the living room.

"Hey, man." He shuts the door and tosses an orange package beside me on the sofa. "Special delivery."

I stare at it. If I didn't feel like such a mess already, the package guarantees it.

"What is it?" he asks.

"It's nothing," I respond flatly.

He chuckles and tugs at one of his short dreads. "Okay. You're looking at it like there's a body part in there or something."

"I'm pretty sure you'd be able to tell if there were."

He shrugs. "I've delivered some pretty messed-up stuff. You'd be surprised what's possible with the right packaging."

"I don't want to know."

He moves to his recliner. "What's up with the map?"

I rub over the creases in my forehead. "Trying to figure out where Keegan might want to meet Simon or vice versa. He's paranoid about where he'll be seen. Rightly so. Any place good for a hit probably isn't a place he'll agree to go."

"So you're trying to get ahead of the game."

"Probably just spinning my wheels until I get my hands on Keegan."

"Oh yeah. How's tomorrow night sound?"

I pause and meet his eyes. "Devon confirmed?"

Makanga grins. "They're on their way to DC right now."

"They?"

I can't mask my alarm, but Makanga only laughs.

"I've had her staying with my sister. It was the best I could offer on short notice. It's a long drive, but they'll be here tonight."

"*Here?*"

"Hell no. I set them up in a room at the Madera."

"We have to be able to get her out of there if Keegan doesn't cooperate."

"You worry about Keegan. I'll worry about the girls," he says.

I rest back on the couch with a stressed sigh.

"You gotta relax, man. We're not there yet. You're going to run out of adrenaline before you get a chance to pop this guy."

"Unlikely."

He runs his fingers over the seam on the armrest. "You hear from Isabel yet?"

"That'd be a miracle since she has no idea where I am. I got rid of my phone before I got here."

He purses his lips. "You think she could be at her parents' house?"

I remember then that Makanga had dropped her there when I disappeared to see my old army friend, Brennan. Against my wishes, but I know better than most that Isabel can be persuasive when she wants something. Makanga knows more than I'd like about her personal life, but I'm short on allies at the moment and he seems like he wants to help.

"It's possible," I finally say.

"Why don't you take a ride over there?"

I lift my eyebrows sharply. "You really think that's a good idea? The last thing I need is the FBI on my ass while I'm trying to pin down Simon."

"Yeah, you're probably right. Just figured it would give you some peace of mind."

"Peace of mind is a luxury I don't have right now."

I can tell Makanga wants to push the issue, but there's no talking me into it. I'd do just about anything to see her— or at least know she's all right—but it's not worth the risk… for either of us.

I fold up the map and grab the package, ignoring the stab of anxiety that lodges in my gut when I think about its contents.

"I'm going out. I'll see you tonight," I say, my tone clipped.

A gleam of mischief hits Makanga's dark eyes.

"Don't look at me like that. I'm not going to see her. She might not even be there."

He laughs and lifts up his hands in mock surrender. "I'm not saying anything. Just figured you might be in a better mood if you checked it out."

"I'm not going, so get used to me being a miserable bastard in the meantime."

He just shakes his head as I gather up my things, leave the house, and toss my bag into the passenger side of the coupe. The engine roars to life when I turn the key in the ignition. Being behind the wheel of Dion's loaner is a nice upgrade from riding shotgun in Betsy. Maybe it'll be the distraction I need to clear my head.

I drive around Arlington, no destination in mind, until I find myself in front of Brienne's old apartment, the place where her life ended thanks to one of Jay's men. The spot where Isabel witnessed her best friend die shows no trace of what happened here. I study the buildings across the street, wondering which window her killer hid behind. I was too busy getting us the hell out of here to care.

I'll never forget the horror of that day. Not for myself but for what Isabel went through. She lost a friend and finally knew what we were up against. Two cold, hard truths wrapped up in the same tragedy. I'd give anything to save her from the memory. Maybe if we'd done things differently, Brienne would still be alive, but that way of thinking is a dark spiral that leads nowhere good.

I drive out of Arlington and get on the highway to go north. Isabel and Simon and the package fill up my thoughts, a nonstop whir of what-ifs and unresolved pieces of this never-ending nightmare.

An hour later, I'm traveling past warehouses that curve along the Patapsco River. I turn before the bridge. Rick's Fish House is just ahead. A few cars are parked outside. I kill the engine, grab the package, and walk toward the restaurant, ignoring my nerves. The deck is empty of diners. String lights swing in the wind, and I recognize the place, but none of the magic I felt here remains.

I walk toward the dock. The rickety little fish feeder is still there. I pass it, stopping at the end of the pier. If Isabel were here, we could toss pellets into the water and dream about our future—a future that's never felt so out of reach simply because she is.

It's strange standing inside a memory that doesn't feel like it fully belongs to me.

Cars drone by on the bridge over the river. Water sloshes up against the pilings. No kids are running and laughing. There's no music. The dream I had of this place was warmer. The people in it had hope even though the future was uncertain, even if the things we felt were new and overwhelming. It's not the only memory I have of us, but it's a good one. I'll never let myself forget it.

I lift the package and study the messy block lettering on it. No return address. I rip open one side. There's a small piece of paper inside with a message written in the same handwriting.

The second vial is a strong sedative. Our mutual friend thought it would help the antidote run its course without interruption. I did my best, but this comes with no promises.

Inside are two vials protected by layers of bubble wrap and elastic bands. A wave of nausea hits me. I don't bother unwrapping them to study them further. I shove the note back inside and stare across the river to the horizon of structures on the other side.

Unlike here, the opposite riverbank is lined with trees and greenery. A park and some nice condominium buildings. I wonder if the view is better from over there. Probably not. They get to look at the ugly gray warehouses and Rick's shack with its cheap Christmas lights.

I don't know where I'd rather be. Standing on this splintering dock where I fell in love with Isabel a little more than six years ago or somewhere that looks better from here but maybe isn't better at all. Maybe all this wanting my memories back is like that. One little piece of endless longing for more than I should.

I've killed people. I've done terrible, unforgivable things. My only purpose in life appeared in the form of a death wish. I could have killed her, but somehow she's the one who saved me. The day I found Isabel was the first time I ever let myself care about my shadowy past. She lit everything up. I didn't believe in miracles or even luck, but she made me want to. Then I fell in love with her all over again. I believe she fell in love with me too. Not just the old me. *Me.*

If I put Mushenko's antidote into my bloodstream, I don't know who I'll be.

3

ISABEL

I check my phone when it buzzes with a text from my father. Rivero pops a peanut into his mouth and casts a bored stare up at the televisions above the bar. It's our second day here. We've spent hours sifting through Knight's laptop documents, aligning them with the parts of the Felix plan we know. I fill in the blanks where I can. Carefully. Strategically. Especially after my father leaves to take his meeting with his DEA contact, leaving me with Rivero and Parish.

"My dad is running late. Do you think you could take me home?"

"Sure. We can hang out for a drink if you want," Rivero offers casually.

My instinct is to say no. But we've settled into slightly

better rapport after another day of chasing the same enemies. He seems more interested in the baseball game than me anyway, and the prospect of being home alone doesn't thrill me. I've also had about six Diet Cokes, and my nerves are akin to live wires.

Parish clicks his computer shut and stretches his arms above his head with a groan. "I'm heading home."

"Long day at the office?" Rivero smirks.

Parish laughs and shakes his head. "Something like that."

He packs up and gives me a little wave goodbye on his way out of the pub. The patrons are livelier at this hour, yelling at the television and swapping stories animatedly. I'm in shock that after a day of drinking, some of them are still able to form sentences.

Rivero saunters to the bar. His arrogance doesn't seem put on but rather stitched into his inherent makeup. Perhaps if we'd met under different circumstances, I could appreciate it more. He's an attractive guy. Strong, dark, and handsome. And smart. Abrasive at times but driven. And when we're driving toward the same thing, I almost think I could like him. After a few minutes, he returns with two pints of beer.

"Pale ale okay?"

"Perfect. Thanks."

"How are things going at home?" Rivero lobs the question casually, like we're friends now. We're not.

"My mom left a couple of days ago. Dad says she just needs time, so I suppose all we can do is give it to her."

He looks me over briefly, a discriminating kind of stare like he's trying to figure out a riddle. Maybe to him I am.

"What?"

"I just keep looking at you and wondering how a pretty suburban girl like you could get mixed up in all this. I mean, I don't know you very well, but Morgan doesn't strike me as someone who'd raise an unruly kid."

I wince. "I'm not *unruly*."

Although maybe lately I am. In fact, if Tristan were here, he'd probably chime in on that. Rivero knows about my situation but not enough to see the full picture. I don't know if it'll encourage him to ease up on me, but I decide to speak up in my own defense.

"I love my parents, but they smothered me. After my sister died, my mom was paranoid something would happen to me too. I didn't understand why until all this happened." I pick at the corner of a cocktail napkin, marveling anew at how dramatically things have changed.

"So you rebelled."

"Striving for any degree of independence was met with strong opposition, but I kept fighting until I finally wore them down. Call that rebellion if you want."

He pops another peanut into his mouth and chews with a sly smirk. "Now you're blowing up buildings and trying to take down an international pharmaceutical giant."

I roll my eyes at his persistence. He's obsessed with what happened in Paris or at least that he managed to loosely connect it to me.

"Are you ever going to own that?" he presses.

I clench my jaw, suddenly regretting this decision to linger here with him. I take a drink and pretend like the baseball game has my interest.

"Are you?"

"No, I'm not." My answer is clipped, hopefully closing the subject.

"If it wasn't you, who was it? Don't think you're fooling me. I've been watching you dance around the truth for two damn days. You're deeper in this than you let on."

"I'm just trying to get my life back."

"What about your boyfriend? How does he play into all of this if you just met him?"

My palms prickle with anxiety. I don't want Rivero getting anywhere near Tristan. "You should leave him out of this, which should be easy because you're never going to find him."

He narrows his eyes a little. "Have you heard from him?"

"He's too smart to seek me out. He knows it's dangerous."

"Funny. I'd been focused on you this whole time."

Our gazes lock. I stop breathing because there's something in his eyes. Knowing. Discovery. Everything I was deathly terrified of when he stopped us at the airport.

"I obviously had to know who was savvy enough to slip through my fingers and make it out of the airport before we even knew he was gone."

My heart starts racing. I keep my lips sealed shut.

"For a second there, I thought he was going to help me fill in the blanks on you, but now that I know you better, it makes sense that you'd link up with someone who operated underground. Someone who could move from place to place without being noticed."

"All he's ever done is try to protect me. And if you want my help to bust this thing open, you're going to have to forget about him." I will my voice not to shake, but I need him to back off. He's trying to draw a line I won't cross.

"I don't think it's that simple. Ethan Gallo's fingerprints didn't trigger anything going through border patrol, but when I ran them through the other government databases last night, I got a hit. You were both traveling under aliases, which wouldn't be especially interesting except Tristan Stone was injured in the line of duty nearly six years ago and no one ever heard from him again. No credit cards. No bank accounts. Zero activity. You've been dead for two months. He's been a ghost for a lot longer. Pretty interesting, don't you think?"

Forget about him. I silently beg him to shift his focus to what really matters. Simon. Felix. Stopping this deadly plan from happening. But the glimmer in Rivero's eyes tells me he's not going to let this go. He can dig all he wants. I'll never do anything to bring him closer to Tristan, and as long as Tristan stays away, Rivero won't have a chance.

I rise quickly. "I'll get a cab home."

He follows me with his stare. He's trying to intimidate me. Turn me inside out. Once upon a time, that may have affected me more, but I've faced off with worse men than him.

"Your father can't protect both of you," he adds, like he's trying to bait me into saying something stupid and incriminating.

"You're confused. Tristan doesn't need protection."

"Then why are you being so careful? What are you hiding?"

I place my hands on the table and bring my face closer to his. "More than you'll ever know. More than will ever matter next to the death and deceit that Simon's orchestrating at this very moment. You have no idea what I've been through, but you can trust that Tristan's kept me alive through all of it. And if you think you can intimidate me into implicating him, you're dead wrong."

He regards me for a few tense seconds before draining his glass and averting his gaze.

Satisfied that I've won the staring contest, I turn to leave. Except I know this isn't over.

TRISTAN

The Madera is an upscale boutique hotel. The man in the dark-gray suit fits right in, twisting his glass of red wine by the base, looking like he's somewhere else in his mind. He barely notices me when I take the stool next to him.

"Senator Keegan."

He straightens his posture and looks me over, suddenly seeming more composed. "Do I know you?"

"No, but I'm a friend of Devon's."

His composure is short-lived. He shoots a panicked look around the bar.

"She's not here," I say.

The blood vessel in his neck ticks rapidly. "If she's not here, where is she?"

I turn to square my torso with his. "I'll tell you, but we need to talk first."

The bartender is chatting up the cocktail waitress at the other end of the bar, ignoring his only customers. Us.

"Is she all right?" he asks, his voice low.

I maintain a calm exterior. I don't want to make him too comfortable or give him too much hope. A healthy degree of fear is helpful in trying to get information out of people.

Keegan licks his lips nervously. "Listen, whoever you are—"

I lean in. "You don't need to know who I am. All you need to know is that Devon's alive because of me. I don't trust you and you don't trust me, but if you want me to protect her, that's going to have to change. I need some information from you."

He takes a few seconds to absorb what I've said. He looks me over again, like somehow he can determine anything about me from the exterior. He can't. He has no idea what I'm capable of.

"What do you need to know?"

"Devon's pregnant." I utter it with a certainty he can't deny.

He averts his gaze and stares at the liquor bottles lined up in perfect rows across the bar. He nods. Shame.

"That's a problem you probably wish would just go away."

"Life is a series of problems we wish would just go away. We can't change the choices we already made," he says quietly.

I'm not sure what to make of his statement except that he's definitely given Devon's condition some thought. The finality in his words could be acceptance or regret.

"Do you wish Devon would just go away?"

He whips his gaze to mine, a wounded look in his eyes. "No. I didn't say that."

I study him. The defensive hurt emanating off him. The way his attention tunnels toward me suddenly, unapologetically. He's telling the truth, even if the truth is colored with shame at what he's done—had an extramarital affair, one that's going to produce a child out of wedlock, which may or may not turn the rest of his world upside down.

"Someone wants her dead."

He stills. "Why?"

"Because she's getting in your way."

He shakes his head vigorously. "I don't understand. That doesn't make any sense."

"You're mixed up in something bigger than I think you realize. And the powers that be don't want anything tripping up what you have to do."

He winces. "The powers that be? I know who I answer to—"

"And you answer to Simon Pelletier."

Some of the blood drains from his face.

"You're helping him out, right?" I push into the truth

I already believe.

He turns back to his glass of wine, not denying it.

"Do you know about felixedrine?"

He shows me his face again, a line forming in the space between his dark brows. "What the hell is that?"

This guy is a real chump. He has no idea why he's pushing this act through, other than the bribes or favors Simon's offering him.

"You probably think you're doing a good thing and scoring some easy money too. It's not like that."

His jaw begins to tick. "Who are you?"

"If you care about Devon and have any interest in calling off the dogs who want her out of your life, I'm someone you're going to help. I need you to set up a meeting with Simon."

He doesn't answer, but I can sense his growing concern. If Simon knows Keegan's turned on him, Keegan will pay dearly for it. He doesn't understand it won't get that far.

"This doesn't come back to you," I say. "I don't care what you're doing. I care about what he's doing. It's a lot bigger than some legislation you're pushing through for him."

"You're not with an agency?"

"I work alone. Simon came after someone I care about. This is extremely personal."

He replies with a short nod. Acknowledgment.

"He paid you?" I ask.

He nods again.

"How soon can you set something up?"

"It depends. I don't have any control over this guy. We both have busy schedules. I can't promise anything."

"Call him now. Tell him there are some complications. Some big players getting in the way. I guarantee he'll be willing to clear a path for you in no time."

"What if he wants names? Do I just lie?"

"Tell him you're not comfortable talking about it over the phone. You'd rather meet in person."

He curses under his breath and looks up at the ceiling like the answers are there. "I don't know about this. My career is on the line if this goes wrong."

I laugh. "Really? You knocked up your mistress. News flash, your career is already on the line. Besides, this isn't politics. This is life and death. Don't be stupid."

He swallows hard. I can tell he's wondering if it's his life or Devon's I'm talking about.

"Set it up, and I'll trust you to see Devon. Underestimate me, and you'll be lucky to see her again."

With that, he slowly pulls his phone out of his pocket. His hands are shaking as he presses it to his ear. Silently I pray he can keep his composure and not sound like he's got a gun to his head.

Watching Devon Aguilera rush into Keegan's arms the second she saw him should affect me differently. Everyone got what they wanted. Devon got her meeting, and I got mine.

After I waited around the Madera another hour for

Keegan to get his message through to Simon and then a call back, the two men agreed to meet at Keegan's hideaway office in the Capitol building in two days. Of course Simon would choose one of the worst possible places. Security. Cameras. Tourists and lots of innocent people.

Seeing Keegan rewarded for being a dirtbag who takes bribes and betrays his family only adds to my frustration. I leave the hotel with a sharp turn.

"Where are you heading?" Makanga is on my heels as I pass through the front doors.

"I don't know." I really don't. I need time to think and plan, now that I have details to work with. I should be wholly focused on the new mission, but I'm not.

"Red. Hold up."

I halt my journey to the car to face him. "What?"

He holds his arms wide. "You on the warpath or what? I thought things were good."

"Everything's fine. Make sure Aguilera disappears again after their little reunion is over."

"That was the plan. But you look like you're out for blood all of a sudden."

My jaw ticks. "That surprises you?"

He shakes his head, the corner of his lips lifting into a half smile. "This isn't about Simon, is it?"

"This obviously has everything to do with Simon."

"No, it doesn't. You're pissed off because the senator is getting laid and you're not."

"Fuck you." I resume my journey to the car, a fresh bolt of rage razoring through me.

"She's home, you know," he calls after me.

I freeze and turn back. "Excuse me?"

He strolls toward me, closing the distance between us. "After you took off yesterday, I asked a friend to keep an eye on her house. See if they saw her coming or going."

I don't even know what I'm feeling. Outrage. Anxiety. Desperation.

"A *friend*?"

"Someone who has no idea who she is or why she's important to anyone. Calm down, Red. I'm telling you so you know. You're wound too tight over this girl. If you don't get your head straight, you're going to end up making a mistake that could cost you everything."

I fist and unfist my hands. "Do you really think psychoanalyzing me is a good use of your time?"

"I think if I'm putting my ass on the line for you, I need to trust that your head is in the game and not twisted up worrying about Isabel and what she's doing. So my professional advice to you would be to figure it out. Tonight, ideally, so we can regroup tomorrow and I don't have to worry about you busting a blood vessel over something that doesn't fucking matter. Like Keegan's evening agenda."

My nostrils flare as I attempt to rein in the verbal tirade Makanga deserves. Except the more arguments I design to prove him wrong, the more I realize how right he is. I haven't been able to think straight without her. I'm always focused when it comes to a job. Eliminating people is what I do. I should be calculating every possible move. Every angle and opportunity. Instead, half my thoughts are reaching for the woman who's been ripped out of my life without warning.

I've devoted countless hours to wondering if she was all right. If she's home, that means Morgan worked something out with Rivero. It's an open door for me to find her, an invitation that's as dangerous as it is tempting.

4

ISABEL

The cab drops me off in the driveway. I've been running my conversation with Rivero over and over again in my head, agonizing over how far he'll take this truth-finding mission when it comes to Tristan. But the second I see my mother's car, all I can think about is getting inside. I pay the driver and rush to the house.

I find my parents in the den. My father is seated on an accent chair, my mother on the couch, their bodies angled toward each other like maybe they've been trying to breach the space between them but haven't yet. My mother's eyes are red-rimmed when she looks up at me. I'm paralyzed in place, unsure how to be or how to act. So much has happened, and I can't know how she feels.

The same hesitation seems to swim in her eyes too. Her

lip trembles as she lifts from her seat and comes to me. Her palms are soft and cool against my cheeks.

"Isabel." Her voice is a watery whisper.

"You're home."

Finally, after two days of wondering and worrying, though I've put her through far worse.

She nods. "We both are. We're both right where we're supposed to be."

"Where were you?"

"I stayed with a friend for a couple days. I just needed to clear my head. I… I was afraid to face either of you to be honest. I'm sorry. I'm so sorry, Isabel."

I let tears of relief blur my vision. She hugs me tightly. Part of me wants to apologize back. Another part of me doesn't want to bother with the guilt when the choices we made were made out of love. We both know it.

My father comes beside us, embracing us both. And in that moment, I know we're going to be okay. If they've survived everything else, my parents can make it through this too. Even if the truth threatened to tear us apart, if somehow it can make us whole again, bring us closer than we were before, it was worth the risk. Worth the pain.

My mother sighs heavily and pulls back, brushing at my tears with her thumbs. "Come sit with us. We have a lot to talk about."

I nod and settle beside my mother on the couch.

"Now that you're home," she begins, "now that we're all together, there's nothing left to keep us from being completely honest with each other. Morgan told me everything that's happening with Chalys. I'm shocked, but of course, I'm not. I knew they were truly terrible people. I just couldn't prove it until it was too late. I never meant for this to affect you the way it has." Her eyes fill with tears again, and she struggles to take her next breath.

"Mom, it's okay. We know enough now. Even if we can't stop the train in its tracks, I think we're going to be able to make a difference."

"I talked to my contact at the DEA today," my father says. "Parish is going to package up what we know about the ports and tip them off about Medina. We can start there and branch out when we know more. But he's on it. I think we'll start looking into Pope next. He's not as elusive as Simon. We might be able to trip him up more easily."

"That's great." His good news is quickly overridden by my worries over Rivero, though. "Dad, Rivero knows about Tristan."

He frowns. "Are you sure?"

"I'm positive. He ambushed me about it as soon as we were alone today. It's like he's determined to turn everything he doesn't know into something bigger than it needs to be. Tristan's hands aren't exactly clean. Neither are mine. But Rivero seems locked into figuring out how Tristan ties into this. He knows I'm telling him half the truth, and he's going to punish me for it."

"Not on my watch, he isn't."

"He can cause problems for both of us. You can't control him if he really wants to make a mess of this."

"We just need to keep him focused on other things.

Did you hear back from your hacker friend yet? My gut tells me that's a lead worth following."

"Landon has the numbers. I'm waiting to hear back, but it should be soon. He works quickly and wants to help. He's been trying to track Simon's movements for a while, but it's kind of a blind spot. However he operates, he doesn't make it easy to follow him."

"I'll talk to Rivero next chance I get. Try not to worry," he says.

My mother takes my hand in hers and gives it a little squeeze. Being in the same room with both of them is a welcome relief, but strange too. We've been at odds for so long. I've been running from Simon's people for even longer. The reunion with my parents heals something in my heart. But not everything. Being without Tristan with no promise of our own reunion feels like an open wound. I'm vulnerable and off-balance. My compass always points to him, except he's lost to me now.

"Have you heard from Tristan?" my mother asks.

I shake my head. "Not yet," I say softly. "I know this is the last thing you want to think about, but if things don't go the way we want... If Rivero stays focused on Tristan and the trouble we've been in, I'm afraid I'm going to have to disappear again. I don't know how easy it's going to be to come back home if I do."

"It won't come to that," my mother offers.

I lift my gaze to my father's. His expression is hard and less hopeful. He knows there's a chance. I expect he's already considered it. If they were scared enough to fake my death, they understand that drastic measures are sometimes the only measures.

TRISTAN

A sound argument could be made that climbing the tree in Isabel's backyard—the one that leads directly to her bedroom window—won't get me any closer to the preeminent goal of eliminating Simon. Every awkward shift toward the darkened glass is a testimony to my lack of reason when it comes to Isabel Foster—the woman I've managed to fall in love with twice.

I drove around DC for hours trying to convince myself I could forget about her long enough to get the job done. But when I turned down her street, the anticipation of seeing her again, holding her, and breathing her in was too overwhelming to deny. I have to see her. I don't care if it's for an hour or a night. It no longer feels optional.

I press my palms against the panels and glide the window up from the bottom, far enough to work my way through it. In the darkness I can recognize Isabel's shape under the sheet, her blanket kicked off the edge of the bed. I can hardly breathe. I've missed her more than I let myself realize. As much as I wish I could go to her and wrap my arms around her this very instant, I worry I'm going to scare her to death if I do. The last thing I need is her parents hearing her scream out in terror.

I hover at the foot of her bed, contemplating what to

do. I shrug out of my jacket, tug off my shirt, and toe out of my shoes. The bed dips as I add my weight and gradually align my body with hers. We've spent nearly every night together since we left Rio. Maybe she'll wake up and forget we've been apart. That's the gamble I make when I feather my fingertips along her jaw, lean in, and gently press my lips to hers.

She releases a little moan. I whisper her name, willing her to rouse enough to know I'm not a dream. I caress her skin softly, slowly. She shifts against me, her eyes still closed. It's all I can do to hold back. I ache to touch her everywhere, to remember every inch of her in the darkness.

"Wake up, Isabel. It's me."

When her eyelids flutter open, I still, waiting for her to react. For her to realize I came for her. That I couldn't stay away.

"It's me," I say again, hovering my lips over hers. "I had to see you."

Her hands curve over my shoulders, then go to my face and slide through my hair. "Tristan... Oh my God. You're really here."

The agony in those last words rips through me, like maybe she thought we'd been torn apart forever. I know the sentiment too well.

"It's okay. I'm here now," I say, hoping to allay her worries.

We have a million things to talk over, but right now all I care about is this closeness. The feel of her. The invisible energy that hums between us that I can't name but crave like it's air.

When I dip to take her lips again, she meets me halfway. The kiss she returns is desperate, nearly bruising in its intensity. She's all-consuming. Every cell of my body wants to reach inside hers. We kiss until we can't breathe, until she's writhing against me. Pushing and pulling, like we're at war. Like I'm her heaven and her hell. I try to keep up and answer every demand, every invitation and needy cry, but she's a mile ahead of me. With a frustrated groan, she pushes me away, lifting her torso up with mine as she straddles my lap.

Our mouths crash together once more. Her taste floods my senses. Her fevered touches and the way she grinds against me are quickly bringing me up to speed. Then I'm in the race right beside her, lifting away her night shirt to get access to more of her delicious skin.

"Now," she whimpers, reaching for the button on my jeans. "Now, Tristan. Please."

I free myself just enough and push her panties out of the way. Her thin cry pierces the air as I ease her down, fitting her around me until there's nowhere left to go. My head is buzzing. Being inside her is almost too intoxicating to bear after this absence.

My hand rests firmly on her hip. I hold her there, savoring the sudden connection, slowing down the moment to simply feel her. This completeness. I've never felt this whole. Until now, I don't think I've realized with such certainty that I can't be without her. Ever. As long as I'm breathing, I'll need her.

When she squirms, I let her move and take the control

she's hungry for. I take her mouth, probing my tongue gently but possessively in time with her movements. I want all her air. Every intimate valley of her flesh. All her desire. The tiny whimpers that tumble from her lips every time I can't get any deeper.

A reminder of our surroundings sobers me just enough to hush her softly, knowing it'll take all our restraint to keep this reunion quiet. More than quiet if we want to see it through. The last time we were alone together in her childhood bedroom, I held back because it was too risky. There's no holding back tonight.

When her eyes close and her lips part, I tip her gaze back to me.

"Look at me." I tangle my fingers tightly into her locks of hair, making it impossible for her to escape the tractor beam between us.

Her thighs tremble as she hooks her fingernails into my flesh, but she doesn't look away. Even in the dark, her eyes shimmer. As the minutes pass, the shimmer trails down her cheeks.

I'm caught someplace between her heart and the needy clutch of her body. Witnessing her tears is an emotional surge I'm powerless against when I'm already drowning in how much I love her.

I taste her tears and nip at her lips. I bind us tighter and faster, intent on driving the pain away. The distance. All of it. Every shred of misery, until there's nothing left but the last cry of pleasure that tears from her. I consume it in the hot meld of our mouths, letting it vibrate into my chest as

I finally let go.

For all the self-control I thought I once possessed, Isabel proves over and over I have so little with her. I hold her against me as we float down from the high. I drag my lips reverently over her skin, because as the euphoria fades, it makes room for the ugly reality that this intimacy is short-lived. Every second is a gift. I have to savor them all.

Gradually I lift her away. We lie down together. I'm still half-dressed, but she draws the sheet over both of us before taking the space in the nook of my shoulder.

I close my eyes, both heavier and lighter at once. "I'm sorry…for leaving you."

"I know why you did."

I'd hoped she would. The possibility that she thought I'd abandoned her has been eating away at me along with everything else. I trusted she knew better, but hearing her say it removes the doubt.

"Are you okay?"

I can feel her shift to look at me. "Are you?"

I feather a touch down her arm, enjoying the feel of her against me. "I'm not really okay when we're apart." I utter the admission, feeling both the weight of our separation and the vulnerability that loving Isabel creates in me. The once unexpected and unwelcome exposure has become something else over time—a circumstance that leaves me unarmed in some ways, stronger in others. But Isabel will forever be worth the risk.

She grazes her palm across my scarred stomach with a sweet affection that sometimes I still can't fully understand.

She does more than accept my flaws. She seems to take them on as her own, turning them into something less tragic and more worthy of the love she offers so freely.

"I'm not either," she whispers.

5

ISABEL

If being with Tristan just now hadn't awakened every nerve ending in my body, I might wonder if his sudden appearance in my bedroom was an apparition. With my body melded against his and his scent all around me, I'm tempted to chase sleep with the fantasy that we don't have to be apart ever again. As perfect as he feels and as blissed out as I am, I can't ignore the sobering truth.

"I don't want you to leave. But I'm so scared of what might happen if you stay."

With Rivero still bent on a mission for discovery, I don't take for granted that Tristan could hide out here with any degree of security. To appease my father, Rivero has to keep me out of this for now. Clearly Tristan doesn't fall inside those boundaries.

"I know I can't stay," he says.

I burrow closer as he tightens his arm around me. I wish I could leave with Tristan tonight. Disappear into the darkness and chase a new life with him.

"It'll be over soon. I promise." His tone is more resolute than hopeful. "What happened with Rivero?"

"When my father finally set him straight, I told them everything that could help start an investigation into Simon's affairs. They've agreed to work together unofficially, off the record, which keeps me out of the crosshairs of the FBI and gives everyone the flexibility to dig deeper without anyone between the two agencies stopping them."

"Are they making any progress?"

"They've found a lot of things on Knight's laptop. I told them I'd help them trace the account numbers. I sent them to Landon. I'm just waiting to hear back. So far, nothing points to Simon, so I'm not sure what to expect. But they have the DEA looking at Medina and ramping up security at the key ports."

His silence worries me. I lift up on my elbow to meet his gaze.

"Where have you been staying?"

"With our old friend in Arlington."

I smile a little, relieved.

He reaches up and tucks a few strands of hair behind my ear. "Simon is having a meeting with Senator Keegan in two days. The one who was having an affair with Devon Aguilera. I'm hoping to drop in on him when the time is right."

The lingering buzz of our lovemaking dissipates with this news. "Are you serious?"

"Unless Keegan screws it up for me, which I'm guessing he won't if he ever wants to see his mistress again. He wasn't behind the hit. They're kind of disgustingly smitten with each other, actually."

"Where is the meeting?"

He lets his hand fall to his head, scrubbing his fingers through his hair with a sigh. "When there's a vote going on, Keegan mostly operates out of an office in one of the lower levels of the Capitol building. It's a terrible place for a hit. If I wasn't so determined to make this Simon's last meeting, I would have put it off. Killing him on a yacht surrounded by guests would have been a walk in the park next to getting it done in a government building with that kind of security. Had I only known back in Miami, I would have finished the job no matter what."

My thoughts spin. A meeting with Simon is a coup, but having grown up in DC, I can understand Tristan's concerns. Security is tight and ever-present in that area of the city, inside and outside the building. Even if he gets past enough of it to intercept the meeting, slipping away unnoticed won't be easy if anyone suspects there's something wrong.

"Can Keegan get you inside?"

"Not unless he wants to go to prison for issuing me a visitor pass to kill his two o'clock appointment."

"Then what are you going to do?"

"Do what I do with the least amount of attention and collateral damage as possible. Keegan has to pretend he knew nothing was amiss. Find a reason to show up late, maybe long enough so I can do what I need to and then get the hell out, hopefully without setting off a citywide manhunt."

Anxiety takes root. This doesn't feel right. "Tristan, there has to be a better way. I know you're determined, but you can't sacrifice yourself to get to him."

"I'm aware of the risks. You can rest assured that however it goes down, I don't plan on getting caught." The rigid tension of his body softens a little. "This has to end, and you know it. Simon's the only one standing between you and me and any kind of normal life. I never thought I could have anything like that before, but now it's all I think about. I'm not putting you through any more of this nightmare, and I'm not staying away from you a day more than I have to."

His words give voice to the kind of hopes I'm afraid to say out loud because they feel too idealist to be possible. Sometimes I forget that I lost everything. My job. My identity. One of my best friends. Maybe I force myself to forget all that so I can keep surviving the way I have. To have it back…my life, my freedom, my happiness… Only my fear of losing Tristan could make me turn away from that dream.

"We could still run. I know my father would help us. My parents already know it's a possibility if Rivero doesn't stick to the plan."

He shakes his head gently. "No more running."

There's no talking him out of it. Part of me doesn't want to either. Another part of me wants to throw myself in the way of anything that would endanger him. Intercepting a meeting with Simon reeks of danger. I used to be afraid of Simon's henchmen, but getting clipped by the authorities is a fresh concern.

"I can't bear the thought of anything happening to you." I can't hide the emotion in my voice. I wish I could pretend to be stronger, but I can't.

"I'll be fine. This is what I do."

Another promise with no guarantee.

"Will you at least talk to my father? He might be able to help."

He tenses again.

"I talked to him about the letter," I continue. "I never thought I'd hear him say it, but he understands now that nothing is going to keep us apart. He's fighting for us. He'll help."

He's quiet for a long time before he finally speaks. "I'll think about it, okay?"

I know Tristan. He's already thought about it. He won't trust my father, no matter what I say.

TRISTAN

I should go. I need my mind sharp to figure out how I'm going to get to Simon, but I haven't slept at all. Isabel is dozing beside me, so at peace in rest that I haven't been able to bring myself to leave the comfort of her presence. As dawn starts to push light through the curtains, illuminating more of her, I promise myself a few more minutes to appreciate her in daylight. Then a few minutes more.

The early morning calm is interrupted by the vibrating buzz of her phone on the bedside table. I pick it up, hoping to silence it before it wakes her up. Except it's Blake Landon's name that shows up on the screen. I swipe the screen to answer.

"This is Tristan."

"Hey. Is Isabel there?"

"She's sleeping." I keep my voice low, but Isabel starts to stir.

"Shit. Sorry. I haven't slept yet. Been at this all night," he says.

"Makes two of us."

Isabel blinks awake and looks up at me. Her hair is mussed and her lips are swollen. Never mind that she's naked and warm with only a little bit of sheet between us. Seeing her this way is worth every minute of sleep sacrificed.

"Banks are opening in a few hours, and I wanted to do my research in the off hours."

Landon's voice distracts me from the visual.

"Did you find anything?" I ask.

"I'm not sure. The accounts are all what you'd expect Knight to set up. Except for one."

I wait for him to continue and put the phone on speaker so Isabel can hear now that she's fully awake.

"Who's Jude McKenna?"

Landon's question is met with more silence as Isabel and I lock gazes. I contemplate how to reply, since Jay's involvement has been complicated from day one.

"She used to be affiliated with Simon's organization."

"Well, it looks like she might still be. There's one account with all the big players on it. Davis Knight, Gillian Mirchoff, Michael Pope. Simon's even listed, which was the first thing I noticed since he's suspiciously absent from pretty much everything else. Then there's Jude McKenna. Except she's not a billionaire captain of industry as far as I can tell. Used to work for the DEA until she started running a rehabilitation center in DC. I went to do some more digging on her, but all her accounts have been radio silent for the past month." He pauses a moment. "Is this making any sense to you?"

"How much is in the account?" I ask, avoiding his question.

I can hear Landon tapping his keys rapidly. "Just over ten million, but there are new deposits going in every day. Random amounts from different accounts. Most are international. I'll need more time to track the sources on those."

"What's the account number?"

He rattles off the same one Mateus was told to deposit his cleaned funds into. Fucking hell.

"Thanks. This is helpful," I say, sidestepping further conversation about Jay.

"No problem. I'll let you know if anything else turns up."

I hang up and drop the phone onto the bed between us. Isabel's worried look reflects my own fresh concern over this news.

"What the hell, Tristan? Why would Jay be on the account?"

I do my best to hide my own outrage at having missed this possibility. It's not like we haven't had enough to worry about, but I'd taken for granted that Jay had extracted herself from Company affairs weeks ago. I have to consider all or at least some of it was a lie.

"Why wouldn't she be? She's been involved with them for years. Until Crow kidnapped her and made her a liability, it would make perfect sense for her to be involved in anything this big."

"Why wouldn't they take her off the account?"

I shake my head. "Maybe they were waiting for her to make an attempt at the funds so they could track her down and take her out. Or maybe nothing really changed between them at all. That's a lot of money to walk away from, regardless of the circumstances."

"But if she hasn't used any of her accounts, it seems like she's still hiding."

Isabel is trying to give my former manager the benefit of the doubt. I can sense her reaching for a way to resolve this in her mind. God love her, she's still trying to see the best in people when we've seen the worst of humanity these past two months.

"I suppose there's one sure way to find out," I say. "I'm still in touch with Townsend. Under the right circumstances, I can get the truth out of him."

"If Townsend knows, though, that means he's been involved too. He'd have to have known this entire time.

Why would he help us?"

"Maybe he knew, maybe he didn't. Jay could be using him."

"But…" Her shoulders soften. I can almost read her thoughts, her shock and confusion painted across her beautiful features.

"I have no idea what she's capable of, Isabel. He may not either. But I'll find out what's going on, one way or the other."

She draws her soft touch up my forearm and back down until we're palm to palm. She already knows what has to happen next.

"I shouldn't have stayed so long. I need to get going before your parents get suspicious." Saying the words borders on painful.

"I wish you didn't have to leave." Her voice is barely above a whisper, like she's trying to hold her emotions in check.

I'm not sure if I can survive more of her tears. I'll barely survive walking away from her today. But I have to finish this. For both of us.

"I'll be back to get you when it's over."

She blinks back tears and crawls gently into my arms. I hold her. I tell her how much I love her. I promise to come back. I'll always come back for her…

I speed away from Isabel's house, my phone pressed to my ear. Leaving her is agony, so I decide to spread the misery. It's early, but I don't care. I need answers, and I need them now.

"Who is this?" Townsend's voice comes through the phone.

"It's Red. New number."

A pause. "Did you get the package?" Townsend's question momentarily distracts me from my original intention.

"I got it."

"And?"

"And don't worry about it. I need to talk to you. In person."

I don't trust him not to disappear forever if he knows I'm onto his or Jay's deceit. However he's mixed up in her scheme, I'll be sure to figure it out as soon as I can get my hands on him.

"Why? What's your problem now?"

"Something came up in Paris. Crow got away."

"Fuck all. Are you kidding me?"

When pure frustration overwhelms his usual sarcasm, I smile to myself, satisfied that I'll be able to twist this development to my advantage. "I think I might know where he is."

"Well, are you going to fucking tell me, or did you call me just to catch up like old times?"

"I need your help with something first."

I hear him exhale impatiently. "Let me guess. You're going to hold out about Crow until you get what you want. That's the way it usually works, right? I'm sick of these games, Red."

"You help me. I help you. That's how it works."

"Or you could hand over Crow once and for all and we can be done with it."

"I know where he might be. I don't have him, so you'll have to chase that lead on your own. Until then, I can't risk you getting distracted. When can you meet? I'm going to be in DC for a few more days."

He cusses under his breath. "Whatever. I can be there tonight."

"Perfect." I smile again, oddly looking forward to seeing him even though it's probably not going to be pretty.

6

ISABEL

My mother is sitting at the kitchen island when I come downstairs. Her palms molded around her teacup, she looks a little rested—at least less worn down than when I saw her yesterday. While I'm truly happy to have her back home with my father and me, my thoughts are solidly with Tristan. In his absence, I'm in tatters once again, wondering if this will be the time he doesn't come back to me.

I could have begged him to stay. All it would have done is weigh on him. He still would have disappeared out my window, leaving me alone to wait and worry while he tries to pin Simon down.

Memories of our night together aren't even enough to distract me from the fear that started working its way through me the second Tristan told me about Keegan's meeting. If anyone can pull off this mission, Tristan can. I just have no idea how.

"Good morning," I offer brightly, though my heart isn't really in it.

I pour my coffee and try to wade past my worries and think about the day ahead.

"I see you had a visitor last night."

Torn from my malaise, I whip around to face my mother.

The corner of her mouth is lifted in a coy smile. "I was up early. I saw him come down the tree. He could have used the front door, you know. You aren't teenagers anymore."

I'm stunned into silence, paralyzed momentarily by a remembered feeling of getting caught with him before and having to face the consequences for it. We aren't teenagers trying to fool around behind our parents' backs, though. There's a lot more on the line.

I smile a little, hoping to hide my prevailing sadness. "I wish things were that simple again. It was good to see him, though. I've been really worried since we got separated."

"I know all about that."

She's talking about me, of course, but I don't have any room in my heart for the guilt of falling out of touch. Especially when circumstances may separate us again soon. I'm bound to Tristan.

My father interrupts the moment when he joins us. He looks like he's ready to say something but stops himself when he sees me. "You look miserable. What's going on?" Frowning, he looks to my mother.

"Tristan was here," she says lightly.

"In the house? When?"

"He left this morning. He just wanted me to know he was okay." I'm not about to imply that Tristan and I did any more. He'll suspect it anyway.

He lets out a tense breath. "Okay. Is everything all right?"

"He's going to see Simon." With those words, I hope to communicate the rest I'd rather not speak out loud—that Tristan has every intention of killing Simon Pelletier the second he gets him in his sights. If my father's passion for justice has dimmed at all, he can't know anything else about it. But for Tristan's sake, I desperately want my father's help.

"How did he manage to track him down?"

"He had someone set up a meeting that he plans to intercept."

"Where?"

I worry the inside of my lip, scared to say too much too soon.

My father places his palms flat on the island and leans in, his determination plain. "Isabel. *Where?*"

"At the Capitol building. Simon has a reputation for taking meetings in public places—or places where it'd be difficult to make a move on him."

He straightens and drags his hand through his short hair. "That complicates things."

Meeting at one of the most iconic and well-protected areas in the country is more than a complication. No matter what he says, Tristan is too driven on this mission to weigh the true risks. His freedom. His life. Our future. We could lose everything if this goes wrong. And even if Tristan thinks he can pull it off alone, I don't know if I can let him. Not this time.

"Dad…I want your help. I can't tell you anything that would compromise him, though."

"Compromise him? Do you have any idea how deep I'm already in this? I'm ready to pull a lifetime's worth of favors to take this bastard down. Tristan's not the only one worried about being compromised, believe me."

I look into his eyes, trying to convey the dark truth of the matter. "You know Tristan's not going there just to talk to him."

He's quiet for a long moment. My mother stares into her tea. They both know this is an ugly mission, but it's one that Tristan won't turn away from, no matter what.

"We all know that bringing Simon into custody isn't going to accomplish a goddamn thing," my father says. "I wish things were different, but that's the unfortunate truth."

Having my father fully on our side is both a relief and a fresh dose of worry. He has age and experience on me, but I'm not sure if he's seen the kinds of things I've seen, even in the field. If anyone ever met their death at the end of his gun, of course he'd never tell me.

"What if you change your mind? I need to know we can count on you, no matter what happens."

He lets out a frustrated sigh, but sadness simmers in his eyes. "I know you've been shell-shocked. I fully admit that I haven't always deserved your trust when it comes to Tristan, but you're my little girl. These people have already taken Mariana away from me. They're done playing with people's lives. I'm going to make goddamn sure of it."

I nod. The break in his composure silences my doubts and reinforces this new, unexpected pact between us.

"If we can get Tristan safely in and out of the building without attracting any unwanted attention, I think that's half the battle. Once anyone realizes what happened inside, he needs to be long gone without any suspicions."

He drums his fingers on the countertop. "Anyone can enter during visitor hours, but sneaking downstairs to the hideaway offices could get him noticed." Frowning, he squeezes the back of his neck. "Damn it. Had to be the worst possible place."

"He won't wait for another chance. Last time—" I stop myself short of mentioning Miami. He doesn't need to know about that. Not now, not ever. "He got past us. Tristan isn't going to let Simon slip through his fingers again. I can't talk him out of it."

My parents share a look, some quiet understanding passing between them. My father's expression is resolute in a way I'm beginning to recognize and appreciate more and more.

"I'll find a way to get him in," he finally says.

"There must be a staff entrance," I say. "Could you get him a pass?"

"Possibly. Can he look the part?"

"If that's what he needs to do to blend in." I've never seen Tristan in anything other than street clothes, but my father has a point. "Then what?"

"Then hopefully he can find his way out."

TRISTAN

Anticipation rushes through my veins like the choppy water flowing under the docks just ahead. I used to enjoy this more. Not knowing the extent of Townsend's deceit takes some fun out of the hunt. I'd like to think the worst of him, but only time will tell.

Hours have passed since I sneaked away from Isabel's house this morning. Each moment apart from her seems to stretch out longer than the last. I'm in a better place than I was before seeing her, but I won't be happy until nothing else can keep us apart. Finding out why Jude McKenna's name is listed on the account Mateus was supposed to wire funds into should be a welcome distraction. Except Townsend's late and I'm growing impatient.

I tighten my grip on the gun tucked by my side when there's a loud rapping on the passenger window. Townsend's face appears through it. I press the button that unlocks all the doors at once. He slides into the passenger seat, slamming the door behind him.

"Nice ride." He glances to me, then squints toward the river and the restaurant. "What's up with this place?"

Even if he knew, he wouldn't appreciate the significance, so I don't bother telling him. "Just an old haunt."

He regards me for a moment before reaching into his

jacket and pulling out a pack of cigarettes.

"Not in the car."

He taps one out anyway and tucks it carefully behind his ear.

"You already looked at the files Mushenko dug up," I say matter-of-factly.

He shrugs. "I took a glance before I handed them over."

"And?"

"It looks legit. Seems like the FDA thinks it is too."

"If that's how you felt, why didn't you just tell us that?"

He exhales an annoyed sigh. "Listen, I'm not a fucking scientist. I don't do what Mush does. I like to work with the shit, not cook it up. I'll be as curious as you are when it hits the market and we can see if it actually does what they're promising."

"Just seems like maybe you were wasting our time."

He releases a dry laugh. "Ah, Red. I'm really going to miss these chats."

"Why didn't you go after Crow yourself when he showed up in Berlin?"

"Don't like planes," he says, his tone clipped. "Anyway, I figured the Company had it handled."

"Seems strange that one minute you're ready to run through a wall for a little revenge, and the next minute you don't care all that much about seeing it through."

His mouth wrinkles into an ugly grimace as he turns his body toward me. "A little revenge? Are you serious? Do you ever stop and think about what they did to her?"

The way he spits it out, I know there's a lot more venom

behind it. Whatever he might know, I trust his protectiveness over Jay is genuine, which may be half the problem.

"What wouldn't you do for her?"

His dark eyes grow darker. "Cut the shit and tell me where Crow is, or I'm out of here."

I'd hoped to talk a little more, but he's not giving me much choice. I reach out and cuff his neck, shoving him sideways against the window at the same time. With my left, I shove the muzzle of the gun hidden by my side into the soft flesh under his jaw. He clutches my arm, but I only squeeze harder. I'm stronger and faster. He knows it.

I take in all his panicked responses. Dilated pupils, slick palms, restless legs trapped below the dashboard that have nowhere to go when I have him pinned against the window with all my strength.

"Red," he croaks past the hold I have on his throat. "The fuck."

"Do you think I'm stupid?" I ask the question calmly. I'm curious what he has to say. Except I'm barely letting him breathe, let alone answer. "Because either you're jerking me around, or Jay's jerking us both around. Neither would surprise me. We're going to figure it out right now."

He tries to swallow but can't. He presses his lips together so tightly they're white.

I tilt my head. "Maybe I should give you a little truth serum. That's what's in the antidote, right? A little bit of this, a little bit of that. Maybe I'll shoot it into your vein instead and see what happens. Seems only fair since that's what you did to me."

His nostrils flare when I let him take in a full breath. The added unease when I mention the antidote reaches into me too. Any doubts I harbored about it are now wrapped in distrust for Townsend.

"I paid a little visit to the Paris lab. Reminded me what a piece of shit you are. I guess that was a good spot to play doctor, huh? You want to talk about revenge? Did you think I forgot you fucking blasted my memories because you helped us out a little bit?"

"Said I was sorry," he grates out. "Hypocrite."

I lift an eyebrow. "You want to test me right now?"

After a few seconds, he shakes his head as much as he can. We're both murderers. I get it. Doesn't mean I have to give him a clean slate after what he did to me.

I lean in so close I can smell the tobacco on his clothes. "I'm going to let you take a nice deep breath. Then you're going to tell me why Jay's on Simon's offshore accounts and anything else you think might keep me from putting a bullet in your head."

His gaze flits back and forth across my face. He's trying to read me. Motherfucker.

I release my grip to gain just enough leverage to slam his head harder against the window. He widens his eyes and tries to twist and look out the window.

"There's no one here to help. I'm your only hope. Unless you have something to tell me, this is probably the last stop for you."

"Okay... Okay. Fuck," he rasps.

After a prolonged moment, I pull away. "Don't bother

trying to bullshit me either."

He blinks a few times before taking in a ragged breath. From the way he glares at me, I don't think the things on his mind at present align much with what I want to know.

He rubs his neck and swallows hard. "Who cares if she's on the accounts? It doesn't make her any less valuable to the Company. Only makes the price on her head that much higher."

"She lied to me. She's deeper in this than she let on."

"Why the fuck would she tell you? It's not like she trusts anyone."

"Because I saved her life. Three times, actually. This is the thanks I get?"

"She's not working with Simon. A long time ago she tried getting out of the Company. He couldn't risk letting her go with everything she knew. She was too valuable, so he got her to double down instead, roping her into this Felix fiasco. She was on the accounts long before Crow snatched her. She hasn't exactly been available for him to take her off it."

"If they're both signers on the account, that means they're partners," I say, furious at myself for assuming Jay's subordinacy to Simon all this time.

"The whole fucking lot of them are in on this. Jay got cut in along the way, and there was no going back. Now she's nothing but a liability. You think they want to get their hands on your precious Isabel. How badly do you think they want Jay?"

Judging by the money on the line, I'd guess Simon

would do about anything to have Jay back under his control, if she isn't already.

"How long have you known she was involved in this?"

"She only told me after Miami. When you got that close to Simon, it wasn't just about hiding out anymore. She realized there was hope of getting out of this mess."

"And how exactly did she think she'd manage that?"

"The second she walks into that bank to make a withdrawal, she's as good as dead. This isn't over until they're gone. Every last one of them." He hesitates. "And you're the best man for the job."

The air in the car is thick with a different kind of tension. Suddenly it all makes sense. Even with Townsend's help, Jay wouldn't be able to get to all of them. It had to be me.

"Why didn't you just tell me? I thought we were on the same team."

"We're in this for different reasons, mate," he says quietly. "There's a lot of fucking money in that account."

"And you want all of it."

"You're damn right I do. You and your girl are on a mission to save the world. I'm not going to sit here and lie to you like I care."

"You think any of that would shock me?"

"No, but if you knew Jay was involved at all, you'd think the worst—the way you already are. I wasn't going to let you make a target out of her instead of Simon and his cronies. I want that fucker Crow gone, but I came to Boston to keep you focused on Felix. I knew you were bloodthirsty for the Boswells and it was just a matter of time before you'd take the last of them out. I was just pointing you in the right direction."

"Away from the money trail."

He shrugs.

"And what about the antidote? You figured I'd jump right on that as soon as Simon was out of the picture?"

He licks his lips nervously, averting his eyes briefly.

I lift the gun and point it at him, my blood pumping angrily through my veins.

"I don't know what's in it, all right? Mush didn't tell me anything. It's a gamble. You knew that."

"Doesn't sound like my odds are very good if you're banking on it taking me out of the equation."

"I don't fucking know!"

His eyes are round, his voice uneven, like he knows he's running out of time. To lie. To tell the truth. To do whatever he needs to do to appease me. I grind my teeth. I should shoot him. Get it over with. If he's not working with me, he's against me. He's getting in my way. They both are.

"Jay knows about the antidote too?"

A resigned kind of laugh leaves him. "You're dumber than I thought."

I tilt my head, the darkest corner of my brain whispering at me to press the trigger. "Sorry?"

He shakes his head, a miserable smile on his face. "She'd never let me kill you. Crow? Now that's another story."

"Right. She just wants to send me to the front lines to do all her dirty work so she can make off with Simon's money. I'm really moved."

"You were going for him anyway. What's the difference?"

"I don't like being lied to. That's the difference. You think I care about the money?"

"Why wouldn't you?" he says in a raised voice of exasperated disbelief.

He doesn't know I haven't gotten close to burning through the money I earned from Jay's assignments. And he definitely doesn't know about the Halo money that flooded Isabel's account after I killed Martine.

"Let's just say I'm comfortable."

He rubs at his throat again, eyeing me warily. "Then finish the fucking job."

Slowly, I lower the gun. "I plan to. And you're going to help me."

7

ISABEL

I zip up my backpack and take a last look around my room. Two months ago, I left my parents' house not knowing when I'd be back. I have that same distant feeling again—like after tomorrow, things won't ever be the same. My gaze lands on the old picture set atop my dresser. I walk over and pick up the heavy ceramic frame that's held the memory of my sister and me for as long as I can remember. I turn it over, lift up the metal tabs holding the photo to the glass, and release it.

Our names are written on the back with the date in my mother's script. She probably thought we'd have so many more photos like this together. What if Mariana had lived? I brush my thumb over her sweet three-year-old face, a mirror of mine beside her. I don't know if I'll ever be Isabel Foster again. She seems like a stranger now.

I'm still me, but I'm not. I'll always have my memories, but maybe Tristan and I aren't so different anymore. Life has carved a cruel line into our psyches, a bloody demarcation between our youthful innocence and the harrowing truth. The warmth of a dream and the harsh light of awakening.

Now we see more. We feel more. And somehow, with everything that's been taken from us, together again, we *are* more.

Newly determined, I slide the photo into a side pocket of my bag and sling it over my shoulder before leaving my room. I'm quiet on the stairs, careful to avoid the creaks and moans I've memorized from a lifetime in this house. I already warned my parents, but no matter what happens tomorrow, if Tristan and I can get away, we should stay away. And I'm not letting him fight this war alone.

My father convinced Rivero to go to Miami to poke his nose into the new DEA investigation around Javier Medina and the port authority there. Hopefully Rivero will forget about Tristan enough for us to disappear and stop looking over our shoulders. If not, maybe my father won't give him any choice once I'm gone.

I leave a note on the counter for my parents—just a goodbye for now—and unlock the front door. A taxi is idling at the curb, waiting to take me away from the place I'll always call home.

Twenty minutes later, the driver pulls up in front of a narrow house. Makanga's unforgettable car and a red BMW are parked in the driveway. I pay the driver and walk up the path to the front door. I knock and wait. Tristan probably won't want me here, but that doesn't slow my heartbeat when I think about seeing him again and spending one more night with him beside me.

After I knock, Makanga answers and opens the screen door with a squeak. He narrows his gaze as he looks past me and cranes his neck to glance around the yard.

"I'm alone," I say, a little disappointed at the less-than-warm reception.

"Who brought you here?"

I huff out a sigh. "I called a taxi and remembered your address. Can I see Tristan?"

I hear footsteps behind him. Then Tristan comes into view as he nudges Makanga to the side.

"Isabel." He takes my bag and ushers me inside, but his expression is no warmer than Makanga's. "What are you doing here? I thought you were going to stay with your parents until I came for you?"

"I figured you could use some help."

Makanga chuckles before walking over to his chair.

"I don't need help," Tristan says. "I need to know you're safe so I can concentrate."

I cross my arms over my chest. "How are you getting into the building tomorrow?"

"The way most people get into the building. Through the visitor center. I can get where I need to from there. Does your father know you're here?"

"No, but he got you this." I pull the staff pass he arranged out of my bag and hand it to Tristan.

He stares down at it, then up at me. For a split second, I

worry I've gone too far. Of all the times I've pushed myself into his plans, maybe this was the time to step aside and let him do things his way. I cross my arms tightly again, a small defense against the hard look he's pinned on me.

"What did you tell Morgan?"

I suck in a breath that's less than steady. "That you were meeting with Simon."

"At the Capitol building."

"Yes. Obviously."

The muscles in his jaw flex. "Isabel, why the hell did you do that? I have this under control."

My apprehension slips, quickly replaced with frustration that we're fighting this battle all over again. "Like hell you do. Walk in the front door, kill Simon, and walk out? That's your strategy?"

When he doesn't say anything, I step around him, taking my bag from him as I move. I settle on the couch and pull out a few visitor-guide brochures, unfolding one on the table in front of me.

"With a staff pass, you can enter through the entrance on the north side. Keegan's office should be close. This way you won't risk anyone seeing you trying to sneak someplace you aren't supposed to be."

He comes closer, hovering above me. "You're worried I won't be able to make my way to his office? That's what this is about?"

I glare up at him. "I'm worried about you underestimating everything because you want this too much. We're talking about the Capitol building, Tristan."

"Which thousands of tourists flow through every damn day. I made it out of an international airport in less than five minutes. You think I can't get where I need to go in there?"

"You also had security immediately looking for you, which isn't something we want. Will you stop being so pigheaded and just let me help?"

He doesn't answer me, which is almost promising. It's not a yes, but it's not a no.

Makanga is wearing a smirk as he leans over to look at the map on the brochure. "Seems like a more direct approach. Is the pass legit?"

"My father assures me it is. He doesn't know I'm going to be there yet, but when he realizes I'm not home in the morning, he'll figure it out. He's not going to do anything to jeopardize this. I promise you."

Tristan's eyes grow wide. "*You* are not going anywhere near this. Mark my words."

I exhale a frustrated breath through my nose and push on. "Where will Keegan be?"

"He's planning to be late for the meeting. I figure I'll have about fifteen minutes before Simon gets restless and leaves."

"Which means that whatever happens, chances are Keegan is going to find Simon after and alert security before you're even out of the building. He won't have any other choice if he doesn't want to somehow implicate himself."

He exhales with a subtle shake of his head. "Not necessarily."

"It's a tight window," I say.

He shrugs. "It's do-able."

"If someone stumbles upon a crime scene, the police are going to be looking for you faster than you can disappear. I'm not talking about getting out of the building, Tristan. I'm talking about getting out of DC before there's a citywide manhunt."

A heavy silence falls on the room. Makanga seems to be holding his breath. I'm waiting for Tristan to react. To tell me I'm wrong or toss me in a cab back to my parents' house. He stares down at the map a moment before taking a seat beside me. He steeples his fingers in front of his mouth, saying nothing, which feels oddly like resignation.

I bite the inside of my mouth to keep from smiling.

"I can come in through the visitor center and, when the time is right, create a diversion. Something that will give Keegan a reason to leave the building instead of meeting Simon as planned. An evacuation will create confusion with all the visitors and staff trying to leave in a rush. No one's going to notice either of us. Security will be too busy trying to get people out. It should be a while before anyone notices Simon after that. By then we'll be long gone."

Tristan is quiet for a long time. So long that I know he's at least considering my proposal. He doesn't want me getting mixed up in this, and he won't want me in the building when it all goes down, but we threw solo missions out the window a long time ago. He could do it alone if nothing went wrong, but I'm convinced we're stronger together.

The look he finally casts my way is filled with frustration—but also, I hope, acceptance.

Makanga pulls the lever on his recliner, elevating his legs with a loud clank. A smirk curls his mouth as he settles in. "I can drive."

TRISTAN

The firm knot pressing against my throat is one more reason for me to silently curse Isabel's plan. I feel ridiculous in the navy-blue suit she picked out for me, except she hasn't stopped looking me over since I put it on at the store this morning.

"You're distracting me," I mutter, trying to ignore her appreciative glances.

She laughs. "Why?"

"Why do you think? Are you focused?"

She slides her hand into mine. "I'm focused. Promise."

"You should probably go now," Makanga says from the driver's seat. "There might be a line to get in."

I check my watch. Simon is set to meet Keegan in fifteen minutes. Isabel needs to be in place before then just in case.

She takes a deep breath and looks to me, her humor faded. "I'll wait for your signal. Then you have to head to the rotunda right away. The staff won't evacuate the same way as the visitors. You don't want to get grouped with them once everyone starts moving."

I hold her stare a moment, wishing I could tell her that despite her obstinance, I'm totally floored by her compulsion to help me, to be with me, to stand beside me at all costs. I lift her hand and kiss the back of it. "I'll meet you back here after."

Her eyes get glassy before she lurches forward to hug me one last time. The next time I hold her like this, we'll be free of Simon. And if we're not, I might never hold her like this again. I close my eyes and push away the possibility. Isabel's plan is a good one. If Keegan doesn't fuck things up, I should be able to get out of this with my freedom and Isabel with hers.

"I love you," she whispers against my ear.

When she pulls away, I kiss her gently, unwilling to say it back but silently vowing I'll tell her every day for the rest of our lives if we survive this. Until then, I just need one thing from her.

"Be careful."

"You too." She touches my face before getting out and walking hurriedly down the path toward the visitor center.

Makanga puts the car into gear and drives us around to the north side of the block. "You good?"

"Never been better." It's a lie, of course.

"You going to make it clean, I hope?"

I meet his reflection in the rearview. "It's going to be what it's going to be."

We've reviewed everything a few times, everything except what'll happen once I'm finally alone with Simon. If this goes sideways, Makanga and Isabel will at least have the benefit of plausible deniability. Besides, I can map everything down to the minute, and something could and very likely *will* change. At the end of the day, all I care about is making sure Simon can never hurt anyone ever again.

The minutes tick by. Simon strikes me as someone who arrives right on time, never late and not a minute too soon, so I plan for that. Five minutes till, I reach for the door handle.

"If I don't come out right away, you get her out of here. Don't wait for me. Got it?"

Makanga doesn't answer, but I know he'll probably err on the side of saving his own ass even if Isabel begs him to hang around. I take his silence as affirmation and start the walk toward the north entrance. Isabel wasn't wrong. Getting into the building with easy access to Keegan's office is the biggest hurdle. As long as Morgan's staff pass does the job, it's one less thing for me to worry about. But I've learned to take nothing for granted. Things could get messy really fast.

Once I'm inside, the security guard checks my pass and waves me toward security. I lay my leather bag on the roller belt and step through the metal detector. No beeps. I wait for it on the other side, hands tucked into my pants pockets, feeling as confident as a slimy politician who pads his government salary with bribes from monsters like Simon.

I collect my bag and meander the halls until I find the maze of underground offices below the Senate floor where Keegan and every other senator can enjoy a meeting place away from their primary offices. The journey is shockingly unremarkable. The cinder-block walls are painted sunshine yellow. The signs are little more than shorthand directions for people who haven't already familiarized themselves with these pathways.

I pause outside Keegan's office, listening for voices inside. All I can hear are footsteps echoing through the connecting halls. The very high possibility that Simon could be on the other side of this door is almost too good to be true. I can still remember when Jay told me he was a shadow. A shadow I've found not once but twice.

My heart beats faster. Not from fear but from something akin to glee. I've never been so invested in someone's demise, and I don't think I ever will be again. No one deserves this more than Simon.

I put my hand on the knob and open the door. From his seat on one of the fancy upholstered chairs, Simon glances up and smiles automatically. It fades quickly as I shut the door behind me. I unbutton my jacket, set my bag on the lacquered coffee table, and take the seat opposite him.

I fold my hands across my lap as a triumphant chorus of trumpets and horns plays in my mind.

"Simon. At long last," I say, unable to school my unabashed grin.

His already pale complexion seems to drain a fraction. "Tristan." He says my name awkwardly, like he's not sure I'm really, truly sitting across from him.

"You remember me. I'm flattered. Have we already met? I probably wouldn't remember if we had."

I'm still smiling, even as the truth burns at the edges of my internal celebration.

"What are you doing here?"

I don't even try to stop myself from laughing. It's loud and feels good and ends with a cleansing kind of sigh. "Sorry. I've just been wanting to meet you for such a long time. This is a real honor."

He doesn't seem to share my sense of humor. He glances to the door.

"Keegan's going to be late," I say, quickly smashing any hopes he might be dreaming up for an escape. "Hope you don't mind if we catch up while you wait. I've been trying to fill in the blanks a little lately."

"I don't know what you had in mind, but this is hardly the time or the place."

I shrug.

"We should take this meeting elsewhere. My hotel is close by. We can discuss business there."

To his credit, his stony expression gives little away. After so many kills, I've gotten used to all the desperate pleas and telltale signs of crippling fear. I'm feeling strangely bereft in the face of Simon's admirable self-control. There's still time to break him, though.

"Not a chance," I finally say.

He doesn't blink. "Let's get on with it, then."

I take a deep breath, all too aware of our limited time but committed to doing this just right.

"You know, you're lucky I never killed Isabel."

"Why is that?" His tone is flat and uninterested.

"Because if I'd gone through with it and then found out what you'd done to me, you'd have been dead three seconds after I walked through the door. Somehow she's managed to convince me that I still have a little of my humanity left, even though you and Jay did your very best to destroy it."

"Your humanity? That's a little too sentimental considering you're lucky to have your life. You were nearly dead when we found out about you. We could have let you die in the ER tent at Camp Dwyer."

"I feel so blessed."

He shakes his head almost imperceptibly. "Think what you want, Tristan, but you were spared a life of inescapable post-traumatic stress. You had no family, no job, no home to go back to. You had no one until you had us."

I hate Simon a little more with every passing second. His subtle arrogance. The surety in his tone.

"You're wrong. I had Isabel. If you hadn't fucked up my memories, chances are pretty high we would have been together." I ignore the pang of emotion that comes with saying those words out loud. "Gotta love when life comes full circle, though."

"Sorry if I don't have time for your trip down memory lane," he says through gritted teeth. "You don't want to be in the Company anymore. I get it. Needless to say, this isn't a good fit. Let's move on."

"Move on? So you're not going to send someone after me every chance you get and hope they'll have better luck than Crow and Web and Townsend and Dunny? It's getting to be a pretty long list at this point."

"Exactly. Enough is enough."

"What about Jay? You letting her off the hook too?"

He doesn't reply, doesn't move a muscle.

Another smile plays at my lips. He wants her most of all. If Townsend was telling the truth, Jay existing outside of Simon's control is far worse than the menace I've become to his operation.

"I bet that really screwed things up for you when she started talking to Crow about your clients. Especially with her being a signer on your supersecret offshore accounts and all."

His nostrils flare ever so slightly. "She's an inconvenience, same as you. Something I can easily work around."

I make a small sound of disbelief because there's no working around people who won't disappear completely.

He pushes his glasses up his nose. "Is it the money you're after? That's an easy problem to solve. We have truckloads of it. Name your price, and let's end this conversation. I have work to get back to."

I laugh. "You think it's all about money, huh?"

"What more could you possibly want?"

I stare at him a long time, knowing I'll never get what I truly want. No matter how much I long for it. No matter what miracles anyone promises.

"I want my memories back, Simon. That's what I really want. I'd do nearly anything to have them, because I have no idea who the hell I really am. My life started the day Jay sent me to Rio. Outside of a few nightmares and flashbacks, there's no going backward from that point."

He has the decency not to feed me any more bullshit about saving my life.

"What would you do if you were me?"

He offers a tight smile. "I wouldn't have made your choices. I would have done my job. We wouldn't be sitting here if I were in your shoes."

"And given the choice, you would have opted for this." I gesture to myself. "This interrupted existence. Years wiped away, just like that." I snap my fingers.

He doesn't hesitate. "I'd take that over death. Any day."

I drag the backs of my fingers along my freshly shaved jaw, contemplating the shrewd, awful human sitting across from me. Then I reach inside my jacket. Simon visibly tenses, which encourages me. I withdraw a thin syringe from my inside pocket and roll it between my fingers.

"Because you supposedly saved my life, I'll let you think it over a little more. You only have a minute because I'm in a bit of a rush. Then you'll have to make a decision, or I'll do what I think is best for you. Same way you did for me."

His eyes are wider. His breathing heavier. It's a heady rush.

"What is that?" His voice is barely a whisper, his gaze fixed on the cheap syringe as I lift it higher.

"Townsend says you call it Elysium Dream."

8

ISABEL

The rotunda is filled with tourists, most congregated around the half dozen or so red-jacketed tour guides speaking animatedly about the history of the building and the activities that go on in the nearby House and Senate galleries. The architecture is impressive. A colorful and awe-inspiring fresco crowns the room. I'm sure it would all be fascinating if I weren't here for a much more sinister purpose.

My heart is in my throat as I wait for Tristan's signal and simultaneously scope out the possibilities. But there are so many people here. No doubt Tristan and I can get lost in this crowd. Hell, we'll be lucky to find each other in it once things start happening.

I check my watch for the hundredth time, then my phone. Time keeps marching on with no word from Tristan.

Hurry up, hurry up.

What could be taking Tristan so long? Did Keegan show up too soon? Is Simon late? Of all the possible scenarios, the worst one is Tristan losing sight of the plan to get in and get out as quickly as possible. He wants this too much. I worry he'll drag it out or make a mistake.

I nearly jump out of my skin when my phone rings. I look down, expecting Tristan, but my father's number lights up the screen. He called a couple of times this morning, but I avoided him. I should now too, but something compels me to pick up.

"Dad?"

"Where the hell are you?" His tone isn't soft or forgiving, which isn't easing the steady rise of my panic.

"I'm...I'm fine."

"Tell me you aren't there with him. Damn it, Isabel, tell me you weren't that stupid."

Lashing back only adds to the threat of discovery. I'm trying not to stand out, even in this busy crowd. Screaming into my cell phone at my father will definitely get me noticed.

"I have to go."

I'm ready to hang up when he yells again.

"Don't you dare hang up on me. You're going to stay on with me until this is over. What's going on?"

"Tristan's with him now," I say quietly. "At least I think so. I'm waiting to hear from him."

"What are you doing there? There's no reason for you to be that close. He can handle this without you."

"Maybe he can, but I wasn't going to risk it. He needs a diversion once it's done. Something that will give us a head start so we can get out of DC before anyone finds out what's going on."

He's quiet for too long, and wherever he is, I'm certain I'm breaking his heart a little more.

"I'm sorry, Dad. You know I can't stay."

"You can always stay. I'll protect you. That's what I've been doing, haven't I?"

"Yes, you have, but you have enough to go on now. You don't need me there to help with an investigation. Keeping me around is only going to remind Rivero that he hasn't unearthed all my secrets."

"If you disappear, he's going to want them even more."

"Not if you talk to him. Keep him focused on the important things."

"Isabel," he exhales tiredly. "We just got you back."

I close my eyes and shake my head, even though he can't see it. "I'm not a little girl anymore. Tristan's my home now."

Even if it means being on the run with him. And if the authorities figure out that we're involved in Simon's death, we could be on the run for a long time.

A large group of tourists meander by, a short brunette guiding them along, pointing skyward toward the oculus of the dome. "You'll see George Washington is one of the figures depicted, and he is flanked by two mythological figures, the goddesses Victoria and Liberty."

The crowd shuffles along as I glance around nervously,

wishing Tristan would show up or reach out. The not knowing is burning a hole through my stomach. Suddenly I'm petrified he didn't even get past security. Was I wrong to push this plan on him?

"Dad, what if this doesn't work?"

"Then you get the hell out of there. You shouldn't be there to begin with. I can't believe he brought you into this."

I can't mistake the anger in his voice—resentment directed at Tristan that I thought I'd never have to hear again.

"I didn't give him a choice. I never do."

He sighs. "God help me, you're just like your mother."

TRISTAN

"You're bluffing." Doubt and uncertainty lace Simon's words.

I lift an eyebrow, amused that he thinks so. "I have one job, and I do it pretty well. Bluffing doesn't have anything to do with it."

A bullet is a bullet. I don't play games. I am enjoying watching the sweat start to bead on Simon's forehead, though. I could spend hours getting off on his fear, and it would never be enough.

"You won't get away with this," he says.

I smile. *Yes, I will, you evil son of a bitch.*

"I'm sure that everyone will get exactly what they deserve. Like all those soon-to-be junkies who are going to be lining up for your new miracle drug before too long."

He swallows hard. "It's a business."

"A business that's facilitating a massive flow of drugs into the US. How many people have to die for you to call it a success?"

"People die all the time. When it's all said and done, Felix will save millions of lives."

"Do you really think so?"

"I know so."

I tilt my head. "Why not let Felix succeed on its own merits, then? Or is that not exciting enough for you? It's not enough to have a win. You had to orchestrate a nationwide crisis to make it a real smash hit?"

"You have a lot to learn about how the world works, Tristan."

I fidget with the syringe. "You're probably right. I'm sure there are a lot of people who are really impressed with this whole operation. That's how you formed your little club, right? Collect a bunch of power-mongering billionaires who don't care about playing with people's lives if it gives them a thrill. Keep moving the line on what's acceptable until you're knee deep in something like this, and it doesn't even feel wrong."

"What you don't realize is that it's going to happen with or without me. Killing me isn't going to change anything."

"I didn't say I was going to kill you."

He looks to the door again, which reminds me of the time. I push my sleeve up to glance at my watch casually. "You're right. We should probably get this over with."

He rubs his hands on his knees anxiously. "What do

you really want, Tristan? I can't undo what's done, and you know it. You need me for something. You wouldn't have come this far for this."

I lift the syringe. "For this? I definitely did."

He looks to the door again, then back to me. I lean forward, and he jolts backward like I struck him.

I laugh. "Are you nervous?"

"Listen, I'll call it off. Is that what you want? Will that make it right in your mind somehow?"

I make him wait a few seconds before I answer. "Do you want to tell me where the leaks at the border are?"

"If that's what you want. If I tell you, are you still going to kill me?"

I pause thoughtfully. I've never wanted to kill someone more than I want to kill Simon. Taking it off the table is disappointing, but he's ready to talk. Plus, I can always change my mind.

"Fine." I pull out my phone and call Morgan. I put the call on speaker as it rings endlessly, finally ending with Morgan's voicemail. I nod expectantly to Simon. "Talk. We don't have a lot of time."

His lower lip trembles as he leans in. He rattles off the names of the ports we already suspected Knight was targeting with his bribes. Simon closes his eyes, and his brow wrinkles as he relays the times and details of the shipments with a degree of specificity that impresses me. He looks at me when he finishes.

"Is that all?" I ask.

When he nods, I end the call and put the phone away.

Isabel is expecting a message from me. The wait is probably killing her, but she'll have to wait a little longer.

"Can I go now?"

I lift my gaze to Simon. "No."

He starts to visibly shake. "We had a deal."

"I said I wouldn't kill you. It pains me to honor that promise, but I will."

He stares at the syringe I'm still holding. "You had real trauma. That's the way it works—"

"I plan on giving you real trauma, Simon. And I know how it works. I can personally attest to its efficacy. I mean, you may get flashbacks from time to time. Those can be disturbing. But you'll pretty much have a clean slate. This is about twice what Townsend gave me, so I think it'll do the job."

"What good will it do? You think you're on some moral high ground because you figured out what we're doing, but you're nothing more than a criminal yourself." He's shouting now, gripping the wooden arms of his chair like a kid hanging on to the bar of a roller coaster as if it would slow it down somehow. "The things I know are worth millions. *Billions.* You're going to flush it just like that? I could tell you things that no one else knows."

"I'm not sure I want to know any more. I hate that you've already taken up this much space in my head all this time. I'm ready to start thinking about something else."

"Then just let me go. You'll never have to think about me again. I'll stay out of your way. Jay too, if that's what you want. I'll walk away from the whole damn thing."

"It's not that simple. The castle is going to crumble anyway. We found your accounts. Your buddy Medina is already getting grilled by the feds. Pope will be next. Vince is dead. Gillian and Davis too. If you really don't want me to kill you, that's fine. But you're too clever for me to leave you to your own devices and trust that more people aren't going to die while you try to get away with everything you can. Because, let's face it, that's who you are."

He opens his mouth to speak but says nothing. It must be a lot to take in. The imminent collapse of an enterprise that's been years in the making. Then the prospect of one's own demise. He can't even deny that he'd try to wiggle out of whatever troubles are coming his way. Of course he would. He'll do anything to survive, just the way he is now.

He pushes up from his chair, a sharp motion like a firecracker launching from the ground. When he goes for the door, I follow him. He's desperate, but I'm faster. I yank him away, and he stumbles backward.

"I won't let you do this," he cries.

"You will."

With that, I take two long strides toward him and give him a shove toward the wall. He stumbles again before bringing his hands to my chest in a feeble attempt to push me back when I'm on him again. He's so weak. He smells like fear. I despise him.

"Tristan, stop. You don't have to do this."

I grasp his face in my hand, forcing his jaw shut. I'm sick of his begging and empty threats. I'm glad we never met until this moment, because already I can't wait to be rid of him.

"Goodbye, Simon."

In one swift movement, I slam his head against the wall. It's hard enough to knock him out but not enough to give him a brain hemorrhage. Sadly, I can calculate the difference.

I drag his limp body toward the door, aligning his new injury with the floor. I don't hesitate or overthink it. I pick up the syringe that's rolled to the floor from our chase and uncap it. I take his hand and find a bulging blue vein. As soon as I puncture it with the needle, I plunge the poison I know too well into his bloodstream.

As I envision the drug doing its silent work inside his body, I do my best to empty myself of emotion, which used to feel like the most natural thing in the world after a kill. Except I'm capable of a lot more now, thanks to Isabel. I'm not sure Simon will be so lucky. He may not feel things for a very long time.

When it's done, I tuck the empty syringe away inside my suit coat. Simon doesn't move. He's no longer a threat. Even after he regains consciousness, he won't be. As much as I'd like to stick around to make certain of it and witness the aftermath, it's time for me to go.

ISABEL

Now

My heart races when I see Tristan's one-word text. I glance around the room, suddenly frantic to find someone to do what I need. A large group of middle schoolers with matching orange T-shirts are huddled together near the middle of the room. One of them lingers behind, staring at his cell phone screen, far enough from the group that I decide he's the one. There's no time to look for a better candidate. I walk over and give a little wave.

"Hi," I say with a forced smile. "Can you do me a favor?"

He looks up at me blankly. "Uh, I guess."

"That's your tour guide, right?" I point to the man in the red jacket who's almost impossible to see through the throng of students.

"Yeah. Why?"

"Could you go give this to him for me? It's really important."

I reach into my back pocket and pull out a piece of paper with my handwriting on it. I don't want him to read it yet, but kids are curious so he probably will. Hopefully he waits until I'm already out of sight.

He takes the paper, frowning as he does. Before he can respond, I turn and walk out of the rotunda, praying this works. Tristan's message didn't say anything about Keegan, but if he hasn't shown up yet, that means we only have minutes. Maybe seconds. I hurry toward the nearest bathroom and shutter myself in a stall. I rip off my long blond wig and peel off the second layer of clothes I wore. Stepping out again, I stuff everything into the trash and take a quick glance at myself in the mirror. If they start looking for the blonde with the bomb threat, they shouldn't be looking for me.

All of a sudden, I hear static from the speakers set into the ceiling.

"Attention, please. Attention, please. For everyone's safety, it has become necessary to evacuate the building. Please leave the building immediately at the nearest exit."

The announcer repeats the message, and voices outside the bathroom grow louder. I open the door as a mass of people are moving toward the visitor center exit. I join them, hiding myself in the center of the crowd. Security guards and guides are shouting from every location, reminding people to stay calm but to keep moving.

Panic fills the air as patrons murmur and complain and worry aloud as we shuffle along. I share their panic, just not for the same reasons. I see no sign of Tristan in the mob. He had a longer trek from the underground offices, so I remind myself to be patient. He'll show up soon.

A minute later, I'm in the open air just outside the visitor entrance with dozens of others who quickly disperse across the greens away from the supposed threat in the building. I hesitate and look around again, feeling more desperate by the second. Where is he?

I don't want to attract attention hanging around, so I walk toward Makanga's car, which I can spot parked down the street. I'm nearly there when I take out my phone and call Tristan. It rings and rings. I'm feeling sick. I should turn back, but that's not what we agreed on. I hang up and am about to dial again when two strong arms wrap around me from behind. I scream as I'm lifted off my feet into the air.

Tristan's laugh cuts through the instant panic that's

flying through me. He sets me down so I can turn around and face him.

I slap his chest, angry and relieved and overwhelmed. "Damn you, Tristan. What the hell? Why didn't you pick up your phone?"

His smile reaches his eyes, as calm as the cool spring sky behind him. "Because I was running to catch up with you. You couldn't wait a few seconds?"

A ragged sigh of relief leaves me. "Not when I'm worried something terrible might have happened to you. Seconds matter. You know that better than anyone."

He closes the small space between us, cupping my face in his palms. The tips of our noses meet. His gentle touch and the air we share are alive with a frenetic kind of energy, a hundred lightning strikes of emotion that bond me tighter to him.

"I love you," he rasps. "I love you so fucking much."

When our mouths collide, I forget the rest. The past. The pain. I let it all go because I feel like under this kiss, Tristan is letting it go too.

"Lovebirds. Guys. Come on. We gotta hit the road."

I break the kiss when Makanga bangs his hand on the roof of the car with a thud.

I gaze up at Tristan. "Where are we going?"

"Anywhere you want," he says, wearing a smile that takes my breath away.

9

TRISTAN

Six months later

With a little effort, I tug open the sticky sliding door that Isabel has been on me to fix. A splash of hot coffee slides down my hand and the side of the mug I'm holding.

"Shit."

Isabel tears her attention from the early morning tide rolling in. I take the chair next to her and hand the coffee over carefully.

"It's hot. Take my word for it."

She grins. "I think I'm going to call someone about the door. It's driving me nuts."

"I can do it. Just give me a few weeks. I'm working my way down the list."

And it's a long list. Of all the places we could go, Isabel's heart was set on Perdido Key. She said it was the first place where she could imagine us putting down roots. Whatever vision she had for us that circumstances interrupted, she was determined to come back and see it through, so of course I agreed. We drove around town and walked the beach checking out different spots, but in the end, she was determined to overpay the owners of the beach house where we celebrated my birthday months ago and call it home.

"You don't have to do everything yourself," she says. "If you won't let me help you, we can at least hire someone for a few things."

"You insisted on buying this rundown house, and I'm determined to fix the damn thing up myself. So you're just going to have to be patient," I say, my tone teasing but resolute.

"We can afford some help."

I shrug. "I don't care. It keeps me busy."

A few months after we moved in, Isabel took a job helping out at a local school. I didn't love the time away from her, but I needed something to fill up the hours. Being idle wasn't an option for someone like me. More than anything, I needed an occupation that didn't involve employing my survival skills.

I don't know much about home repair yet, but dedicating myself to the myriad projects that are needed here gives me a chance to do something constructive. In truth, it feels good turning something ugly and neglected into something nice again. Plus, every time I conquer something new, Isabel's eyes light up in a way that almost knocks the wind out of me. Making her happy is addictive, and selfishly I want all the credit for putting that look on her face. Not some sweaty contractor who will do almost anything on the list for fifty dollars an hour.

Isabel is entranced by the water again. The sky is a hazy lavender, and the waves are calm. We spend all our mornings this way. I don't crave routine now that we're not running for our lives, but I like this one because we share it and an unspoken gratitude seems to exist inside of it. We watch the birds skim above the water and the clouds roll along. Life keeps on moving, and we get to be a part of it.

I reach over and take Isabel's hand in mine. She turns her head, and the way her expression softens, she must recognize the reverence in mine.

"What do you want to do today?" I ask.

"We don't have to pick my parents up from the airport until after dinner. I have to run a few errands if you want to come with."

I register a little knot of anxiety at the mention of her parents, but I don't show it. Every day, I feel like I'm retraining my brain to accept normal, uncomfortable things. Isabel's patient with me about it, especially when it comes to being around other people. She's starting to make friends. I worry I'm a long way from getting there, but I'm trying. Errands, though, I can do.

"Count me in."

The next morning, I find Morgan in the kitchen screwing new handles onto the cabinetry. We have to talk. I'm tempted to wait until he and Lucia are ready to go back home, but I'm also too anxious to put it off anymore.

"Morning," I say. "Do you need some help?"

He glances up at me briefly before returning to the task. "I'm good. Just saw these on the counter and figured I'd take care of it quick."

"Thanks. By the time I get to everything that needs to be done here, I'll have to start all over again."

He chuckles quietly. Morgan isn't much warmer to me than he was before. We aren't at odds, but we're both guarded. I suspect that's how he's always been, which is fine by me. It's a language I can speak, even if it requires very few words.

"Where's Isabel?" I ask.

"She and Lucia went out furniture shopping. We wanted to get you something for the new place. Knowing Lucia, it'll be an all-day affair."

Having the house to ourselves all day might not be ideal after he hears what I have to say, but I've already decided it's going to be now.

I lean against the counter and brace my hands against it. "I want to marry Isabel."

He tightens up his screw and checks out his work as if he didn't hear me. I know he did. Finally he sets down the screwdriver and looks at me.

"All right."

"I wanted to run that by you before asking her. Out of respect," I add, trying to ignore the fact that he'd been instrumental in dividing us all those years ago.

"Have you two talked about marriage at all?"

"Not a lot. She mentions little things here and there. We're obviously committed to each other. It's just a formality, but I think it's something we both want."

He nods but doesn't seem convinced. The knot in my gut doubles. Not because I need his permission but because I don't want friction with him over this. I'm asking out of respect, but I'll marry her no matter what his thoughts are on it.

"This is nice what you're building together here, but it's still new. Things are a lot different when you're not dealing with life-and-death situations all the time. Once the adrenaline wears off, people change."

I frown, my invisible defenses shooting up rapidly. "What are you trying to say?"

"Did Isabel ever tell you how Lucia and I met?"

I shake my head.

"She was still living in Honduras. The CIA had a pretty big presence there at the time, and I was in the field. Suffice to say, it was a mess that we were both eager to get out of. When it was time for me to go, we agreed that I would take her with me. Get married, get her citizenship, the whole bit. But falling in love with someone in that kind of environment is a lot different than figuring out how to play house in the suburbs for the rest of our lives. Things change." He rubs his forehead. "And some things don't."

"Are you saying you aren't in love with each other anymore?"

"I'm saying that you can play handyman here all day long, but you're never going to be able to walk away from who you were, Tristan. Lucia put on a good show, but I knew she and Gabriel were doing things behind my back that they shouldn't have been. I just didn't know why."

"You lost a child, and the people behind Chalys were responsible. Do you really think she would have taken up a mission for justice if that hadn't happened?"

"Losing Mariana was the worst thing that had ever happened to either of us. It set off a chain of events we could never have predicted. I won't deny that. But Lucia's always been restless. Fierce and determined. Loyal too. All those things drew me in, and yes, I am very much in love with her even after all these years. I'm just telling you, it hasn't been an easy road to walk together."

I take a moment to absorb all he's said. His cautionary tale is unexpected, but the lesson isn't hard to relate to. The process of trying to jam our new lives into some kind of typical mold these past several months hasn't always been smooth. We're figuring it out day by day. I have no idea what challenges the future holds, but I'm determined to face them.

"I want forever with Isabel enough to walk that road no matter what it's paved in. If we can survive everything we have, I think we can stomach a little domesticity. I know we'll never be like other people, but that doesn't mean we can't be happy."

"And you want my blessing," he says after a long moment.

"She'll marry me no matter what you say. But giving us your blessing is probably the best gift you could give her. All things considered."

His eyes darken a little with the challenge, but he's challenged me too. Neither of us has forgotten his hand in all of this. I'll love Isabel until the day I die. If he hadn't tried so hard to turn me away from her, I'm certain I still would have found my way back, more dedicated to being with her than ever.

Gabriel marries us on a Sunday in November, just as the Southern heat starts to give way to cooler weather. We make the sandy beach our church and the winding path through the dunes our aisle. Her parents are here—a nonnegotiable term of Morgan ultimately giving his blessing. I wasn't allowed to whisk her away and leave them out of it.

Skye, Zeda, and Noam, who all have started to become more regular fixtures in our lives, made the drive from New Orleans too. With Karina by his side, Mateus, who'd championed for us harder and longer than anyone, wouldn't miss it either.

I may not have been keen on sharing our wedding day with anyone else, but the minute I see Isabel, everyone else ceases to exist in my mind. Even her father, who clutches her arm possessively before relinquishing her, couldn't distract me from the breathtaking woman who is about to become my wife.

She looks like an angel in her white dress, an uncomplicated gown that leaves her shoulders bare and ripples in the breeze as our bare feet sink into the powdery sand. With a little laugh, she pushes from her face the tiny wisps of hair that fall free. I help, using it as an excuse to touch her since I can't kiss her yet.

Our vows are simple but absolute, a testimony of the unbreakable bond we forged long before this day. She cries, and I brush away her tears with a trembling hand, not caring who sees us so vulnerable. I can only marvel at the enormity of it all, the profound gift I've been given after all the wrongs I've done.

Gabriel ends the short ceremony with a prayer in Spanish. Words that are only important to me because they are important to her. Her eyes glitter with emotion as he speaks, and I make another vow in my heart that I'll worship her the same way some people give themselves over to God. I'll let her carry my sins away and dedicate myself to the love between us. And if I do all this right, maybe I can walk through this life with her for the rest of my days a better man.

ISABEL

Wind whips the ocean against our windows in loud torrents. The waves are angry but barely lick the stilts that hold the house above the shore. The news is going in the background, trying to predict where the hurricane will make landfall. Tristan is at the kitchen table with a fully disassembled ceiling fan that hasn't worked since we moved in. His features are scrunched in concentration.

I need a distraction, but once he zeroes in on a project, I've learned to just let him be.

I rub my arms and stare out at the rolling waves, tinted green under the stormy sky. This is our first big storm since we've been in Perdido Key, and my nerves are already shot. I have to do something, or I'm going to worry myself into a frenzy.

I go into the bedroom and start tidying up. I fold a pile of laundry and start putting it away, which leads to a total overhaul of our dressers, including the one that holds Tristan's endless sea of black T-shirts. I empty them onto the bed, intending to refold them. Once I do, I notice a stack of paperwork in the bottom of the drawer. I pull it out carefully, casting a quick glance out the bedroom door. The weather reporter is broadcasting from a pier about an hour away, repeating the same things they've been saying for the past hour. I'm sure Tristan is still in his own little world.

I set the contents atop the dresser. A ripped yellow package is held to a manila folder by a rubber band. Tristan's name is written on the package above a DC post office box. I pull off the rubber band and tip the package so its contents fall out. They're wrapped in several layers of bubble packaging that I quietly unwrap until two vials roll into my palms.

If I thought I was on edge before, my nerves are rioting now. I swallow over the knot of anxiety in my throat. I read the writing on the masking tape stuck to each one. One is marked "antidote" and the other "sedative." I place them carefully on top of the plastic wrap for fear I'll drop them.

Tristan never heard from Mushenko again. That's what Tristan's always told me. But if this is what I think it is—a recipe to reverse the memory loss he sustained—then it could have only come from one person. I'm angry with him for lying to me, but why would he hold on to it? We've been here for months. We're building a life. I don't want to change anything about it, least of all the man I'm completely dedicated to.

I push the vials aside, feeling sick at the mere sight of them. They're an ugly reminder of the life we left behind along with a thousand memories that will haunt me forever. I'm still too curious not to open the folder. Inside it, I recognize the files Tristan stole from Jay's apartment. His whole history is spelled out, from the enlistment letter my father penned to the brief about the bloody mission that changed Tristan's life forever. Set atop the papers is his red notebook. The ledger of lives lost at Tristan's hand.

I pick it up and thumb through the pages. Seeing the names and the numbers beside them doesn't help the sickness roiling through me. I get to the last page, where I'd written my own name once upon a time. Tristan since scratched it out so it's barely legible. The last entry is the one name neither of us will ever forget, though.

Simon Pelletier.

He's the one who's responsible for all the others. He'll never be able to mark someone else for death. Those days are done. It's not justice, but it has to be enough.

Tristan walks in, startling me so hard I nearly scream.

He looks between me and everything laid out, then back to me.

"What are you doing?"

I clutch my lower lip between my teeth. I learned a long time ago he's not a fan of me going through his things, but that was before we agreed to share a life together.

"Sorry. I was reorganizing the drawers, and I found these."

He moves between me and the dresser. He replaces the vials in the package and binds it back to the folder the way it was before I started snooping.

"Is that what I think it is?"

"It's nothing you need to worry about," he says quietly as he stashes everything back into the empty drawer.

"I'm your wife. I think if you've been holding on to an antidote, it's my business."

"They're my memories."

A spike of fury runs through me. "And what about the ones we're making now? Isn't this enough?"

He turns toward me, his brow angrily furrowed. "Obviously it's enough. I haven't taken it, have I?"

"If you're keeping it, that means you're not ruling it out."

"That's a pretty big assumption, Isabel."

"Is it?"

He works his jaw, avoiding my penetrating gaze. "I have no intention of taking it. I'm happy with our life. I'm happy with everything the way it is. It's just…" He closes his eyes a moment before lifting them to me. "I'm afraid to get rid of it. I'm afraid I'll change my mind and wish I had it. That's all."

I don't know how I feel. Betrayed that he kept this from me. Heartbroken that he's had this choice hanging over him. Most of all angry because the choice isn't mine.

"Don't you think I should have a say in this?" Tears spring to my eyes. "You're everything to me. You're my whole world. What if you have a bad day or are feeling impulsive and you decide to take it and…" I can hardly breathe at the possibility that Tristan could lose more than just his memories. I'm so overwhelmed by it, I rip the package out of the drawer and storm out of the room.

"Isabel! What the hell are you doing?"

He catches me in the kitchen on my way to his tool bag, where I have every intention of finding something to help me destroy the godforsaken vials. He grabs my wrists, but I twist away. He catches me again in the living room, but I trip and we stumble to the floor. I stretch as far as I can to keep the package out of reach. His body covers the length of mine. He's bigger and stronger, so it's only a matter of seconds before he tears the package from my hand. A furious cry leaves my lips as I try to get it back to no avail.

He takes my hands and pins them to the floor above my head. "What is wrong with you?"

I'm breathing hard, and so is he. Maybe I'm being crazy and erratic, but if it means saving the man I love from an uncertain fate, I'm only getting started. I'll fight until I'm bruised and bloody. I'll fight until I win.

"I won't let you take it. I want you to get rid of it," I say between ragged breaths.

"You're saying that now. What if you change your mind?"

"I won't. I won't ever change my mind."

He searches my eyes like maybe I don't mean what I say. "You used to want my memories more than anything."

"I want *you* more than anything. The man you are. You can't…" I swallow hard, and tears stream down the sides of my face. "I can't lose you again, Tristan."

He lowers his forehead so it touches mine. "I won't let that happen."

"Then get rid of it. Please."

He doesn't move for a long time. Finally, he drags his palm down my arm, still keeping me trapped to the hard floor with his other hand. He feathers his fingertips across my lips before kissing me lightly. His gaze is a tractor beam of intensity, so focused that I hardly notice when he reaches to the side and slams his fist down against the package. The sound of breaking glass is unmistakable, loud against the quiet roar of the waves crashing onto the beach below. More tears slip from my eyes, but these are different. They're tears of relief and acceptance and love.

"Thank you," I whisper.

EPILOGUE

SIMON

The four white walls I call home don't bother me too much. It's a strange comfort…the blankness of this place. The people here add the color and the substance with their storied pasts. For the most part, I'm silent. I watch. I learn. For others, the long road of confinement causes trouble. They grow angry and act out. We're all surviving here, paying a penance one way or the other, but I do my best to follow the rules—the official ones imposed on us and the ones we impose upon ourselves.

I quickly figured out how to use what little I have left on the outside to buy my safety on the inside. Determined to do things a little differently than I used to, all I bargained for was my own security. Eight more years and I can start fresh and worry about creature comforts. I don't know what

I'll do then. I'm still learning about myself and what I'm good at. Maybe by then I'll be good at something that won't land me back in prison.

Two years ago, I woke up—a forty-eight-year-old man who had everything and nothing. I had a beautiful, charismatic wife. More money in my bank accounts than anyone could ever hope for. All the fun, expensive toys. Boats, cars, houses. Interesting, powerful friends. To some it looked like a dream life, but I soon learned that having nothing is a lot less complicated than having everything.

The days after they found me were a confusing blur. Doctors were everywhere. My wife was hysterical. I just wanted to go home, wherever that was, so I could get back on solid ground. Someplace where things might make more sense.

A few weeks at home did nothing. Athena went from manic to detached. Our friends weren't sure what to make of it all. People I'd done business with didn't trust me. After the neurologists confirmed the concussion I sustained when I fell during the evacuation destroyed my memory, the circle of people in our lives got smaller and smaller.

Then the investigation started and there was no one. Athena left. My attorneys did their best. Having a client with no recollection of his wrongdoing wasn't a terrible circumstance, but it couldn't erase the things I'd done. Suddenly the dream life was all trash. Every time more information came forward and new accusations were made against me, I felt like I was watching my past unfold on the screen like a movie. The star wasn't me—just a doppelganger

I shared everything with.

Apparently I'm a terrible person. Or at least I was. If I hadn't hit my head, I think I could have found a way out of all those troubles. I could have implicated some other people and skimmed some time off my sentence or maybe gotten away with doing none at all.

I'd never say it out loud, but I like it better on the inside. I like the routine. The monotony. Outsmarting people and sidestepping trouble is a game I've learned to play, and I think I do it well. I don't have a lot to compare it to, so it's enough to keep me entertained for now.

I don't feel like I'm missing anything, which is probably a good thing. Because deep down, I know I'm missing so much.

AUTHOR'S NOTE

When Tristan and Isabel introduced themselves to me many years ago, I couldn't have known then that the story would eventually unfold during such a meaningful time in my own life. Any book I write is in some small way a reflection of my current reality. The Red Ledger has been more than a winding romantic journey toward a happily ever after, quietly echoing some elements of my personal life. It's been a much louder, bloodier, and twisted tale of two lost souls navigating an ugly, unforgiving world. And for my own survival, I needed to live inside this world with them for a while, as unpleasant and hopeless as it sometimes felt.

My first thanks go to those characters in my own life who have offered such rich inspiration during my creative process. Without your immaturity, malice, and pettiness, this story simply would not be possible. Every moment of outrage added valuable fuel to my hate fire, which I then poured directly into the book. As a writer, I couldn't have pushed myself as far without your help.

Thank you to Jonathan, my mom, my children, and my loyal friends for being emotional lifelines. I'm forever grateful to the Waterhouse team for restoring my faith in what I've built and lifting my spirits simply by being yourselves. Thank you as always to my readers, for your

patience and continuous support.

Special thanks to Kirk Overhoff for your insights about the pharmaceutical development process, and Brian Saady, whose book, *The Drug War: A Trillion Dollar Con Game,* played heavily into the themes that emerged in the series.

Lastly, to my characters, who after all this time together feel quite real, thank you for waiting for me and for coming to life precisely when I needed you to.

ABOUT THE AUTHOR

Meredith Wild is a #1 *New York Times, USA Today,* and international bestselling author. After publishing her debut novel, *Hardwired,* in September 2013, Wild used her ten years of experience as a tech entrepreneur to push the boundaries of her "self-published" status, becoming stocked in brick-and-mortar bookstore chains nationwide and forging relationships with major retailers.

In 2014, Wild founded her own imprint, Waterhouse Press, under which she hit #1 on the *New York Times* and *Wall Street Journal* bestseller lists. She has been featured on *CBS This Morning* and the *Today Show,* and in the *New York Times,* the *Hollywood Reporter, Publishers Weekly,* and the *Examiner.* Her foreign rights have been sold in twenty-three languages.